The Madam

m. robinson

Hannah,

Mine.

M. Robinson

xo

Dedication

To my VIP Group!

Acknowledgements

Ben: I LOVE you. You are my everything. Thank you for always supporting my dreams and pushing me in the right direction when I need it the most.

Dad: Thank you for always showing me what hard work is and what it can accomplish. For always telling me that I can do anything I put my mind to.

Mom: Thank you for ALWAYS being there for me no matter what. You are my best friend.

Julissa Rios: I love you and I am proud of you. Thank you for being a pain in my ass and for being my sister. I know you are always there for me when I need you.

Ysabelle & Gianna: Love you my babies.

Jettie Woodruff: You are forever the PP of my life a from here to Ur-anus.

Rebecca Marie: THANK YOU for an AMAZING c Madam. I wouldn't know what to do without you and y creativity.

Jamie Carollo: Thank you for the love and support with everything you have done for me.

Alexis Moore: Your brutal honesty and our witty interesting conversations.

Jennifer Mirabelli: My dirty girl undercover! Love you.

Hetty Whitmore Rasmussen: The support and enthusiasm you share with me.

Heather Harton: My GILF and my friend.

Kathy Coopmans: Mom!! Love you for being you.

Karen Hick Benton: I LOVE YOU. The end.

Barbara Johnson: You always make me laugh.

Shannon Vincent Franco: My cousin, thank you for supporting me.

Kimberly Lenae Stewart: The friendship that we share is one that I cherish.

Mary Beth Witkop: My beautiful girl. I love corrupting you and shocking you.

Veronica LaRoche: The way you promote me is unbelievable.

Ashlee Marie Dirker: You are awesome!

Julie Kerr: Your honesty and friendship mean everything to me.

To all of my family; Rios, Robinsons, Ubillus, Barhoums, Sabis, Britos, etc...I never imagined that I would have the support that I have received from you guys to follow this career. It has meant everything to me to have the love and appreciation you have shown me. I am very lucky to be able to call you my family. I love you and thank you.

To all the blogs A HUGE THANK YOU for all the love and support you have shown me. I have made some amazing friendships with you that I hold dear to my heart. I know that without you I would be nothing!! I cannot THANK YOU enough!!

To all my new author friends that I have made! That has most definitely been a privilege!

Last, but most definitely not least, to my VIP GROUP. Oh my God ladies…words cannot describe how much I love and appreciate every last one of you. The friendships and relationships that I have made with you are one of the best things that have ever happened to me. I wish I could name each one of you but it would take forever, just please know that you hold a very special place in my heart. You guys make my day, every single day. THANK YOU!!!

To all the fans that have shown me an outpouring of love and support. I would be nowhere without you. You are forever my VIPs!!

Authors Note

When I started writing VIP I never imagined that I would turn it into a series. I poured my heart and soul into writing that book. The characters became like my children and family, I love them. I never understood how authors would say that their characters become real people to them until I started writing. It's amazing how much of yourself you pour into a story. You miss time with your loved ones because you just need to finish one more chapter...a couple more words...just one more scene...etc...etc...etc...

Writing The Madam was a unique experience for me that I will never forget. I love this bitch so much! She is hardcore and I wouldn't have her any other way. Her story is intense, dark, erotic; it's a roller coaster of emotions. The way I heard her voice in my head is exactly how I have portrayed her in her story.

After I started receiving the outpour of fans wanting Sebastian and Ysabelle's story to continue, I immediately knew that The Madam needed her own story for the series to click together. I cannot tell you how much it has meant to me to be accepted in the indie world by each and every one of you. I am incredibly lucky to be able to do what I love and have it be received with such kindness and admiration.

I wrote this series for you.

PROLOGUE

You can call me whatever you want, I've heard it all before. But the truth is the first time I saw money, I fell in love. Money makes the world go round. It's the root of all evil. It gives you both pleasure and pain. Greed is one of the seven deadly sins, along with envy, and my personal favorite...lust. God said thou shalt not covet thy neighbor's wife; well God never met one of my VIPs.

I'm not an evil woman, but I want what I want, when I want it. I do whatever the fuck I please, and at the end of the day, if you fuck with one of my girls then you fuck with me. You don't fuck with something that belongs to me and if you do, I'll make sure to make you pay for it. I fear nothing. Fear makes you weak and I am not a weak woman. I can be your most treasured jewel or your worst nightmare. The choice is yours.

I don't depend on anyone other than myself, because at the end of the day that's all I have. I rely on no one and that's what makes me incredible at what I do. I live in a man's world and I fucking own it. Women rule this world and the only reason we let men believe they do is because they lead with their cocks. Our pussies hold the power. We give life and are the only living organism in this world that can bleed for seven days and not fucking die.

Love is a figment of your imagination; it's right up there with monogamy. It's a platonic state of mind that you program yourself to be in. It's an illusion. The mind is the most powerful tool one can have. They say we only use 10% of our brain and if that's the case, could you imagine what it would be like if we were capable of more?

I'm not a selfish woman, I do share my things with others but they need to be returned to me in the exact same condition as borrowed. You break it you buy it. You think you may know me but you have no fucking idea. My namesake, I am a powerful, sexual woman. I am an enchantress on a good day, a demon on the bad, and an Illusionist for all the days in between. I am a lot like Ysabelle in the sense that I show you what I want you to believe. That's maybe why I wanted her, why I still want her. Ysabelle really is a stupid fucking woman, but I don't want to talk about her and her fucked up decisions. We will get to that; we will cover everything.

I am a no holds barred type of woman. I have no secrets to keep. But a lot happens behind closed doors, and I'm about to open those doors for you. Give you a glimpse of what and who I am.

My name is Lilith Veronica Stone, AKA Madam, and this is my story.

CHAPTER

The first written text of prostitution can be dated back to 4000 B.C. I've always hated the word "prostitution" but it truly is one of the world's oldest professions. Women from all over the world knew early on the power that they held between their legs. They were a force to be reckoned with even back then. It's interesting to see how the world has evolved since this taboo profession began. But of course, back then it wasn't prohibited, it was called bartering. I'll give you something if you give me something in return. This is how I've lived my life. It has been my motto, my creed, my oath so to speak.

The psyche of the human mind is a fascinating concept. God gives us freewill, he gives us instincts, survival skills, he sets the stage and you pull the strings. One may think he is the puppeteer but the reality is, you have to blame someone for your mistakes, so why not him right? It's so much easier that way. Although, God is a bit of a voyeur in my eyes as he likes to watch. He also sets the rules; look but don't touch, touch but don't taste, taste but don't swallow.

This is where he and I differ. Temptation is an alluring son of a bitch. I'm not a religious woman by any means, but I have been called God a time or two. I prefer Madam though. They say you learn a lot about a person through their name; my given name is Lilith meaning "of the night". Legends say Lilith was Adam's first wife, sent out of Eden and replaced by Eve because she would not submit to him. I was pretty much fucked the minute I was born.

I was born June 6, 1960; yes, I know you see it, 666 the sign of the devil. Is that me? I think not, although, one can dream can't they? That would make me fifty-four years old. I don't look it by any means. In my eyes I don't look a day over thirty-five. Trust me, I can fuck anyone under the table in more ways than one. Everyone has a creator and we are put on this earth for a purpose; some believe that once that purpose is served, you're done. Game over, do not pass go; do not collect $200.

I say fuck that. Women are put on this earth to be cherished and treated as a queen; men are our worshippers and will do anything by whatever means possible to make our wishes come true. If they don't, we deserve the right to make them suffer; after all, we did create them. Doesn't that give us leeway?

I know what you're asking yourself. What made me this way? Why am I a sadist bitch? It's all right; you can say it. I actually prefer it. I am a sadistic bitch, but get one thing straight; I am "the sadistic bitch". When I walk into a room I expect you to turn and watch, when I talk I expect you to listen, when I say something I expect you to do it, no questions asked. It's all very easy; you just need to follow my rules. I set the guidelines.

In my mind, I am your God.

I may be coming on too strong, but like I said, I will share everything with you. I have nothing to hide or to be ashamed of. The decisions and choices I made were given to me, I was not forced, I was chosen. Just like I choose my girls.

For you to understand my life you need to live it. I don't know if reading about it will do it justice, nonetheless, I am going to try. There are always three sides to every story, yours, mine, and the truth. I deserve a chance to explain myself. Love me or hate me, it's who the fuck I am. The Madam.

VIP can be dated back to the prohibition. When alcohol and VIP took over the world. It has been in my family for decades and generations have run it since the 1920s, all handed down from woman to woman. Never has a man laid his fingers on VIP; many have wanted to, offering millions upon millions of dollars, never standing a chance to control it. Not one piece of the action. My great female ancestors saw an opportunity with their pussies; one that many women bartered for food, clothing, shelter, my family decided that money would be the key.

Money controls the world. And guess what? Sex sells in every language. Everyone and anything has a price. You'll sell your first born if the price is right; trust me, I speak from experience. I do not lie. I am a lot of things, but I am not a liar. Withholding the truth is not lying, neither are secrets, or skeletons in your closet. Everyone has them; it just comes down to how good you are at keeping them there.

VIP started like any other business; from nothing. A woman had an idea and went with it, slowly but surely, it became something greater than she could have ever imagined. It blossomed into a life of its own. Men came from all over the world for a taste of a VIP. It's not named Very Important Pussy for nothing. The women were not created, it was in their blood, like they were born and put on this earth to serve that purpose and that purpose alone. It was innate to them, each and every chosen VIP is never taught to please, they are guided.

Not just anyone can be a VIP; it's not an organization that is based off interviews or applications. You're chosen, selected, picked, and taken; you are the elite. By the time I was born, VIP was a multibillion-dollar corporation. What started in salons, alleys, and vehicles, became mansions, private jets, yachts, and every motherfucking luxury known to man. My mother was the owner at the time, and she was the strongest woman I have ever known. My father was a very high profile businessman, and he had another family of his own, but my mother was his vice. My father was a devastatingly handsome man. He had jet-black hair with emerald green eyes, a strong jaw line that accented his thin lips and perfect white teeth. He was muscular, fit, and nearly cleared 6'3. He wore business suits every time I saw him, and never drove his own car. From afar, my parents looked like they were meant to be in magazines and print out ads; they looked perfect together. The embodiment of the perfect Miami power couple.

My mother never saw herself as the other woman though. She used him. He was her play toy to do with as she saw fit, and growing up I saw her use and abuse him daily. My mother loved four things; VIP, herself, money, and me. She was an amazing mentor to me, taught me everything I know. I was born into a life of luxury. I never had to want for anything, never had to ask for a goddamn thing. It was all handed to me on a silver-fucking platter with a bright red bow.

I never took anything that I had for granted. My father played an active role in my life; I knew what he and my mother were to each other. That had nothing to do with me. See, my father's other family had all boys; I was his only girl, his princess. Both my parents loved me in different ways and they both said it often. I wasn't born into a hollow existence. My parents never played me against each other and they never pretended to be something they weren't.

I never met my other siblings and I was my mother's only child. The first time I realized that my life was different, was when I was five years old. I was like any other little girl, very curious of everything around me.

I secretly watched through the gap of my mother's bedroom door with my doll in my arms and my hair in pigtails. She sashayed across the room in her black knee length silk robe, pulling her hair up to expose the crook of her neck as she perched herself on the corner of her king size bed.

"I told you time and time again, Vivian, that I don't want Lilith exposed to this lifestyle," my father stated as he ran his fingers through his hair.

"And I've told you that I don't give a flying fuck what you want. Lilith is mine and you're lucky that I even allow her to be in your life," my mother carelessly said, leaning back on one of her elbows, looking calm yet threatening at the same time.

"Allow her? Vivian, you can play this Madam card with everybody else, but you can't fuck with me. If I wanted to take her from you, I could. Nobody in their right mind would leave a child to be raised in this environment."

My mother viciously laughed. "And what environment may that be Charles? The one you partake in any chance you can get? The place where you can get fucked in the ass with a strap on and no one will think less of you? Or where I sometimes bring you a man? Is that the environment that you speak of, because from where I am sitting, you have more to lose than I do. Your bi-sexual tendencies will be the end of you, darling, we always knew that. Now get one thing straight, Lilith will take over one day. The faster you realize that she is my heir to this 'environment' the better it will be for all of us," my mother threatened with intensity that I had never seen or heard before.

My father shook his head and folded his arms. "Jesus, Vivian. Lilith has a chance of a real life, why on earth would you want this for her?"

"Charles, this is where you and I differ. I don't have to explain myself to you. Your job is done. I agreed to you having an active role in Lilith's life if you wanted, because I think children should have their father present. As far as any decisions based on what her life and upbringing will be, can be checked at the door. End of conversation." My mother stood sharply and glared him in the eye, threatening him with just one look. She then turned suddenly to where I was standing.

She cocked her head to the side and replaced her intense stare with a loving one. "My Lilith," she beamed as she welcomed me with open arms. I went to her with innocence and devotion like any other five year old child.

"Mother, why are you and Father fighting?" I questioned.

She smiled. "That was not a fight, darling. You will know when Mother is fighting," she whispered in my ear as she pulled my pigtails out of my face.

She resumed her composure and looked at my father. "Charles doesn't know what's good for him and he keeps throwing his opinion in when it doesn't matter," she stated, bringing her loving gaze back to me. "You are your mother's girl, that's all you need to remember, my Lilith."

I smiled bright and wide. "Is Father leaving now?" I asked as I looked at my father, who looked like he wanted to say something but knew better.

"Charles has his other family, Lilith, you're not his priority, you are mine. Always remember that. Men are good for nothing but sperm," she laughed; it must have been a joke, but I didn't understand it. My father didn't seem to find it too funny either.

"Fuck you, Vivian," my father spewed before he gathered his coat and left; my mother laughed the entire time.

"So dramatic, Lilith," she proclaimed in a high pitched voice with her hand on her chest. "Thank God you have most of my genes, I can't stand pussies."

She rose from the bed and removed her robe as she walked into her closet. My mother was the most beautiful woman I have ever seen. Even to this day her beauty haunts me, her bright blonde hair that came past her shoulders and layered her face, the porcelain white skin that made her blue eyes vibrant and only refined her impeccable facial structure. She had these dark black eyelashes that looked fake and made her eyes look alive. My mother was tall at 5'7 and built like a model; she had legs that went for miles, and a tiny waist that accentuated her 34D breasts. I never once saw my mother without makeup or put together. She was always picture perfect.

A shy woman she wasn't; I think I saw her naked more than I saw her clothed. She emerged, holding a pantsuit and laid it on her bed. I watched her flawless body move so effortlessly; she always entranced me. I wouldn't learn till later that my mother would be my mentor, my maker, my Madam.

She must have caught me staring. "Lilith, come here," she called with a malicious smile.

Crouching down to my level, she looked me straight in the eyes. "One day you will look just like me. Do you want to be like Mother?" I nodded.

"I will teach you everything you need to know. Lilith, you will be Madam. Men and women will bow down to you. You will hold so much power in your hands that the world will be your kingdom. Do you understand me?" With inquisitive eyes, I eagerly nodded, not knowing what it all meant but liking the sound of it anyway.

My mother contentedly sighed. "You were made for great things, Lilith, know that now," she stated, kissing the tip of my nose. I had no idea what my mother meant at the time, but this was a phrase that I would hear throughout my entire life, one that I repeat to myself often.

"Now, enough of that. How about we go shopping!"

Even at the age of five, I knew that my mother was an intimidating and fascinating woman. She had a presence about her, a certain aura that surrounded her and anyone could see it. She could do whatever she wanted, never had to ask permission, and was always granted instant access to anywhere she wanted to go. I grew up on private planes, a chauffeur drove me everywhere I went, and had private tutors that came to my home.

I was taught how to play the piano, the violin, and was fluent in six languages all before the age of ten. Any and all personnel that were to interact with me had to pass a thorough background check and extensive interview by my mother and her "team" of associates. My mother wouldn't allow anyone to corrupt my way of thinking. She had her own plans and motives for doing that. I never associated with other children my age either, my mother hated children. She wouldn't allow me to use poor vocabulary or to get dirty like other people's children; I didn't grow up eating hotdogs and hamburgers, I ate caviar and sushi. I was always around adults and those adults didn't have children. I was a porcelain doll in my mother's eyes; she dressed me like one, and expected me to act as one, absolutely perfect on the outside.

The Madam

I never had a hair out of place; I was always dressed in designer clothes, and was never allowed to leave the table without being excused first. I was even slapped on the hand when I didn't say "please" or "thank you". My mother wanted me perfect. There was no baby talk in my house; I never crawled, I went from sitting right to walking. My mother wouldn't have it any other way. I had only the best of what money could buy around me.

I was never coddled, my mother was insistent on that. She showed me love in other ways. Once, when I was six, I slipped on the freshly mopped floor. I started to cry and my nanny had rushed to my aid.

She grabbed me in her arms and swayed me back and forth.

"Shhh, baby, Lily, it's okay. You're all right, I got you," she lovingly reassured.

"What the hell is this?" Startled, we both surprisingly looked up to find my mother watching from the doorway with her arms crossed and her face appalled.

"Lilith, her name is Lilith! Not baby Lily. Let her go this instant." My nanny removed her arms from around me and I swear I could hear her heart beating through her clothes.

"I fell and hurts myself, momma."

"I fell and hurt myself, Mother," she corrected. "Come here to me."

I went with trembling limbs to my mother's side. She carried me and placed me on the granite countertop where she inspected my knees.

"Lilith, you are fine, you do not cry; do you understand me? You never show weakness, I don't care if you are bleeding, you hold it in. The next time I see or hear you cry, you will be punished. Am I clear?" I heard my nanny gasp as I nodded my head, trying to hold back the tears that I felt in my throat.

"You're late for your art class. You're excused, but first go change your stockings; throw those away, they are ruined." I eagerly nodded, wanting to please her. She placed me down on the floor and I left, trying not limp because I feared the repercussions if I did. Before I got to the stairs I heard my mother's wrath, and it was enough to freeze me in place while she screamed at my nanny.

"Get your belongings, you're fucking fired."

"But Madam…I-"

"Save your excuses! You know my policy. She is not to be treated as a baby. Your work here is done. And since you're headed to the servant quarters, make sure to tell Maria she's fired too. My child could have been hurt from her negligence of leaving the floor so damp." I heard the click of her heels before I hightailed it to my bedroom.

CHAPTER 2

That wasn't the first or last time that my mother fired my nanny. Let me rephrase that, that wasn't the first or last time my mother fired someone who worked for her and had to "assist" her with raising me. There was never anyone good enough for her, she always wanted more, always wanted better, but could never find it. Nothing was ever good enough for "her Lilith".

By the time I was eight, I had gone through seven nannies, eight violin instructors, four tennis coaches, nine linguist professors, and that's just the tip of iceberg. For a while, I thought my mother's favorite phrase was "you're fired", she was the Donald fucking Trump of the Upper East Side. I learned early on to not get attached to people; they could leave just as fast as they entered my life. I also learned how to keep secrets at an entirely young age. My nannies always felt bad for me and I learned how to manipulate that feeling early on. Manipulation is the key to getting what you want; always remember that.

I had them eating out of the palm of my hand and all it took was a "please", "thank you", and a smile. They would sneak me chocolate, let me eat cheeseburgers, and ice cream quickly became my favorite obsession. I wanted Barbies, charm bracelets, an easy bake fucking oven. Would my mother allow that? Hell no! Did I have it? Hell yes! I was lucky enough to have a mother who traveled at any point in time, for days at a time. It was easy to hide things. She had no idea where my sock drawer was, let alone where I hid my treasures. I had them scattered in different places and not ever did I get caught.

My most valued memories were when my nanny would take me to the local park. It became our secret pact. She knew that I controlled her paycheck and I knew she controlled my freedom. You could say that I was an honest and upfront little girl.

They say children have no filter and repeat everything they hear.

"My mother told me that what I have between my legs can control you bowing at my heels," I carelessly told the boy next to me as we continued to build in the sandbox.

"Really, let me see!" he enthusiastically shouted as he threw down his shovel to face me completely.

"Okay!" I screeched in return as I turned to face him to pull up my dress to expose my white ruffled panties.

He cocked his head to the side while confusingly studying my underwear. "There's no candy. That's just your no-no place." I shrugged and we returned to playing.

My mother loved me; she cared about me and made sure that I had everything I "needed". Yes, she could be the ice queen of all ice queens. She made me aware that I was the center of her universe in everything she did. I observed everything she did for me. I think I was maybe nine, the first time I'd really gotten into trouble. It was late on a Saturday night; my nanny had already retired for the evening and had left me alone. I wasn't tired yet and I wanted a drink. I wandered down the hall and descended the stairs in my satin nightgown and fuzzy slippers. I knew I wasn't allowed out of my room that late, especially on a Saturday night. The rule was that I needed to call my nanny if I needed anything.

As I came down the last step, I could hear a humming sound and my mother talking. She was speaking in a low sultry tone, and I was sure she'd gotten me a kitten or something.

"That's it, yes, Jasmine, rub it right there; just like that," I heard her say.

I had to look; the excitement got the better of me. I'd been asking for a kitten for months. What I saw made me gasp. My mother instantly turned in her black pinstriped suit, as did the naked woman on the couch who immediately covered herself. My mother on the other hand cocked her head to the side, raised one hand to her hip, and smirked. I turned around and took off running. I shut my door and quickly covered myself with my blankets feigning sleep, quietly praying that my mother would not approach me about what I had witnessed.

20

Moments later, I heard the door open and her heels tapping on the tile floor. I closed my eyes tight and swallowed the saliva that had formed in my mouth.

She sighed. "Lilith, I know you're not sleeping," she said calmly.

"Turn and face me, NOW!" The tone in her voice made me jump. I slowly took off my blankets, scooted to the end of my bed where my legs dangled off the edge. I cautiously looked up at my mother sitting on my chase lounger, arms to her sides, resting on the back of the settee.

"You have been a very bad girl, Lilith. What are the rules past nine?" I didn't say anything; I was scared shitless.

"I asked you a question and I expect an answer. Do not make me ask you again," she threatened in a voice I had never heard before.

"I-um-I'm-I…" I mumbled and my mother's irritation grew.

"What the hell? You are further pissing me off. Now you're showing me weakness. What are the rules in this house, child?" she questioned, raising an eyebrow.

"Do not cry, show no fear or weakness, always say please and thank you, and never leave my bedroom past 9 pm," I said, just above a whisper.

"Yes, those are the rules until you hear otherwise," she reminded me.

"You're going to be ten this year and I know that there will come a time when I will need to inform you of everything that you are meant for, Lilith. Now is not that time. One day what you saw will make sense to you. I promise. As for right now, there are consequences to every action and this one is yours. Come to me. Now!"

I gathered my emotions one last time before approaching my mother, mere inches away from her face.

"Remove your panties." I took a deep breath before I nodded and did as I was told. She grabbed my upper arm and moved me to lie over her lap.

"Bend over, do not arch your back, and don't you dare try to cover yourself, or cry."

She raised her arm high above her head. "Count."

SLAP! I gasped from the surprised shock of the pain. "One…" I barely let out.

SLAP! "Two," I said through gritted teeth.

SLAP! "Three. Please, Mother, no more…please!" I pleaded.

"Two more for begging."

SLAP! "Four, four, four," I shouted in misery.

SLAP! "FIVE!" I yelled, trying to hold the tears at bay. When I didn't hear or feel any movement from my mother, I shuddered in relief allowing my body to go lax from the stiff position. It was over; I had survived the first physical punishment my mother ever handed me. I attempted to try to soothe my ache and my mother immediately grabbed my hand.

"Don't do it," she reminded in an agitated tone. "Sit down, Lilith." I closed my eyes and bit my lower lip as I removed myself from my mother's lap to slowly descend on the couch.

She shook her head, "Tsk tsk tsk, Lilith, sit on the floor." She must have sensed that I was about to plead with her. "Don't," she repeated with a pointed finger.

When I finally sat on the tile floor, I had to push my fingernails into my skin to stop myself from crying. I knew if I cried I was done for, this was the first test of control my mother showed me, not just for her, but for myself as well.

"I'm proud of you, darling. You will sit like that for the next hour, then you will brush your teeth again, and you will go to bed. Do you understand me?" she patronizingly asked and I nodded.

"I love you, Lilith."

"I love you, too." She kissed my forehead and left me to wallow in my own misery without so much as me shedding one tear.

❊VIP❊

I should have been thinking about the stinging on my ass in the months that followed. Instead, I wasn't thinking about that. I was thinking about my mother and that woman. I couldn't help where my mind went when it wandered, or when I was dreaming. I had woken up with a tingling feeling in between my legs more times than I could count. A few weeks after my tenth birthday, I awoke from the most intense dream I had ever had. It was similar to what I saw the naked woman doing to herself. I had this burning feeling in my private area. They say curiosity killed the cat; well I fucking murdered that pussy. I discovered myself when I was ten years old. My hand wandered and took over of its own accord. I didn't see a happy ending by any means, but I did figure out that if touched correctly, eventually something would happen and it could be mind-blowing.

I tried hard not to defy my mother after the night she waylaid my ass, but I was still a child, and sometimes the curiosity got the better of me. I remember the first time I knew I wanted to be just like my mother, not just in little girl terms. I knew at the age of eleven, I wanted to be just like her. She was out of town. I knew she wasn't coming home that night, she'd already called to tell me goodnight. I quietly crept out of my room and tip toed to my mother's bedroom, which was all the way across the other side of our mansion.

When I finally made it to her bedroom door, I could feel the nervousness and anxiousness in my stomach. I felt as though I might throw up. I was never allowed in my mother's room without her being present. That was another rule that was added on my eleventh birthday. I mean seriously, who specifically tells a child they can't go into a room and expects them to listen? I just wanted to see why she didn't want me there.

I took a deep breath and reminded myself that everyone was asleep and my mother was not home. There was no way I could get into trouble. I opened the door, making sure not to make a sound as I closed it behind me. Once it was shut, I locked it and only then did I take my next breath. I turned on the lights and the whole room illuminated like I was in the center of a museum. There were dimmers, low and high lights, spotlights; it was insane how much perfect and specific lighting there was in this room.

I started my mission easily enough; I just looked around, running my fingertips along the furniture and bedding. No harm right? My mother's room was spectacular! The bed was almost like a black mirror. I could see my reflection in the headboard as I ran my fingers across the shiny footboard. I lifted the hem of my nightgown to wipe away the fingerprints I'd left. At the corner of the headboard, there was this button that I had never seen before. One couldn't see it unless you knew it was there.

I ran my index finger in a circular motion around it while biting my bottom lip. I pushed it before I gave it another thought and the corner wall unit on the other side of the wall opened. I had no idea that was even there. I started biting my nails as I walked the fifty feet to the opening; I know it was fifty feet because I counted. After that, my feet moved on their own accord as I walked into a room where all the walls were painted a deep burgundy and everything else was black. I had never seen anything like it, not in movies, or in magazines, or in books. There was funny looking furniture everywhere and all sorts of sticks and leather contraptions on the wall. There was something that resembled a cross in the center of the room and straps coming off the ceiling.

It looked like a dungeon and I was terrified that I was going to find a dead body. At the same time, I felt empowered being in this room. I loved that feeling; it was the first time in my life that I felt powerful. I don't know why I felt that way, just that it was there. I had to find out what was in the dresser; it was calling my name. I opened the first drawer and there were these toys that looked like swords. I picked one up and turned it on and the strong vibration made me drop it on the floor.

I put it away as quickly as I grabbed it and opened the next drawer that held silver metal tools that looked painful and scary. I didn't like that drawer, so I moved on to the next one. It had items that looked like mushrooms inside. The last drawer had leashes, collars, and necklaces that had balls in the middle. I scratched my head because I didn't understand the concept of this cabinet or room. I took one last look as I walked back into my mother's bedroom, stopping, I made sure to close the door of the secret room.

I went to her desk next and all the drawers were locked.

"Hmmm if I were my mother where would I hide the key?" I asked myself.

I began frantically searching until I finally found it hidden in a compartment in the corner under the desk. I quickly opened the first drawer and there was a huge black binder that had the inscription "Cathouse" written on the top. I pulled it out and put it on the desk. The first page had a table of contents like the books I read. It listed women's names, medical information, addresses, and a whole bunch of other information I didn't understand. As I kept turning the pages, I would see pictures of beautiful women, both clothed and nude. These women were gorgeous, some of them I had seen before and others I hadn't.

I became bored with the book rather quickly and put it away. What I found in the middle drawer really caught my attention. It was a big black book, and "VIP" was etched on the top. I had heard my mother say VIP all the time. I had no idea what she meant. The book looked like an organizer with thousands and thousands of men's and women's names in it. I hadn't realized how heavy it was and had to use all my strength to put it away. I returned the key to its rightful spot and continued my journey of discovery.

I made my way to the closet, which could have been a large bedroom on its own. I had seen my mother's clothes before, but never like this. It was breathtakingly beautiful how all the colors and styles were organized. Everything had its place.

At that exact moment, I wanted to be just like my mother.

I wanted everything that my mother had and was.

I wanted to be her.

All it took was one night alone in her bedroom for me to want what I didn't know would inevitably become mine.

CHAPTER 3

Two more years went by with not so much as a hint of what my future would hold, but that all changed on a private jet ride to Switzerland.

"What the fuck do you think we are going to Switzerland for, Daniel?" I continued to listen to my mother yell into the phone.

"Yes, I'm fully fucking aware that I needed to be there yesterday. I had other business that needed my attention…you know VIP doesn't run itself. I need to speak to the President, not the manager of the bank. I am not about to place $25 million dollars in the hands of some fucking manager. Make it happen or I will find someone who will," she aggravatingly roared as she hung up.

"Why do I leave things in the hands of a man, Lilith?" she questioned, looking at me adoringly as I looked up from my book.

"Especially when a woman would do it right the first time," I repeated what I heard her say time after time.

She smiled and nodded.

"Mother, how much longer?"

"Not long, darling. Once we get there, you will go with the nanny to the hotel and I have some business that I need to handle. I'll come get you later and we will go to dinner, yes?" I nodded and smiled wide. I loved spending one on one time with my mother. It was the highlight of my life.

I excused myself to go use the restroom but was grabbed by the hand before I could take another step.

"Lilith…turn around." I did and I will never forget the look on my mother's face that afternoon. She looked like she had waited her entire life for that very moment.

"My Lilith. You're a woman. Jesus Christ, you are finally a woman." She looked as if she'd just witnessed a miracle; glee covered her perfectly polished face.

I turned around to see for my very own eyes what she was talking about.

"I'm bleeding! Oh my God, I got my period, Mother!" I screamed, joining in on the excitement.

"You sure did, darling. Let's go get you cleaned up." She beamed reassuringly.

Once we were seated, my mother said to the stewardess, "Open a bottle of Dom Pérignon; two glasses. Thank you."

"Hand a glass to Lilith." The stewardess looked at mother like she had lost her damn mind. It was blatantly obvious that I was a minor. But my mother didn't care; she always did what she wanted.

"Raise your glass, darling. I toast to you and your newfound power. There is much for us to discuss. You have no idea the grandeur that will rightfully be yours one day, today marks the day that you are that much closer to becoming what you were made for." I raised my eyebrows, not understanding a word my mother was saying.

She clinked my glass and downed her entire champagne with one sip.

"Take a drink. We're celebrating the beauty that is you." I sipped my glass, thinking that it would taste much worse than what actually touched my taste buds. It was good and I tried to keep drinking but my mother took away the glass.

"Ladies don't gulp, Lilith," she said condescendingly.

"You just did." I giggled, feeling more empowered in my newfound womanhood.

She grinned. "Do as I say, not as I do. Are we clear?" she teased and I nodded.

The next two years changed drastically. No longer did my mother try to hide things from me, I wasn't excused when she would take certain phone calls, my nanny didn't have to follow me everywhere, and I met more gorgeous women than I thought possible. At one point, I questioned my sexual preference because I would find myself fantasizing about what it would be like to be them. To look like them, talk like them, act like them, just to be one of them. I needed it, I wanted it, I couldn't think of anything else.

I still didn't understand what any of it meant. I knew better than to ask questions. If my mother wanted me to know something, she would tell me; that's how she operated. Several other things started changing after I became a woman; my body being one of them seemed to change overnight. I went to bed a little girl and woke up a teenager; I had developed 34C breasts and curves in places that weren't there before. The years of playing tennis had allowed me to develop a toned physique and I grew to be 5'7, just like my mother. My body matured to a young woman. My mother loved long hair and never allowed the stylist to give me more than a trim, but for my fifteenth birthday, she permitted sun kissed highlights. It made my straight waist length hair platinum blonde.

I got attention everywhere I went and I fucking devoured it! I ate it up like it was my last meal; I flirted like I knew what I was doing, and paraded myself around any chance I could get. I didn't go to school, so that only left boutiques, shopping plazas on South Beach, restaurants, and parties my mother would allow me to attend, both at our home and other invitations. Believe it or not, some of the parties that my mother and I attended had other kids my age. I met this girl named Alexandria at a banquet benefit for cancer. I was still fifteen and she was a few months older than me; we made friends fairly quickly due to our upbringings being similar.

She was the complete opposite of what I looked liked. I think her parents were Latin; she had a tan complexion with dark chocolate doll eyes and curly unruly hair, her facial features were much more pronounced than mine. Our heights were the same and every time she talked, I couldn't help but stare at her pouty mouth. The slight accent she spoke with was just as addicting. She was picturesque.

She was also my first kiss.

"I fucking hate these stupid benefits. Like my parents give a shit who's dying from cancer today; it's just an excuse to look charitable, and my lush of a mother to get drunk," she proclaimed as I followed her through the back gardens of this house I'd never been to.

"You sure you know where you're going? It seems like we've been walking forever."

"Yeah, my dad does business with the owner. I can't wait to show you the garden! It's perfect and quiet and I got us a surprise."

We walked for another five minutes before I saw exactly what she had been describing. It was astounding how all the flowers and trees blended together. It looked like we had walked into The Secret Garden. I walked around in a daze, looking at all the different types of plants that I had never seen before.

"Lilith!" Her excitement broke the trance I was in and I turned to look at her. "Look what I've got." She pulled a pint of whiskey from her purse. "I stole it from

the bar when the bartender wasn't looking," she proudly stated.

"Let's get toasted!" She took three huge gulps before handing it to me, "Ugh…it burns all the way down, but it will be worth it."

I wasn't much for peer pressure and my mother would have probably shit herself, not at the situation, but the fact that I was the follower not the leader in the scenario. I took some sips, keeping in the back of my mind that ladies don't gulp, and before we knew it, we were both drunkity, drunk, drunk.

I couldn't stop laughing, I had never been drunk before and everything around me was hilarious. Alexandria was a bit more in control of herself, although she was still all over the place. She had fallen over laughing with her hair scattered all over her face. I started moving pieces of it away until she suddenly grabbed my wrist and we gazed into each other's eyes. My first thought was if my eyes resembled the glossy mirrors of hers. She licked her lips, and my very next thought was that I wanted to lick them too.

We both moved simultaneously, me advancing and her ascending, to each other's mouths. I had never kissed anyone before, but I had read enough about it to know how it worked. The moment her lips touched mine I moaned. She tasted like whiskey and peppermint Tic Tacs, her lips were soft and smooth. We were completely and utterly in sync with one another. Our movements paralleled what the other was doing and the second I felt her tongue in my mouth my lower abdomen tingled. We effortlessly moved together and my mind didn't have any thoughts, other than the sensations I felt in my pussy.

She was the first to break away from our kiss and I will never forget the teasingly erotic grin she displayed. I know we were only fifteen, but it doesn't matter what anyone says, women are born with their sexuality. It's this unknown gift we have, this ability to say so much without having to say one word.

The rest of the night proceeded without any problems, everything returned to the way it was, except sometimes I would catch Alexandria smirking and looking at me. It didn't make me feel uncomfortable; it made me feel powerful, like this surge of adrenaline I didn't know I had. I was like a bird in a nest ready to fly. When I went home that night, I thought about that kiss and how much I loved it. When I was younger, I use to wonder about my sexuality, I was always attracted to the female body, starting with my mother's. I hadn't been around many men growing up, and my sexuality was once again questioned.

At this point, I didn't give a fuck!

To each their own, right?

I fantasized about Alexandria for months; I fondled, and pleasured myself to that kiss- it was the first time I ever came.

❖VIP❖

My sixteenth birthday came faster than I had anticipated; the year just flew by. My mother threw me the most lavish sweet sixteen party money could buy. It was actually quite interesting seeing as I didn't have any friends, yet there were teenagers everywhere; I had no idea who anyone was or how my mother found them. All I know is I had an amazing time and I soaked up all the attention I could get. I love being the center of attention. The party dwindled down after midnight and that's when my father showed up. I would see my father here and there as I got older, but I always saw him on birthdays and holidays.

"I can't believe how fast time goes by, Lilith; you're a woman now," my father said as he pulled the hair away from my face and placed it behind my ear.

I smiled. "You missed my party," I reminded him, even though I'm sure he knew it.

"He wasn't invited," we heard my mother say from behind us. My father didn't pay her any attention.

"I got you something. Would you like to see it?" he asked and I eagerly nodded. I always loved my father's presents.

He grabbed my hand as my mother followed to the front driveway. There, with a huge red bow, was a brand new red BMW.

"Oh my God!" I shouted in surprise.

"Happy birthday, baby," he said softly as he leaned in to kiss my forehead. He handed me the keys and I ran to my new prized possession.

"A BMW? Really, Charles? What did that set you back, 40 grand? Is that all she's worth to you?" my mother taunted him.

"It's her first car, Vivian. It's plenty for her," he replied unapologetically.

"I'll make sure to tell her that when I hand her the keys to her McLaren F1."

"Are you fucking kidding me?"

I saw her smirk deviously as she turned to face him and she leaned forward to grab his tie. "Did I stutter? You heard me," she murmured, just loud enough that I could still hear.

"Do you want to play, Charles? Because I want to play. I'll let you put it anywhere," she said and I saw my father grin.

"Lilith, darling, your father and I have some things to discuss. I will see you in the morning," she said with a smile and started moving toward the house.

"Thank you, I love it!" I said to my father as he pulled me into a hug.

"I love you, you know that right? You're one of my proudest accomplishments," he whispered in my ear.

"I love you, too." I repeated.

My mother grabbed his hand and I watched them leave as if they were a happily married couple.

CHAPTER 4

After I got my car, I had more freedom to do what I wanted. My mother wasn't always on my ass about what I was allowed to do and I took full advantage of the freedom. Alexandria not only introduced me to drinking, but I also became formally introduced to Mary Jane, otherwise known as marijuana. She bought me my very own bag and pipe that I carelessly hid in my nightstand.

For the first time in my life, I walked into my bedroom one night to find my mother sitting at the end of my bed waiting for me.

My heart dropped.

"Mother," I gasped in surprise.

"Lilith. Where have you been all night?" she interrogated in a calm, soothing voice.

"I just hung out with Alexandria."

She slowly approached me from the bed. "The next time you come home high, darling, try putting some Visine in your eyes. Follow me, NOW!" I was terrified; my mother scared the shit out of me sometimes. I followed closely behind her to her office.

"Take a seat, Lilith, it's time we had a little chat." She sat in her leather chair and I sat in one of the seats in front of her desk. My mother was dressed in a crisp white suit; she untied her suit jacket to expose the cleavage of her corset top.

She sighed and folded her arms. "Do you have any idea how disappointed I am in you, Lilith? Is this how I raised you?"

"No, mother. I am sorry," I stated, trying not to sound weak. The last thing I wanted was to further piss my mother off.

She pulled out the bag Alexandria had purchased for me and threw it on the desk.

"This is bullshit." She unlocked her top drawer and pulled out another bag of marijuana. I had never seen anything like it. It was bright green with red hairs and white crystals all over it. I could smell its potency from where I was sitting.

"After everything I have ever given you. It has always been nothing but the fucking best money could buy." She shook her head in disgust. "I don't know what came over me, Lilith, but I decided that I wanted to scope out your room. To my surprise, I find that my daughter smokes weed; not only that but she has her own bag, and it's fucking bottom grade hash."

She grabbed both bags, one in each hand.

"This," she stated, moving her right hand, "is garbage. It's what homeless people smoke, lower income individuals, people who live off the fucking government. How do you live, Lilith? Huh?"

"Now, this," she stated, moving her left hand, "is top quality, medical grade marijuana. This is what people who live like you do, darling, smoke."

She threw my bag in the garbage, opened her bag and started to roll a joint. I had seen Alexandria do it many times before.

"If you're going to do something, Lilith, then do it fucking right the first time. Don't ever let me find anything but the goddamn best anywhere near your pretty little face again. Do I make myself clear?" she questioned.

I nodded. I couldn't say a word. You would think that this should shock me. In reality it didn't. My mother was not your average PTA parent, as you can see. If I was going to do anything, then it needed to be the best. Period. She finished rolling the joint, bit off the end, and lit it up. She took three hits and handed it to me.

"Take it and hit it," she instructed, waiting for me to do the same.

"Hold it in for as long as you can," she demanded, and I did until my lungs burned and I couldn't hold it in anymore, which made me cough for a minute straight. I heard my mother laugh.

"Do it again," she insisted in a lighter tone than before. I smoked half the joint before I passed it back to my mother. She hit it a few more times and put it out.

"How do you feel?"

"Fucked up," I replied without thinking, making my mother laugh.

"Mother-daughter bonding at its best," she added, comically laughing.

We spent the next few hours talking, laughing, and eating. It was one of the most memorable times I had with her. But this was just the beginning.

✳VIP✳

After that night, my mother allowed me to come to some of her smaller parties at the house. At first, she watched me like a hawk, but after the first few times I didn't see her as often. It was difficult to be the center of attention when my mother was around. She always owned the room wherever we were. I found myself getting bored and I would retreat to our boat dock to watch the yachts go by.

"What's a pretty little thing like you doing back here by herself?" a deep, dark, sexy voice said from behind me.

I turned to find an older, attractive man. He was dressed in a suit, similar to what I had always seen my father wear. His hair was blonde and combed back in a slick style, with bright green eyes, and a narrow jaw line. He had both hands in his suit jacket and he was leaning on the railing with his legs crossed. He looked ready to attack and I jumped on the opportunity. You can't really blame me, I was never around men my own age, and I had somewhat of a daddy complex.

"What's your name?" he questioned with his head cocked to the side and a shit-eating grin on his face.

And…this is where shit hit the fan in my brain. He had no fucking idea that I was Madam's daughter. I jumped on the opportunity like a fish does to water.

I stood up and walked toward him. "Veronica," I replied, using my middle name as I extended my hand to shake his. I was wearing four-inch heels and I came up to his chin, he must have been 6'4.

"Julian," he responded as we shook hands.

"To answer your question, I was admiring the view," I said, trying to sound confident.

"As was I." He grinned.

I batted my eyelashes and grinned right back. Julian and I talked about meaningless things as we watched the endless ocean, flirting and laughing until it was well past one in the morning. I knew my mother would come looking for me soon and I did not want her to catch me with Julian.

"It's getting late, I have to go," I stated, getting up as he grabbed my hand to stop me.

"I'll take you wherever you need to go."

I smiled. "I don't need a chaperone."

"How about a companion?" I could almost pick up a hint of desperation in his question that lit my insides on fire.

"Companion, hmmm, I might like that. I'll see you around, Julian." I gave him my best seductive smile and walked away with sway in my step.

❊VIP❊

A part of me always knew that my mother ran a risky business. I knew that beautiful women belonged to not only The Cathouse, but also my mother. I guess I even knew sex was involved somehow. I lived in the same house, saw beautiful women enter rooms with my mother. I had to be pretty naïve not to know. I didn't really know the extent of my mother's business until one afternoon when my mother took a call during lunch.

I listened attentively as she set up an appointment for a male physical with Dr. Casler, whom, I'd also come to know over the years.

"Why would you be making a doctor's appointment for a client, Mother?" I curiously asked.

She looked up from the paperwork in front of her with a raised eyebrow, "My my, Lilith, what big ears you have?"

"Just curious," I responded boldly, showing her no fear.

She removed the paperwork from her desk and replaced it with the VIP book that I had snooped through years ago.

"I've been meaning to have this conversation with you. I just hadn't figured out the right time to do so. No time like the present." She hit the intercom button on her phone, "Madelyn, I am not to be interrupted for the rest of the afternoon. Have Philippe bring the 1961 Chateau Palmer Margaux. Thank you."

She sighed and looked at me. "Darling, you have no idea how long I have waited to have this talk. From the moment you were born, you were meant for greater things, things that the average person will never be able to achieve. A lifestyle made only for a VIP."

"How do you think you live like this? What do you think I do? Let's start there," she suggested.

"I'm not-"

"Bullshit," she interrupted me. "Lilith, have I ever taken my eyes off you? Do you honestly think that you can do anything in this home and I not see it? I have eyes everywhere, darling. For example, look behind you, Lilith," she instructed with a point of her finger. I turned to see a framed picture of a man and a woman.

"Do you see that painting? I know you do. That painting has a hidden camera. I have cameras all over the house. I don't have one in your room, but that doesn't mean for one goddamn second that I don't know what you do in there. Now…let's try this again, shall we?" she questioned, again pausing. "What do you think I do?"

I licked my lips in nervousness. My mother had seen everything throughout the years, and I had no fucking clue. I fought the urge to pick through my memories for the things she could have caught me doing, but knew I didn't have enough time for that. She asked a question and needed an answer.

"I know it has something to do with VIP. I don't know what it means, but I know that you're called Madam. You only have women that work for you or with you. I know that it involves sex and stuff."

"Mmm hmm…and what exactly do you know about sex and stuff, Lilith?"

"I know that it's supposed to be intimate and with a man and a woman who love each other." I responded with the best answer I had; it wasn't like we'd ever had the birds and bees talk.

"Mmm hmm…and what if they don't? Huh? What if they just want to fuck? Is that not all right? Tell me the rules here."

"Mother, I-" I started to say, unsure of how to respond.

"Enough," she reprimanded as she handed me the glass of wine that Philippe had poured. I took it without hesitation, needing something to do with my hands while we had this vexatious conversation.

"You are nervous, Lilith. Why? I'm your mother. There is no need for fear here. I want you to just listen. I'll do the talking, all right?" I nodded; thankful I could just sit back and listen without having to answer any more of her disturbing questions.

"Lilith, what I do sets me apart from the rest of the world. I have the liberty to do something that makes a difference in people's lives. I provide a service for those who need and want it. In return, I get the luxury of living a life most people only dream of." She smiled tenuously as she sensed my confusion.

"VIP stands for Very Important Pussy. You do know what pussy means, right?" she asked me.

"Yes." I felt the unfamiliar blush on my cheeks.

"Lovely. Say it," she nonchalantly demanded.

"Excuse me?"

"Say the word pussy," she repeated, this time with more authority.

I swallowed the saliva that had formed in my mouth. "Pussy."

She grinned. "Do you see how easy it rolls off the tongue? It was meant to. Pussy should be a word that is celebrated! It could have several meanings, but the bottom line is, pussy is meant to be shared. Sharing is caring, darling," she explained.

"I own VIP, which means, I own pussy. Since I own it, I cherish it, I take care of it, and I provide for it. VIP is a multibillion-dollar organization that is run by me and only me. Before it landed in my hands, it was owned by your ancestors, all of who were women. This mansion, it's The Cathouse; it's the headquarters of where everything gets started. Questions?"

"What does any of it have to do with me?" I asked.

"It has absolutely everything to do with you. I am going to make you a VIP...once I feel that you're ready, of course. It's illegal before the age of eighteen to have consensual sex with an adult, but...a lot happens behind closed doors. I made you, therefore I get to get to decide what's appropriate, not the state of Florida," she professed as she sipped her glass.

"Do you mean, like prostitution?"

"Child, do I look like the type of woman that could be a pimp? My girls are treated for what they are, very important pussies. They have the best of the best, sleep with only the best, and have total control, to a certain extent that is. I of course have to have the final say. These girls are paid thousands upon thousands for an hour of their time. You'll never see one of them giving a hand job in the back of a car or standing on some street corner waiting for someone to choose them.

"Men...and women, pay immense money for their time. You'll learn, Lilith, you'll soon find out that the pussy between your legs is golden," she stated, pointing to in between my legs. "You'll learn to use it to your advantage."

"You want me to sell myself?" I asked in shock.

My mother laughed. "Say it, Lilith."

"Say what?" I asked in confusion.

"Say pussy. You can say it, use it freely, embrace it and the fact that your little pussy is going to make you a very happy girl," she clarified.

"What do you mean?"

"Lilith, my dear. Don't play coy with me. It's in your blood, it's who you are, it's what you were made for. I don't have to watch to know that you've played with your own pussy. It's an ache, a calling, a motherfucking throbbing need for you to want to pleasure yourself; it's what you are bred for. I know you know how good it feels. You have no idea what you're in for or how good a man, or even a woman, can make your pussy feel." When I felt my cheeks burn, flaming with embarrassment, she yelled, "LOOK UP!"

I was startled but she continued. "Don't you ever turn away from me when I am talking to you. You have nothing to be ashamed of. You're beautiful. You have a beautiful pussy and I'm going to teach you how to use it. Are we clear?"

"Yes, ma'am," I replied, trying to find my inner strength.

"Are you scared, Lilith? Are you hearing that voice in the back of your mind? It's telling you all sorts of things. Well, that voice, it's not your conscience; it's fear. Don't ever let that voice be heard. Do. You. Understand. Me." I nodded in silent agreement.

She smiled. "Great! Question portion can begin; I know you have them. Let's hear them."

I had absolutely no idea where to even begin. My head was spinning with the revelations of what my mother had disclosed. I felt anxious, nervous, intimidated, but most of all, I felt liberated. I had always felt different, and it wasn't from my upbringing. It was from something inside of me, a feeling, a presence.

My interests, motivations, and aspirations from the time I was child always led back to sex. I dreamt about it, and pleasured myself to something I had no idea about. It was just an ache. I had hundreds of questions for my mother, and I knew she would have answered them.

I didn't want to ask…I didn't want her to tell me….

I don't ask questions, I make my own answers.

The Madam

I wanted to feel it.
I wanted to experience it.
I wanted to learn it all on my own terms.
I didn't want to wait.
I wanted to be a VIP now.

CHAPTER 5

In the weeks that followed, my mother began molding me into a VIP. Of course, I was still only sixteen, but it started innocently enough. My daily wardrobe changed, my heels got higher, and my dresses and skirts shorter. I had everything below my eyebrows waxed, and a new colorful drawer full of lingerie. My mother called it baby steps.

I followed all her directions and guidelines. Little did she know I had my own agenda. She planted the seed and I was going to water it and watch it grow. I had to take matters into my own hands, literally. I waited till my mother was out of town to execute the first part of a very thought out plan. It took me a while to find a place where they sold such toys, but never underestimate the power of a curious woman.

As soon as I had everything, I went back home, had myself some champagne, and went up to my room. I made sure to wait until all the staff had left or was asleep to make sure that I wouldn't be disrupted. I wanted complete privacy for what I was about to do.

The apple doesn't fall far from the tree. I wanted complete control over myself and everything around me; remind you of someone?

I went to my new lingerie drawer and grabbed a white silk teddy, a virgin was being sacrificed, by little ole me. I felt sexy and sensual when I had it on and understood why women buy lingerie, it's never for the man, it's for them.

I pulled out my new friend, The Legendary Silver Magic Wand, and proceeded to my bed.

Go big or go home right?

I made sure to put a towel down first, Alexandria had told me what happens when your cherry breaks.

I poured some lubricant on my index and middle finger and massaged it on my clit and entrance. I wasn't a fucking stupid girl; I was going to get myself in the mood first before I took my own virginity.

I started feeling around my body, beginning with my neck and then my breasts. I cupped the sides and moved to tease my nipples. I pulled and kneaded them, my right hand moved toward my inner thigh until I made my way to the lips of my pussy. I gently stimulated around my clit, rubbing my slippery fingers around the bundle of nerves that were becoming heightened and sensitive. I massaged it slowly, gradually building up the intensity of my touch. I could feel my heartbeat getting faster, and my pussy becoming wet.

I focused on nothing except what my hand was doing. I touched my clit harder but not too firm; with my other hand, I teased my opening. I slowly pushed in two fingers, never letting up on my clit. At first, it was awkward and uncomfortable, but after a few minutes of my fingers pushing in and out, it started to feel better. My breathing became elevated, and my body started to shake. I finger fucked myself until I couldn't take it anymore and grabbed the silver wand and eased it into my opening.

I stretched myself inch by inch until I felt the barrier.

I took a deep breath and shoved it in.

�֍VIP�֍

Now that I had my pesky virginity out of the way, the next part of my plan could go into effect. "The Madam" was throwing a Halloween party.

"Lilith, I don't want to hear any more. You're staying at the condo for the evening. Maybe when you're seventeen I will allow you to observe a party, however, right now is not the right time. The driver will take you wherever you want, darling. I even bought you a bag of Blueberry Kush, it's all for you. Smoke till your heart is content. I'll see you tomorrow. Goodnight." She kissed my forehead and left my bedroom.

I played nice, packed my bag, and went to the condo. I waited till it was midnight before I took a cab, dressed like a white sexy kitten. I thought it seemed fitting. I had on white lace panties and a matching bra, thigh high stockings, and fuck me heels. I had a mask to cover my eyes, and I added ears and a tail. If my mother had seen me she would have been proud. I'm sure of it.

Once I made it back to The Cathouse, it was fairly easy to go unnoticed. There were hundreds of people everywhere. It took me a while to find exactly what I was looking for, or should I say who. I didn't know he would be here, but I took a chance.

He was dressed as a devil and I took it as a sign. I blew him a kiss, made a finger gesture to follow me, and placed my index finger on my lips in a shhh motion before walking away. I could sense that he was following me; I didn't have to turn to know that he was there. I walked us back to my mother's sixty-foot Hatteras yacht. I had stolen the keys earlier and I knew for a fact she wouldn't find us there.

I let us both inside and made sure to lock the slider behind me.

I seductively walked over to the dining room table; it was the showpiece to the room. Making sure that he had a clear view of what I was doing, I crawled to the center of the table, turned to face him, spread my legs, and meowed.

I saw him take a deep breath, while his eyes roamed my entire body.

He lifted an eyebrow. "My, what a pretty pussy you are," Julian huskily praised. I purred in response.

"Is this how we are going to play it, Veronica?"

I meowed again.

He shook his head and laughed. "This is the second time that I have seen you. Madam hasn't had the pleasure of introducing you to me yet. Are you a VIP?"

"In training," I responded teasingly.

"Oh! The pussy finally speaks, and I didn't even have to pet it yet."

I smirked. "Would you like to make it come?"

I knew I had him when the corner of his lips turned upward. "How old are you?" He may have well been asking my breasts since that's where he planted his gawking eyes.

"Just turned eighteen," I replied.

Fuck it. I lied. Don't judge me, like you've never lied about your age before...

"How old are you?" I didn't really care since he looked old enough, but figured I'd ask anyway.

"Thirty three," he retorted. Like I said before, I had a daddy complex. Why would I want my first fuck to be with a seventeen-year-old boy that barely knew how to hold his own cock, let alone please a woman, when I could have sex with a man and know that he would get the job done, the first time. I didn't want the pathetic, cliché, PG-13 version. I wanted the NC-17, mature audiences only, no one under the age of eighteen prohibited version.

"I don't want to talk anymore, Julian."

"There's a monetary conversation that needs to be had between Madam and I. I don't want to break the rules. Madam doesn't like that," he declared.

"Fuck Madam, and just fuck me," I insisted.

"You have a mighty big mouth for such a little thing."

This is the exact moment that my life changed.

It wasn't my mother's talk, it wasn't her plans, and it wasn't my future.

It was that moment that changed it all for me.

He pulled out a stack of bills and placed it at the end of the table.

"How about I just pay you?" he suggested. I wasn't about to say no; he wouldn't be getting this for free. I didn't know how much sex cost, but I knew I was worth a lot.

I had never seen so much money before, it was thousand dollar bills, one right after the other, and it was that instant that I fell in love with the almighty dollar.

"Take off your bra and panties, everything else stays on," he ordered in a sexy, demanding tone that made me tingle in all the right places.

I provocatively removed my bra, making sure that each strap fell slowly off my shoulders as I licked my lips and reached around to remove it from my breasts. My pink nipples were at attention immediately. I cupped my breasts and moaned. I grazed my hands down to the edge of my panties and bit my lower lip as I removed them slowly, inch by inch, until I was left in nothing but thigh highs, and fuck me heels.

All of this came naturally to me. It just further established in my mind that this is what I was made for. This was my destiny and I wanted each and every single part of it.

I reached to remove my mask and ears but was stopped by his husky male voice. "Leave them on, spread your legs wider kitten; I want to see that pretty pink cunt." I spread my legs as wide as they would go, giving him full access to my most sacred area.

He unbuttoned his shirt and left it hanging open, his abs were hard and extended all the way down to his V shaped torso. He pulled off his belt and snapped it on the table, bringing my attention back to his face.

"Have you been a bad pussy, kitten?" he goaded. I grinned and nodded.

He unbuttoned his slacks and pulled out his big, hard, thick cock. I had never seen a dick in person before, but for some reason, I knew they all didn't look like that. I panicked for a second thinking he was going to rip me open, The Wand was nowhere near his size.

"Come here and get on your knees;" he urged me into submission.

I looked at him through lust filled eyes, I wanted him, and I wanted him bad. I made my way to him and he roughly grabbed the back of my hair as I moaned loudly. My spine shivered from the anticipation of having him in my mouth, which sent a quiver all the way to my pussy. I could feel myself getting wetter.

"Take my cock to the back of your throat. I'm going to fuck your face." Before I could give it a second thought, he shoved his cock into my mouth and I gagged at the sensation. He groaned in response and started to move in and out of my mouth. I didn't do any of the work, just kept my mouth open as he used my hair to guide himself in and out.

They say giving a blowjob is all for the man, well I beg to fucking differ. Having a cock in your mouth is one of the most dominant, in control acts that can leave you feeling extremely empowered.

After a few times, I got used to the response that his cock had in my mouth. I tried to make it tighter for him and I could taste his salty flavor that came off the head of his cock.

"Use your hand and glide it up and down my shaft, and play with my balls," he instructed in a domineering tone. I wrapped my hand around his cock and followed the same momentum and pace as my mouth; my other hand tugged and massaged his balls. His dick got even larger and I could feel a vain throbbing above his shaft.

"I'm going to come. I'm going to come so hard. Swallow all of it. Not one drop comes out of your mouth." The tone in his voice had me weak in the knees I was beyond turned on. The smell and masculinity of his arousal drove me insane. I moaned in the anticipation of what was to come. He dove in one last time and a warm, thick, saltier taste exploded in my mouth, his dick pulsed until I had swallowed every drop that I could milk out of his cock.

He pulled out and I wiped my mouth with my hand. Not realizing how much saliva and come had accumulated there. To my surprise, he picked me up from my waist and sat me on the edge of the table.

"That was fucking amazing," he whispered in my ear, trailing kisses on my neck to the side of my mouth. He jerked my head back by pulling my hair and kissed me with much more intensity and passion than that night with Alexandria. Kissing a man was much different than kissing a woman. It was powerful, demanding, and rough.

When I felt his tongue in my mouth, I tasted the scotch, peppermint, and come that still lingered. He kissed me like he had something to prove. I kissed him back with all the passion I could conjure, but all I kept thinking about was the ache that so badly needed relief.

"I want to taste you. I'm going to make you come all over my face," he declared as he moved to lie on the table. "Sit on my face."

I had no fucking idea what I was supposed to do. He must have sensed my confusion because he grabbed my hand and led me to where he wanted me. To my surprise, he actually wanted me to sit on his face.

I eased my way down till I felt his warm, wet, soft tongue at my opening and I whimpered in excitement. He pushed his tongue as far as it would go and my back arched and head fell backward. His tongue glided its way to the top of my pussy and he circled my clit.

"Oh my God, Julian," I half pleaded, half moaned. I thought I was going to pass out from the desire. When I felt him suck on my clit, my hips took to their own accord and slowly moved forward and backward.

"Please don't stop, please keep doing that," I shamelessly begged.

He reached up and cupped my breasts, rubbing and teasing my nipples. I couldn't take it anymore. He hummed and moved his head up, down, and side-to-side. Once he grabbed my hips to move them quicker and more forceful, I started to shake, and my vision began to blur, it got really hot, and I couldn't help the noises that were coming out of my mouth. I finally felt myself come apart, and I came so hard that I fell forward and had to grab the table to support myself.

He removed himself from under me and immediately shoved his tongue in my mouth. I had never tasted myself before, and the taste of myself, of each other, made me grow even wetter. We kissed, devouring each other's mouths, trying to capture every feeling, every taste that lingered between us. It was erotic and mind blowing.

He was on top of me within seconds and I could feel his cock at my entrance. I didn't have time to think about anything, I was too caught up in the moment.

He thrust all the way in on one push and I silently screamed in my head. The years of conditioning to not show weakness from my mother paid off. He instantly stopped and hid his head in the nook of my neck. I panted in and out trying to diffuse the pain with my breathing. It burned; I had literally just been ripped open.

He didn't move for the first few seconds, I moaned, and it was then that he started to move. I bit my lower lip trying to hold in the tears and throbbing, I was lucky his face stayed in my neck, and he didn't see the distress written all over my face. I played my part amazingly, if I do say so myself. I could have won a goddamn Academy Award. This was completely different than what I had done to myself. He wasn't gentle or easy, he fucked me with raw passion.

After the first few minutes, the pain was replaced with mild comfort. His hand reached down and grabbed the back of my thigh, it moved my angle and the first time he thrust back in, my back arched and I moaned for real.

"Holy fuck, you're the tightest thing I have ever felt. Does that feel good?" he groaned with desire lacing his masculine voice.

"Mmm hmm," I mumbled erotically.

"Move with me. Move your hips as I thrust in and out…fuck yes, like that. Ride my cock, yes…just like that."

We moved together, I rotated my hips in when he would thrust in, and slowly the feeling of wanting to pee subsided. It felt warm, like something was building in my lower abdomen.

"Jesus…your pussy is like a vice. I didn't think it could get any tighter. I can feel you about to come, kitten. You've got to relax, just feel, I'm going to go faster and harder, and you're going to come on my cock," he huskily demanded.

He proceeded to do exactly what he just described and I couldn't control it anymore. The second he eased out, my walls contracted, my back arched off the table, my mouth fell open, and my eyes rolled to the back of my head.

"Agh...yes...yes...fuck..." he exclaimed, just as I felt his cock pulse deep within my core. A wave of tingles flowed from the center of my body out to the tips of my hands, my feet, and even lips. I felt total relaxation and weightlessness. I could feel my pussy throbbing from the aftershocks and it made me chuckle.

He kissed my mouth one last time before we both went our separate ways; the only difference was, I was $20,000 richer.

CHAPTER 6

This may be the only cliché thing I have ever done in my life, but when I got back to the condo that night, I went straight for the mirror. I wanted to see if I looked different, older. I checked every crevice of my body and although I didn't look any different, I felt unbelievable. It was as if I was born again, like I was a butterfly that was finally out of its cocoon. I never wanted this feeling to go away, I wanted to bottle it up, and hold onto it forever.

The months that followed were uneventful, or so I thought. My mother had suggested that it was time that I go on birth control and the pill was just being introduced to modern day American life. The doctor came to The Cathouse like they always had. I hadn't met this doctor before, though I had heard the name, Dr. Casler.

Dr. Casler performed specific procedures and my mother took a phone call when he started to ask me questions.

"Are you sexually active?" he questioned, not looking up from his chart.

"No," I responded, keeping my eyes on my magazine.

"Have you ever been sexually active?"

"No." I felt him look up from his chart, he knew I was lying and I didn't have the nerve to look at him in his face.

He sighed. "What was the date of your last period?"

"Ummm…like three weeks ago."

"Anything seem abnormal?"

"Not really…they've been lighter than usual."

"How long have the lighter ones lasted?"

"A day or two, I didn't keep track," I responded, flipping through my magazine.

"All right, Lilith," he said as he handed me a cup. "Take this cup into the bathroom, and I want you to pee in it. Bring it back to me when you're done."

I cocked my head to the side. "Why?"

"It's a necessary precaution before I can give you the prescription. Go on," he insisted.

I handed the cup back to him when I was finished and my mother walked in just as I was sitting back down on the couch.

"We are almost through here, Madam. I'll need a few more minutes."

"Thank you, James."

We waited until Dr. Casler came back into the room. I will never forget the look on his face. He looked concerned, but most of all, he looked scared as fuck; for whom I didn't know, but I would soon find out.

"Madam, I need to talk to you. In private please," he announced without looking at me.

"James, I don't have time for this. What's going on?" she demanded, showing her lack of patience. I stood up from the couch trying to walk over to them but my mother raised her hand in a stopping motion.

He looked at me, then once again at my mother, pulled a stick out of his lab coat and handed it to her.

My mother's face turned white as a ghost, and before I could even interpret what was going on, she rushed over to me and backhanded me right across the left side of my face. I felt her knuckles pound into my cheekbone. My entire body flew to the ground. I didn't have time to acknowledge the pain before she came at me again. She slapped me across the face again and this time I saw stars.

She grabbed the lapels of my blouse and jerked me forward. "Get the fuck up before I fucking kill you." My face was on fire and my body was going into shock from the pain and nerves.

"If you so much as shed one fucking tear, Lilith…" she threatened as she roughly let go of my blouse to stand up.

Dr. Casler reached out his hand to help me up and my mother shoved it away.

"Mind your own fucking business, James, and get the fuck out. Lilith, get your ass off the floor before I really make you sorry."

"Madam, there are things that need to be discussed before I can ethically leave."

"There is nothing that needs to be discussed, James. She's having an abortion, END OF FUCKING DISCUSSION!" my mother violently yelled.

"It's too late, Madam, by my calculations and her responses, she's probably around three months. No one will perform an abortion; she's too far along. If you find someone to perform one at this stage, she could die. It's too complicated," he calmly explained.

My mother ran her fingers through her hair in a frustrated gesture. "So what you're telling me is, my sixteen-year-old daughter got knocked up and now it can't even be taken care of? Am I hearing this correctly, James?" He hesitantly nodded.

"FUCK!" she shouted.

She looked over at me with disgust. "Lilith, if I have to tell you one more fucking time to get your ass off the floor, I will personally escort you off; and trust me. You. Do. Not. Want. That. To. Happen," she roared.

I grabbed whatever big girl panties I had left and picked myself up off the ground. I could feel my left eye starting to shut and I focused on trying to keep it open. My whole world came crashing down on me in less than five minutes. The feelings of being empowered, a woman, a VIP, slowly left my mind. I felt like a child. I was a fucking stupid naïve child. Not once did I think about protection or pregnancy. It hadn't even crossed my mind.

I was pregnant and I had no idea what to even think. I felt empty, alone, and utterly fucking confused. I couldn't be a mother, I was sixteen, and I couldn't get rid of it, what other options were left? All I wanted to do was breakdown. I knew better than to allow it, the mere thought of it would have my mother beating the fuck out of me, again.

I did the only thing I was conditioned to do, I held it all in.

"Go get yourself cleaned up, Lilith; James, follow me."

What happened next, I still remember as if it were yesterday. I spent as much time as I could changing my clothes before making my way into the bathroom. I turned the faucet on, avoiding looking at myself in the mirror. I soaked my washcloth, took a deep breath, and finally looked up. I had no idea who was staring back at me. My eye was almost swollen shut, it had already started turning purple and blue, and there was a cut on my cheekbone, probably from one of my mother's rings.

I brought the washcloth up to my bruise and I yelped in pain. I couldn't regulate the tears that uncontrollably came down my face. I threw the washcloth across the bathroom and unconsciously put my hands on my stomach. There was a person inside of me. I couldn't fathom how I could have let it happen. I felt weak and out of control. I once again looked at my reflection, and it further ingrained how weak I was, how weak I looked. I wanted it all to go away, I needed to be in control, I raised my fist and punched the mirror as hard as I could. It shattered all around my fist; I cocked my head to the side, watching the blood drip off my knuckles.

I don't know how long I stood there wallowing in my own self-pity.

All I know is that my life had changed forever, with or without my consent.

❊VIP❊

I didn't see my mother for the next few days. I know she was avoiding me; there was no doubt in my mind that she really wanted to kill me. I still wasn't truly convinced that she wouldn't try…after the third day of her being MIA, she made her appearance as I was eating breakfast.

She looked right at me. "Have you been icing your eye? And applying cream on that cut? I don't want it to scar," she questioned without looking away from me.

"Yes," I whispered.

"Madelyn said she cleaned up glass from your bathroom. How did that feel on your knuckles? From the looks of it you did quite a number on them."

"I'm fine."

"Finish your breakfast and meet me in my office. You have fifteen minutes." And with that, she was gone.

Ten minutes later and I was knocking on her door.

"Come in," I heard her say. I walked in and she was leaning against her desk, arms and legs crossed. My mother looked extra intimidating that day.

"What a pleasure you could finally join us," she announced.

"Us?" I cautiously responded.

"Oh yes." She nodded while looking behind me.

I turned to find Julian sitting on the couch, leaned forward with his head in between his hands.

My jaw dropped and I had no words.

"I'm to assume you have been properly introduced...Veronica?" she facetiously asked.

"The Madam" was not only going to beat the shit out of me, she was going to embarrass the fuck out of me too. Which was a far greater punishment than her putting her hands on me.

"You know, I kept wondering why a client of mine would keep calling to ask for another date with a Veronica. Who the fuck is Veronica, I thought to myself. Then, when your bastard decided to make its presence known, it all clicked. Your baby's daddy is looking at mandatory jail time for knocking up a minor, darling," she revealed with a giddy smile.

"The Madam" was enjoying each and every part of my humiliation. She was getting off on the power and control, as well as scaring the shit out of Julian.

"Please, the expectant mother should have a seat. I wouldn't want anything to happen to my grandchild."

"That's fucking enough, Madam!" Julian shouted, getting up off the couch.

"You know as well as I do that I am not serving jail time. Your precious VIP organization would be held responsible, because I will sing like a motherfucking cannery if you so much as try to put this on me. The stories I have would put VIP in ruins. She's a child. What the hell did you expect would happen? I'm held responsible for this, not her. I was high as a fucking kite that night. I barely remember any of it," he responded, putting my mother in her place.

I knew he was doing it for my benefit, but I didn't think it was possible for my dignity and heart to break any more than it already had.

My mother cracked her neck and moved to grab a file off her desk.

"I made some calls. There's a place in Vermont that will take her for the duration of her pregnancy. It's a five star resort for expectant teen mothers that are high profile. No one will find out, and the second she delivers, the child goes up for adoption. I need you to sign off on this form before I can proceed." she handed him a file.

"It's a confidentiality agreement. You agree to not speak a word of this and to sign off all rights to the child." He nodded and immediately signed the last page of the document. He threw the file on the table and acknowledged me for the first time.

"Oh, and by the way, you're no longer a client of VIP. Now get the fuck out." He didn't address my mother's malicious words or even look at back her. He walked over to me and grabbed my chin to make me look at his eyes.

"You will understand this one day, kitten, I am so sorry." He kissed the tip of my nose and left.

And I never saw him again…

CHAPTER 7

In the weeks that followed, my mother made preparations for my "mini vacation" as she called it. I started to experience pregnancy symptoms and to this day have no idea why women consensually put themselves through that. I loathed being pregnant, all I wanted to do was get high or drunk and I couldn't do that either.

I was in an auto pilot state of mind.

"This will be over before you know it, darling. Then you will return home good as new, and we can move forward toward your destiny. This is just a speed bump in the road." She pulled me into a tight embrace.

"Will I see you while I'm there?" I asked, burying my face in her neck.

"Of course, I will come see you as often as I can. I will also be there for the delivery. This will be done and over with before you know it, Lilith, I promise," she said.

She pulled away, grabbed my face, kissed my forehead, told me she loved me, and sent me on my way.

My mother wasn't lying when she said The Oasis was a five-star resort, it was the Betty Ford Clinic for expectant teenage mothers. I made friends with some of the girls, but I mostly kept to myself. My mother sent me all sorts of books to keep me entertained and my pregnancy wasn't bad, just the typical symptoms; at least that's what the doctors kept telling me.

I turned seventeen when I was five months pregnant. I spent it alone; my mother sent me a gift basket and a card, stating she had to leave the country, and that she would make it up to me on my eighteenth birthday. I only saw my mother three times while I was there, each time she didn't stay long, and all she talked about were the plans for the future. I tuned her out half of the time, I didn't know if it was pregnancy hormones, or the fact that I was a fucking teenager, but I couldn't stand to be around my mother. Let me rephrase that…I couldn't stand to be around anyone.

I was fucking miserable. My pregnancy might have been good to me, but I got fat, my back hurt all the time, I couldn't see my feet, and any food that smelled like grease made me nauseous.

Now, here is where you need to pay close attention to my story. On September 9, 1977, I went to bed with horrible back pain, I didn't sleep an ounce that night and when morning came, I was screaming in pain. The nurses came rushing to my aid.

"Shit…she's bleeding. I think she's going into labor. Get the doctor STAT, we need to move her into the delivery room," the nurse demanded.

"Labor? I'm not due for another six weeks. What's going on?"

"She's a minor we need to get her mother here immediately," she said, ignoring my question.

"What the fuck? Answer me! What is going on?" I yelled.

"Honey, it's all right. Everything is going to be all right, just trust us to do our jobs. We are going to take you into the delivery room; the baby is coming. But we have it under control. What is your pain level from 1-10, 10 being the worst."

"Ahh! I don't know? A fucking 12!"

They moved me onto a stretcher and rushed me into the delivery room.

It felt as though hours had gone by. "I need fucking drugs! Get me the fucking drugs. What the fuck are you waiting for?"

"Honey, calm down," the nurse said, grabbing my hand.

"You calm the fuck down, is there a baby trying to coming out of your pussy right now? Go fuck yourself and get me the drugs! Oh my God I need drugs… please…"

"You're too far along. We can't give you anything." She brought a cold washcloth to my forehead.

My head jerked back and hit the pillow. "Ahhh! Then what the fuck are you good for? It hurts so bad…it hurts so fucking bad…"

I hadn't realized the almighty doctor had finally showed up until I felt his hands go up my vagina.

"She's 9.5 centimeters dilated," he announced to the room. "You need to start pushing. I need you to push hard."

I started to push and I felt like I was being ripped open, which I was.

"Ahhh! I can't push...just have the baby stay in my belly. I don't care...I don't care..." I yelled.

"Lilith, I need you to push. You can do this, you need to push," he urged.

The nurse held my hand the entire time; I leaned forward and pushed with everything I had.

"Fuck. The baby is pushing the placenta out and it's in pieces, it's ripped. She's losing a lot of blood." He told the nurses, "Check her vitals. Okay, Lilith, keep pushing. You can't stop pushing, we need to get this baby out quickly, understand?"

I started to feel dizzy and the room started spinning.

"The placenta is out; I see the baby's head. Stay with us, Lilith, you need to have one last final push," the doctor coached.

I pushed one last time and I heard a baby whimper.

"It's a girl. You have a girl," the nurse said.

"Wait, where are you taking her? I want to see her! I want to see her!" I begged.

I started to shake and it was the last thing I remember before I passed the fuck out.

❖VIP❖

My eyes began to flutter and I saw my mother's profile with the doctor facing her. The doctor said something and she turned to look at me. She said one more thing to the doctor and came over to me. I noticed it immediately, her face was flushed and her make-up was smeared. I know she would deny it till the day she died, but my mother had been crying.

"How do you feel, darling?" she asked, grabbing my hand and kissing it.

"Sore and groggy," I whispered with a dry mouth. She grabbed the cup of water and brought the straw to my lips. I drank the entire thing.

"Where's the baby?" It was my very first question.

"It's being taken care of," she said, placing the cup on the counter and grabbing my hand again.

"I want to see her."

She shook her head no. "That's not a good idea."

"Mother....please. I want to see her."

She sighed. I could see her battling something internal.

"All right," she conceded.

They brought over a wheelchair and we made our way to the ICU unit.

I saw the tiniest baby I had ever seen in my life. She was on all these machines that looked painful, but she was sleeping.

"Is she going to be okay?"

"She's in the best hands possible. She will be fine," she calmly stated.

I have no idea what happened next, but my emotions got the best of me, and I broke down crying. I didn't care that "The Madam" was standing next to me. I felt my mother's hand on my back, soothing and comforting me. I cried for what felt like hours, when finally my mother crouched down in front of me and grabbed the sides of my face.

"Listen to me; I will only say this once. Lilith Veronica Stone, none of this is your fault. The baby will be fine and she will be adopted into a family that will love and cherish her. You were meant for greater things. Children are not in your future."

"What?" I sobbed.

"They had to perform a hysterectomy and remove your uterus, there was too much damage and bleeding. It was the only way you would survive. They did what they had to do to save you," she explained and I immediately bawled my eyes out.

She placed her forehead on mine. "Do not let this be the end of you. Do you understand me?" she whispered.

I nodded and let my tears flow. My mother permitted me to cry that day. She held me the entire day and comforted me the only way she knew how.

I cried for everything…

For my past…

For my present…

And most of all.

For my future…

❋VIP❋

Two weeks later and we were on a private plane ride home. My mother insisted that I stay until I was 110% better. Physically I was fine; emotionally I was a hot mess. The doctors said it was perfectly normal to be hormonal and it would be a few months before it would go away. I did the best I could with holding it all in. My mother would permit weakness once, but never twice; she didn't have to tell me to know that.

After three months, my hormonal imbalance had not changed, although, the painkillers helped. "The Madam" had requested my presence in her office; I took two painkillers before knocking on her door.

"Lilith, I have a treat for you. Would you like to see it?" she goaded.

"Sure," I replied. She pulled out a mock invitation for my eighteenth birthday.

"The newest member of VIP, Lilith Veronica Stone" read the first line.

"Coming out eighteenth birthday party" was the second.

"It's nice mother," I replied, faking a smile.

She roughly grabbed the invitation from my hands and ripped it in half.

"This," She stated, pointing at me with her index finger and roared, "is fucking over."

"I think I have permitted this to go on long enough, don't you think, Lilith?"

"I have no idea what you're talking about."

She cocked her head to the side. "Oh really…lie to me one more time, Lilith, and see what happens," she threatened in a mocking tone.

"What are you going to do, Madam? Sell my first born…" I retorted; see, I had lost my shit.

She laughed, "Wow, Lilith…those painkillers make you all big and bad, honey. Maybe I should get you a permanent prescription. But first, we should probably try to remove the stick that has been placed in your ass for the last three months," she teased.

"You want to go toe to toe with me, Lilith, then bring it the fuck on. Say what you want to say."

"All right, I'm going to be eighteen and a VIP soon. I want a say, I'm not a little girl anymore and I'm over you pulling the reigns. You're done making decisions for me; it's something we discuss together from now on."

She giggled; I had never heard her giggle before.

"My, my, my...you think because the decisions you've made have worked so well for you? Let's see huh...you decide to have sex, not only do you get paid chump change, you also get knocked up. Oh, and we can't forget good ole Julian, who at the first chance he got threw you away like you were yesterday's garbage." She paused to let her words sink in.

"But you want to know what really pisses me off, is that he doesn't fucking remember even being with you. Darling, you're never going to make it in this business if your pussy is that forgettable," she sadistically mocked.

I smirked. "Well you know what they say, Madam, like mother like daughter." I waited for the blow across the face that never came. My mother threw her head back and laughed. I mean laughed like she had gone mad.

"Lilith," she said in between laughing. "How refreshing...you really are my daughter and all it took was you squirting out a kid. God, if I would have known that, I would have put a bastard in you sooner. I mean Jesus...where the fuck has this woman been hiding for the last seventeen years? I can honestly say I'm so unbelievably proud." She stated and clapped. "Bravo, encore, let it all out for the cheap seats in the back."

She wiped away the tears from laughing, "Oh...I needed a good laugh. Feel better now?" she questioned.

It was now or never. If I could stand up to my mother, I could stand up to anyone. I stood to stand right in her face.

"I'm not fucking around. I will let you guide and teach me, but you will NEVER make another decision for me. You will not talk to me like a child, you will treat and respect me as your equal. You are no longer My Mother; you're My Madam. Are we clear?"

She grinned. "Crystal."

And thus my training began...

CHAPTER 8

Six months went flying by. Madam developed a whole regimen for me, beginning with my diet and exercise. The baby weight flew off and I didn't have a mark on me, it was if I had never been pregnant and it was all a dream. I put that memory where it needed to go, far away in the back of my mind, where I wouldn't think about it. I programmed myself to pretend as if it never existed; it was all a figment of my imagination. You wouldn't believe what the human mind could do if you tried hard enough.

I also watched an enormous amount of porn; all kinds, male on male, female on female, threesomes, orgies, and good ole fashioned one on one. I watched so much damn porn that I was dreaming about it. Let's just say that my hand grew tired over those six months.

I met the other twelve VIPs; I was lucky number thirteen. They were all drop dead gorgeous, some of them I had met before and others I had never seen. They were all uniquely different, but had one thing in common, VIP. They were welcoming and assisted with my training as well. I attended parties, met future prospects, and Madam explained the ins and outs of VIP and how everything worked.

The VIPs taught me how to entice, flirt, tease, and seduce. It was then that I realized how easy men were. If given the chance, a woman could make any man cheat. Men fuck, just like a VIP.

No remorse, no guilt, no regret.

On Tuesday June 6, 1978, I turned 18.

"Wake up, darling," I heard Madam say. "Open your beautiful bright blue eyes for me."

I did. "What's going on?" I questioned half asleep.

"It's midnight. You're officially a VIP. Do you feel it? The world is at your fingertips, it's right there, right in front of you. It's your time, Lilith," she vowed as she lightly pressed her lips on mine before she left.

I rushed to my mirror and touched the skin on my face.

I was a woman.

I was a VIP.

❖VIP❖

My coming out party was the following Saturday, the theme was Masquerade. I wore a white lace corset that came up to my ribs- my cleavage busting at the seams- a white thong, a silver chain garter belt that held up white thigh highs, and silver four-inch heels. My hair flowed loosely down my back and I wore a glitter white mask that covered my eyes.

I watched myself in the mirror for a few minutes, admiring the beauty that was I. I couldn't remember a time where I didn't admire my mother's VIPs, they were everything I wanted to be, everything I knew I could be. The day had come and it was my turn to shine, I had my moment in the stars, where everyone would only look at me. I wasn't scared or nervous, I felt comfortable in my own velvety white skin. It was my night and I was going to make sure that it was unforgettable.

I finished smoking a Lime Haze joint, Madam had marijuana delivered from Amsterdam that afternoon; it was one of my birthday presents. I also finished my celebratory glass of champagne that Madam had brought me to toast. Keep in mind that the legal drinking age in Florida in 1978 was eighteen.

Just another reason to go all out, right?

I took one last look at myself and made my way downstairs. As soon as my foot stepped on the stairs, everyone turned to look at me. I stopped dead in my tracks.

"I'd like everyone to give a warm, loving, welcome to the newest member of VIP; it's also her eighteenth birthday. Let's make it a night she won't soon forget...shall we? On the count of three, everyone sing happy birthday," Madam stated in the microphone.

I was at the last step when they finished singing and there was a cake with eighteen candles waiting for me. I blew them out and then I was pulled into hugs and kisses on the mouth from everyone in attendance. I took the opportunity to look around me and I had never seen anything like it before. There was translucent lighting everywhere. Half naked women dancing on poles that were set up in several places around the open room, food laid on naked women and men, and waitresses walking topless with g-strings. But everyone was wearing a mask, so I couldn't see their faces.

"Lilith, go explore. Just remember one thing, don't do anything I wouldn't do at least twice." She grinned deviously at me.

I walked through the house as if I was Alice in Wonderland; except I hadn't fallen down the rabbit hole; I jumped right the fuck in, head first. I went into our theatre room and there were clips of the VIPs on a reel, the girls with clients, the girls together, and some of them alone, pleasuring themselves. I heard a loud moan and turned my attention to the naked woman lying on the floor, her hands and ankles were bound separately, and she had a blindfold on. There were two males, each holding a candle. I watched as they poured wax all over her skin, she moaned loudly when it did. Her pale skin turned red in seconds, and their erections would bounce in the anticipation for it. They were all getting off on it, as was I.

It was as if I was watching it in slow motion, I could feel the allure, the magnetism pulling me forward. I had the candle in my hand within minutes and I crouched down to lightly touch her. I started at her cheek and her head leaned toward my touch, she licked her lips in an unspoken gesture to keep going. I moved my fingers to her neck and rubbed up and down on her windpipe, I was in complete control over everything I did, and she had absolutely no say. My panties got wet. I squeezed a bit firmer, not enough to stop her breathing, but enough to know that I could, and she moaned loudly.

My hand cupped her breast and I pushed it upward, I gently poured wax on her cleavage and her breathing escalated in anticipation of what was to come. I moved forward to lick the edge of her lips, and her tongue peeked out to touch mine. I moaned, and we erotically moved our tongues together, tasting and feeling the thirst for it all. I pulled away and licked and sucked on her nipple to make it hard as stone. Once it was, I leaned back to watch her face as I poured wax all over it. Her back arched off the ground, and she whimpered in a satisfying desire.

I didn't stop there; I kept moving the wax down her stomach, right to her inner thigh. I looked back at her face and saw her bite her bottom lip. I smiled deviously and poured wax right at the top of her mound, she gasped in surprise, and I leaned forward to kiss her passionately. We moaned into each other's mouths and I could feel her trying to rub her legs together to relieve the ache that I had caused. I moved my hand toward her pussy, and with my palm, I lightly moved circles on her clit. Not enough pressure to make her come, but enough to drive her insane. I kissed her one last time and moved away, and she whimpered at the loss.

I giggled, and noticed that both men had their cocks in their hands.

"You think you guys could finish the job?" I questioned with a raised eyebrow.

Before I closed the door, I watched one move in between her legs, while the other went for her mouth.

I saw two women exit the next room that caught my eye; I made my way over to it, and opened the door. It was dark and the lighting was dim, there were a few people in that room. I saw two males in the corner, kissing and touching each other's dicks through their pants, while another one watched, stroking his hard dick in his hand. To my surprise, I was growing wetter by watching it unfold. The masculinity and dominance over one another was entrancing and provocative.

There were other people talking as if nothing were happening in the corner of the room. My eyes caught the table that had an endless amount of white lines of powder. I had no idea what it was, but it sure as shit didn't mean I wasn't going to find out.

"You want a taste?" a dark voice whispered in my ear.

"I can smell it on you, Angel, you want it and you want it so fucking bad. Let me be the one to give it to you. You want to feel like a queen?" he provoked as he moved to face me. His hair was blonde, long, and shaggy. He had hazel, dilated eyes, and a smile that could make any girl wet. The facial hair on his face immediately made me wonder what it would feel like between my legs. His body was covered in tattoos and muscle. He looked like a bad boy that drove a motorcycle, and said the word cunt at dinner.

He grabbed my hand, kissed my inner wrist, and escorted me to the table.

We sat down on our knees and I watched as he picked up the $100 bill, bringing it to his nose. He bent forward and snorted two lines up each nostril.

He jerked his head back and sniffed harder cleaning his nostrils with his fingertips.

"Ugh! Burns like a motherfucker, but goddamn that's good shit. Madam has this shit imported from Columbia, only the best. Your turn." He grinned and handed me the bill.

"All right, virgin Angel, I guess I'm going to be the one that takes your wings. Don't do more than one in each nostril and sniff hard to make sure it all goes in."

"What is it?" I questioned.

He smiled. "Your new best friend, Snow White."

I proceeded to do exactly what I had just witnessed and not even ten seconds later, I felt a drip at the back of my throat.

What does cocaine make you feel like? It makes you feel like doing more cocaine.

It's a helluva drug. The second it hit my bloodstream I was alive. It felt like I could walk on water, run a marathon in five seconds, pure mental clarity, I was watching and experiencing everything around me like a newborn does.

But most of all, it made me feel confident, seductive, and horny as fuck.

"You should see your eyes right now. They're piercing. So birthday girl, did I pop your cherry all right?"

I laughed, "Enough to make me come back for more, no pun intended. What's your name?"

"Mika," he replied with an edge to his voice I hadn't heard before.

"Lilith, right?" he asked with a smirk, I nodded.

As much as I wanted to talk to Mika, I wanted to roam a lot more; Snow White had piqued my curiosity. I needed to move.

"Need a babysitter?" I asked.

"A babysitter, huh, no I do just fine on my own," he teased, licking his lips. I watched his tongue make its way back in his mouth and I wanted it to be in mine. Lucky for me, he made the first move. His thumb traced my bottom lip, and the tip of my tongue grazed it as he pushed into my mouth. I seductively sucked on it and hummed.

"Fuck I wish that was my cock," he sighed.

He roughly grabbed the back of my neck and shoved his tongue into my mouth. I sucked on it as I did his thumb and he groaned. His hands cupped the sides of my face and it intensified our lip movements.

"Spread your legs, Angel, open your knees," he huskily demanded. I moved my legs apart, sitting on my ankles, and he eagerly moved my panties to the side to rub my pussy forward and then backward with the palm of his hand. I moaned and he bit my bottom lip.

"Jesus…you're soaking wet. You like that, huh? You want me to finger fuck you, don't you?"

He pushed two fingers inside of me, in an upward motion, and moved them back and forth. I shamelessly moaned.

"You feel that?" he goaded as he pushed on the spot that drove me wild.

"Answer me," he stated, pushing on the same place that made it almost impossible for me to answer.

"Yes…yes…fuck yes…" I let out.

"Ride my hand, Angel, ride my hand like you would ride my cock," he suggested as he continued to torment my g-spot.

I sat up higher and rode his fingers like it was the last thing I was going to do. He never once stopped kissing me; the coke, his kissing, and his fingers in my pussy were enough to drive me to euphoria. I never felt myself that wet before and I could hear the noises I made as I continued to fuck his hand.

I brought my fingers to my clit, making my way closer to the edge of release.

He sensed that I started to play with myself and stopped kissing me to watch.

"Open your eyes," he said in a pleading tone. I did and was smacked in the face with everyone's eyes on me, and that's all it took for my head to fall back and come.

CHAPTER 9

What felt like minutes later, I came to when Mika put his fingers in my mouth. He moved them in and out like he would his cock and I licked them clean.

"You're a dirty girl, Lilith? You know what men like me do with dirty girls?" he questioned in a condescending tone.

"They punish them. Come on, Angel, it's time you see where bad girls go." He grinned at me, sending an electric current through my body that made me want to do anything he said.

We did a few more lines of Snow White and I was beyond fucked up, but it was a different kind of messed up. I was thoroughly in control of my surroundings, but my body felt high. I felt sexy, wanted, desired. The second we stepped into my mother's bedroom, I knew exactly where we were going. I took the lead and pushed the button that opened the hiding door.

Mika folded his arms and smiled. "She has a little devil in her I see."

I seductively walked over to him and placed my hand on the tip of his cock. I rubbed up and down through his slacks, and he grunted. "Want to put something else in her?" I whispered pulling his earlobe into my mouth.

"More than you fucking know, Angel. Let's see if you feel the same way after I beat your ass," he stated as he slapped my ass, making me yelp.

I followed him into the room that I had seen when I was eleven years old and nothing had changed, other than things being added.

"Are you scared?" he questioned.

"Should I be?"

He shook his head no, walked over to the bed that had black silk sheets, and patted it for me to follow.

I sat down next to him and he kissed me. I kissed him back with the same desire that had been lingering between us all night. I felt him start to untie the strings of my corset top until it was completely undone. He effortlessly removed it from my body, throwing it across the room. His hands roughly cupped my breasts, bringing them together and kneading them. I moaned in satisfaction as he pinched my nipples, making them hard pebbles.

He kissed all the way down my neck to my breasts, bringing my nipple into his mouth; he sucked and teased me into submission. I would have done anything he asked, and I did.

"God your tits are fucking delicious. There's no coming back from you, is there?" he groaned.

"You want to play, Angel? Say yes, and we will play all sorts of games. You know what a safe word is?"

"No," I replied.

He looked me right in the eyes. "Whatever happens you can stop it at anytime, say the word vanilla and it's over." I nodded.

"Take your panties off, I want to see your cunt."

I got off the bed and slowly removed my panties, Mika grunted something about my cunt being fucking beautiful and he smacked both my ass cheeks bringing my pussy directly toward his mouth.

He went right for it, he didn't ease me into it; he went right for my clit and sucked with everything he had. He moved his head side to side and my legs started to give out. My pussy pulsated, dripping wet, and he pushed his tongue into my opening as far as it would go.

"Hmmm…you can't come, Angel, not until I say you can. If you do, you'll pay for it," he threatened, devouring my clit again.

I couldn't control it, I tried to move away from him but he held my hips firmer, holding me in place. The asshole moved my hips in the opposite motion of his tongue, making the sensations intensify and there was nothing I could do. I grabbed a hold of his hair and he hummed making me come all over his tongue.

"Bad girl…" he teasingly threatened as he wiped away all my wetness from his mouth.

"Turn around; you see that wall that has those paddles? Go get one. NOW!" he yelled.

His demeanor had completely changed, his eyes got darker, and I could no longer see color in them, they were black irises.

I tried to get my composure but I walked on wobbly legs, not sure if it was from the orgasm, or the fact that I had no idea what was next. I grabbed a black leather paddle, and took a deep breath.

"Go to the middle of the room," I heard him say.

I anxiously awaited and he approached me with ropes and a blindfold.

"X marks the spot, Angel, don't make me tell you again. Go bend over the bench," he demanded.

I could smell the intensity radiating off of him like an animal in heat. I was his prey. I slowly made it over to the bench and leaned forward; the position wasn't entirely uncomfortable. I watched Mika tie my wrists to the bars, he then proceeded to do the same with my ankles. My body was bound and I couldn't move if I wanted to. The anticipation of not knowing what was to come was enough to have me chomping at the bit, and then he blindfolded me.

"Lilith, tell me why you've been a bad girl. Why are you getting punished?" he asserted, as I heard him walk around me.

"Lilith…answer me. Don't make me ask you again," he threatened me.

This is probably where a submissive person would bow down to their Dominant. Hmmm…have you not learned a damn thing about me?

"I came in your mouth, asshole, after I was told not to. But didn't I taste motherfucking delicious?" I taunted.

I heard the paddle before I ever felt it; my body jolted, and I screamed. I was not expecting pain like that. It was way worse than what a hand could ever do.

"Are you ready to play nice, Lilith?" he asked with a satisfied tone.

"What do you think?"

Another smack, harder this time. I wanted to jump up and down to relieve the pain.

"Is that all you got, Mika?" I implied, waiting for the smack.

I heard him shuffling around. What happened next I would have never expected.

"You know what happens to bad girls who can't follow direction, Lilith?" I could feel his breathing close to my ear. "They get fucked."

His fingers touched my clit, gathering up the moisture, and he roughly pushed two fingers inside me. I moaned.

"But not here, Lilith." He pushed harder on my g-spot. "Here," he stated as he rubbed around the pucker of my anus.

I didn't have time to acknowledge before he struck my ass with the paddle again, much harder than before. I screamed in pain.

"Have nothing to say, Angel? That's a shame; but it doesn't mean I'm going to stop either," he said as he smacked me again.

My ass was on fire and there was no denying that there would be welts. He smacked it seven times repeatedly and I thought I might pass out from the pain. My body was sweating and my throat felt raw from yelling. I was on the verge of saying "vanilla".

He lightly smacked my ass with the palm of his hand and it felt soothing. He would caress slow circles after each smack, and the familiar yearning arose.

I couldn't comprehend how my body could react from pain to pleasure, but it surely did. It was as if I had no control over my emotions, my wants, my needs; he had completely taken over my body.

"I will fuck your ass, Lilith, but not tonight."

He carried me over to the bed, after removing the straps, and laid me flat on my back. I yelped from the contact.

"I have a surprise, Angel; want to see what it is? Be a good girl and I will show you."

He removed my blindfold and it took a minute for my eyes to adjust to the lighting. Little by little, I realized we weren't alone in the room, there were at least ten male bystanders. All of them standing around the bed watching me.

My mouth parted and I licked my lips. I watched as they made room for Nakita as she walked by. She was another VIP; twenty-one and came directly from Russia. She was gorgeous, her red hair made her small facial features more prominent, and her bright blue eyes stuck out from a mile away. My eyes devoured her ridiculous body; at 5'8, she had creamy legs that wouldn't end, a small waist, and 34D breasts.

She crawled over to me, running her fingertips on my body.

"Lilith's been a bad girl," she mocked; just like Alexandria, her accent was hypnotizing.

"Turn around, Lilith, show her my handy work," Mika demanded.

I got on my hands and knees and Nakita caressed the welts on my ass.

"Awe, poor baby VIP...let me make it better," she teased.

She slowly began to kiss the welts and moved her way to the crevice of my anus. She smiled deviously, as she looked me straight in the eyes before taking her tongue and licking from my clit to the ring of my pucker. I slightly jolted from the initial contact to my most private place.

"You taste as good as you look, Lilith," she groaned, proceeding to attack my ass with her fingers.

"She's an anal virgin, Mika. What am I suppose to do with that? Maybe just a finger," she taunted as she pushed her index finger in, making me moan and squirm.

I was in the middle of some warped version of an initiation and it was then that I realized The Cathouse was like the cities of Sodom and Gomorrah with valet parking.

But how can something so wrong...feel so fucking right? I embraced my turn, my legacy, and my chance. It was my opportunity to prove myself to everyone that I am and will always be a VIP.

I watched as Mika removed his slacks and it was the first time tonight that I saw his cock. My initial thought was if there was some unwritten rule that the clients of VIP had to be hung, because Mika was just as, if not more, impressive than Julian. His cock stood at attention; long, hard, and thick. He wrapped his hand around the base of his dick and brought it over to my mouth.

He shoved it to the back of my throat and groaned. He pulled my hair back with his hand as he pumped in and out of my mouth. I sucked his cock, as Nakita finger fucked my ass. I didn't pay any attention to what the voyeurs were doing, but I'm assuming they were participating in their own way.

I could feel the throbbing of his cock as he violated my mouth with everything he had. I wasn't far off from my own ecstasy, but I wanted more. I sucked him one last time before removing him out of my mouth and making my way over to Nakita. I still had the taste of him in my mouth and I wanted to share. I kissed Nakita and we twirled our tongues, masking Mika's arousal.

Mika started playing with both our pussies and it only increased the need of release.

"I want to see you girls fuck each other. Put on a show for me," he huskily urged.

Nikita unexpectedly pushed me back on the bed and then she spread my legs. She positioned herself in front of me and placed her pussy on top of mine. We sat with our legs entwined with each other. I followed her lead as she moved her hips front and back like she would if she were riding a man.

The pooling wetness, the uncontrollable moans, and the visuals of everything around us were comparable to a mystical divine awakening. We rubbed our pussies together, faster, harder, urgently wanting to come.

"Fuck yes," Mika grunted, as he pulled Nakita away from me and I whimpered at the loss. He placed her on all fours and violently thrust into her, shoving her forward from the momentum.

"Lick her pussy, Nikita; make her come in your mouth."

She rested on her elbows and devoured my clit, moving her head side to side, as Mika pushed in and out of her, making her mouth move faster on me. Her moaning felt like a vibrator and she sucked on my nub never letting up.

I grabbed the sides of her face to keep her in place and locked eyes with Mika, we all came at the exact same time.

I came to when I heard familiar moaning. I opened my eyes; on the wall in front of me was the recording of what just happened being displayed. All of a sudden there was clapping and the voyeurs began moving to the sides of the bed. I saw the shadow of Madam clapping and walking toward me with a satisfied smile on her face.

She handed me a black silk robe. "I'm to assume you would like some modesty, although from the performance you've given all night, I could be mistaken." She helped me put on the robe and tied it in the front for me.

"Darling, you passed with flying colors," she stated, smiling brightly.

"Excuse me?" I responded with confusion.

"The birthday party was all a ruse, Lilith. It was never about your birthday. It was a test."

"Are you serious?" I continued, shocked.

"Of course, I choose my girls, Lilith. You, my darling, are different. I wanted to make sure that I was not wrong," she gloated, pulling the hair out of my face and I slapped her hands away.

She laughed. "Don't bite the hand that will feed you." She proceeded to push the hair out of my face, turning me to watch the screen.

"You see that woman on display; you see her eyes, her face, her skin; she's beautiful.

She's whatever she wants to be.

She owns everything and anything around her.

She's a vision.

She's wanted and needed.

She runs the show.

She is in control of it all.

She will be Madam one day...

She is you."

CHAPTER 10

Three years fly by at an incredible speed of light. It's 1981, and I am twenty-one years old. My life completely took a 180 turn and I sat in the drivers seat without a goddamn seatbelt on. I sat in the lap of luxury while everyone else was living paycheck to paycheck. I had no idea what it meant to not have what I want when I wanted it. In my world, there were no laws; rules did not apply to me. You have no idea the lengths people would go to for just a taste, a sample, of what I could offer them.

There are VIP tables all over the world. You may think you have sat at them. You may think you have seen them. You may think you have heard of them. But you have no idea. It's the table that no one sees, the table that no one knows about. It's the table in the back with dim lighting, in a secluded corner. Where you can see everyone, but no one can see you.

That's the VIP table.

You may also think that drug dealers live behind closed doors, the bottom feeders of the world, preying on the weak and helpless. That's a bunch of bullshit. The true drug dealers are the ones that have "Doctor" right before their last names. They're the ones that go to medical school for years to educate themselves on "helping the ill". They're the suppliers. I'm sorry to burst your bubble, but the more money you have, the more drugs you do. Why not? There are no consequences, the world is at your fingertips, you have nothing to lose. You would be shocked at the lives people live behind golden gates.

In my society, drugs and sex are a part of our culture.

There were a few behind-the-scenes "discrepancies", as Madam called them, that she only allowed me see. VIP is an extremely lucrative organization. It's for the Crème de la Crème; though that doesn't mean things don't fall through the crevices. Madam controls everything whether that is before, during, or after a date.

I met with Anderson Richard for our first date at a medical banquet for Leukemia. He was charming and handsome in an older way; he must have been in his early forties. His salt and pepper hair distinguished the light wrinkles in the corner of his chocolate brown eyes. He was 6'0 and had a toned muscular physique; always sporting a five o'clock shadow.

The banquet went without any issues as they always did. I played the part of the doting companion in front of the cameras, while he mingled with high profile future clients. He owned a software manufacturing company. It was interesting to see the two sides of every man, and he was no different. He'd shake the hands of clients, with the same hand that mere seconds before were rubbing the folds of my pussy under the table. I believe he got off on the fact that he could do it, and that I would allow it. Most women aren't as accommodating, which further proves that VIPs are one in a million.

We made it back to his suite around midnight, and as soon as the door closed behind us, out came the vulture.

"So, you little slut, what will I make you do for me?" he questioned with revulsion lacing his voice, catching me off guard.

I turned and cocked my head to the side. "What do you want me to do?"

"Whatever the fuck I want. That's what I'm paying you for, isn't it? So you can be my fuck toy for the night? You're a bad girl, Lilith; I didn't want a bad girl. I wanted a good girl. That means I'm going to have to hurt you," he stated deviously.

"Letting me do all those nasty, vile things to you, knowing that I would be touching other people with your juices still on my hand. You filthy disgusting cunt; now take off your fucking clothes before I take them off for you," he demanded.

At twenty-one, I had already lost count as to how many men I had been with, and Richard was just another client who liked kink, another form of foreplay; or so I thought. I proceeded to do exactly what he wanted me to and I left the suite with bruises all over my body and a bloody nose.

I had never felt that violated before, and it only further ingrained in my mind that men are animals, and if given the chance they will cheat, beat, hurt, abuse, humiliate, and fuck anything that walks. I went straight home to my condo and soaked in a warm bath for the next two hours. I tried to cover my body as best as I could, the last thing I wanted was to get Madam involved. She would beat me further if she knew I permitted it to happen.

I sat with Madam at lunch the next day, while she added dates into my appointment planner.

I stood too fast and my right leg gave out.

"Are you all right?" she asked, showing a hint of concern.

"Mmm hmm, I've just been working out too hard."

She nodded. "Uh huh, how was your evening with Anderson?"

"Fine," I stated.

"He called wanting another date. He requested another VIP, why is that?"

"I don't know. He was thrilled when I left."

"Hmmm…" she replied.

I got up off the table to make my way to the kitchen.

"Lilith." I stopped dead in my tracks. I knew that tone.

"Lie to me once, shame on you; lie to me twice, shame on me. It would do you good to remember that I don't do shame very well." I kept walking, not turning around to look at my mother's observant face.

❄VIP❄

A few weeks went by without so much as a warning of what was to come, but that all changed one afternoon. Madam called first thing that morning letting me know that my presence was requested in her office at 3:00 pm. Judging by her tone on the phone, this was going to take the better part of my afternoon. My bruises faded, but my anger grew. I made sure to cover that up with picture perfect makeup and outfit. Not letting one ounce of my outside demeanor reflect what I felt on the inside.

At 2:55 pm, I knocked on her door with an uncontrollable eerie feeling.

"Come in," I heard Madam say from behind the door.

I walked into a scene from The Godfather. My mother was sitting on her desk with a gun in one hand and an extremely large knife in the other. Three bodyguard type men, whom I had never seen before, stood behind Anderson. He was in nothing but boxers, tied to a chair. His face badly beaten and his body was blackened with bruises.

"Holy shit," I whispered to no one in particular.

"Lilith, darling, so happy that you could make it to our little party," she proclaimed.

I immediately put my hand over my mouth. "What the fuck?! What are you doing?" I shouted through my fingers.

She smiled. "Whatever the fuck I want. Now it's your turn."

I shook my head back and forth.

She raised her eyebrow. "Let me make sure I understand. Anderson decided that he was going to get fist happy with MY property, and you don't bat an eye. Now, I take care of what is mine. I did my part, Lilith. Now it's your turn. I mean, unless you'd like to play Russian roulette with me."

"Madam-"

"Don't Madam me anything. Men like Anderson need to be put in their places. They don't understand that MY pussy will always be smarter than their cocks."

"He could report this. I mean, what are you doing? You could jeopardize everything," I tried to explain in the calmest manner I could muster.

She threw her head back and laughed. "By whom? Lilith, I have politicians, detectives, the motherfucking D.A, and Chief of Police on my speed dial. Just because they wear a badge, darling, doesn't mean they don't like to get dirty. Learn something now; keep your friends close, and your enemies much closer."

"I can't-"

"You repeat that word one more time, I will turn this gun on you. What have I taught you, Lilith? You. Do. Not. Show. Weakness. Ever!" she yelled.

"What do you think? Huh? That pretty face of yours will run my empire. I am showing you the way, Lilith. Now, follow the fucking yellow brick road toward me and take your pick; gun or knife?"

I stared back at the face that would one day be me. Could I do this? Could I protect what's mine...I took one look at Anderson as he pissed himself in the chair. I thought back on the way he ripped my dress, how he bit me until I bled, how even days later, I could still feel his fingers around my neck. That every time I said "no" and "stop", he would thrust harder to the point where I felt like he was ripping me open. But most of all, I thought about the look on his face when he was about to come, and for it to happen, he had to punch me in the face.

I thought back on how many women he had done this to, how many more times would he do it. What if next time he kills one of them and I had the chance to stop it?

To make it all go away.

To make him go away.

I vindictively smiled and walked over to Madam. I grabbed the gun and she smiled proudly, her eyes were gleaming with anticipation. I slowly strolled over to Anderson, who was screaming into the mask of tape and thrashing around in his chair, trying to get loose. I raised the gun and pointed it to his head, his eyes widened in fear. I moved the pistol to his forehead and placed my finger on the trigger, pulling it toward me.

Then I heard it click. I pulled again and again...*click, click, click.*

Madam's clapping broke me away from my thoughts.

"You do have it in you," she said, smiling proudly at me. "Good to know." She grabbed the gun from my hands and brought it down to his temple, knocking him out.

"Get him the fuck out of my office," she said to the guards.

She placed the gun in her safe, along with the knife, before turning to me.

"It's game over, Lilith. You win. Don't ever let me find out that I have to clean up your mess. You want to be Queen Bee? Don't ever take shit from anyone. I don't give a flying fuck who they think they are. Understood?" I nodded.

"Good, now get the fuck out of my office."

✳VIP✳

Time went on and I continued to hear I love yous, marry mes, and let me take you away from it all. But like anything, the first time is always the best and most memorable.

Remington Cooper was the rock star of the eighties. He had the ego of well, a rock star, and the cock of a God. He was known for doing an incredible amount of drugs, and had been to rehab a couple of times. Like any artist, he was exceptionally talented and had a dark soul.

Remington was 6'1, had jet black hair, tattoos and piercings all over his body, hazel eyes that always wore more black eye liner than I ever did. He dressed in ripped clothing and his net worth was $30 million; he was only twenty-five years old. I met him at Club 54 and was his for the next week straight; drugs, sex, and rock roll baby.

This was the sixth or seventh time that I was his companion. He always requested me when he was on the road; I would stay with him days at a time.

"Damn, you're fucking gorgeous," Remington grunted as he finished snorting the line of coke off my ass.

"Remy…" I retorted, trying to get up to go to the shower.

"Don't call me that. I didn't say you could get up either," he urged.

"You're my muse, you know that, Lilith?" he whispered, kissing me all over my face.

"Mmm hmm…" I replied, soaking up all the attention.

"I love you, you know that, right?" he confessed; it wasn't the first time I heard it and it wouldn't be the last.

"Mmm hmm…"

He looked deep into my eyes. "Marry me."

I laughed. "Remy, you're fucked up. You have no idea what you're saying."

"I don't give a fuck. I know right now you're mine and I want to keep you that way. Marry me." He was practically begging, annoying the fuck out of me.

Marriage has always been a huge question mark for me. I don't care enough to go into it; obviously, I think it's a load of garbage. People get married because they're lonely, they think they're supposed to, they don't want to die alone…the list goes on. Don't think for one second that I'm cynical, or I'm bitter, I'm a realist.

I probably didn't pick the right time to laugh in Remington's face, but I did.

"Are you fucking laughing at me?" he shouted, getting close to my face. I pushed at his chest to get him off.

"You need a serious reality check! You may need to go to rehab again because you've lost your goddamn mind. Do you honestly think I'm going to say yes?" I yelled, trying to find my clothes.

He forcefully grabbed my upper arm and my first reaction was to punch him in the face, making him stagger back.

"Don't you ever put your hands on me," I angrily stated.

He shook his head. "You stupid cunt. Do you honestly think you're better than me? Well…you better get off your pedestal, Barbie, because you're a fucking whore. I have a true talent, while yours is in between your legs."

I seductively walked over to him and started to trace the outline of his dick with my fingers, instantly making him hard. "And it always makes you come back for more, darling." I grabbed a hold of his shaft and lightly moved up and down. "Doesn't it?"

He moaned in my ear. "Go fuck yourself, Remy," I stated in his.

He pulled my hair at the nook of my neck and licked my lips.

"I'd much rather fuck you," he proclaimed as he threw me on the bed.

Why be tied down with a ring on my finger, when I can be tied up with a dick in my pussy? To me, the choice is obvious.

I snuck out the next morning, making sure to have the pictures that I needed. See, Remy also had a wife. Oh! Did I not mention that part?

I mailed a few pictures of our escapades to Rolling Stone, and let's just say, his wife took him for half.

Lesson learned, Remington Cooper.

Don't fuck with me.

CHAPTER II

After I turned eighteen my father was pretty much non-existent, I knew it was because he didn't agree with my life choices. My father had been an active member of VIP since before I was born...can we say hypocrite? Nevertheless, anytime he wanted to meet with me I would make time in my schedule for him. He was the only "man" in my life.

We ate lunch at a café on South Beach.

"How are things going?" he asked with trepidation in his voice.

"Things are amazing," I answered with none in mine.

"Is your mother looking out for you?"

"My Madam always does. You should know that. I'm sure she's looked out for you too, given your life choices," I challenged, staring him in the eyes.

"Lilith-"

"Save it. I know you have always preferred your other children over me. It's blatantly obvious, it always has been. So let's not play the doting concerned father, it's a waste of both our time. Don't you think?"

"Vivian has always been adamant about the specific role I would play in your life. It was established before I decided to give her what she wanted. It doesn't change the fact that I am your father; I do love you, and I worry every day about what she has you doing."

"First off, I'm not a child. I'm twenty-three years old. Second, she doesn't make me do anything. I love doing what I do, and I wouldn't have it any other way. And lastly, you should worry about what you're doing every day...daddy," I argued with a satisfied smile.

"I didn't come here to fight with you, Lilith. If I could take it all back I would, but I can't. I was young and stupid, and regardless of what you think, your mother and I did share something special."

Now that caught me off guard. "What do you mean?"

"We loved each other, Lilith. I loved your mother very much," he declared almost knocking me out of my chair.

"That's a load of bullshit; don't you think I'm too old for fairytales?"

He looked stunned. "She's never told you?"

"What the fuck are you talking about?" I aggressively questioned.

"Jesus…Vivian and I were high school sweethearts. We were married for three years before-"

"You're lying!" I shouted, standing up and knocking my chair over.

He grabbed my wrist. "Sit and calm down. Why would I lie to you? I have nothing to gain from lying."

I sat back down with caution.

"Vivian always knew she was going to be a VIP, she knew she would take over it eventually. At first, it was phenomenal; I loved being a part of the lifestyle, Lilith. Your mother is gorgeous, she always has been. But after a while I could only take so much; the parties, the other clients, the drugs, it all got to me. I woke up one morning and I couldn't live like that anymore. I felt as if I was losing my soul, and I begged your mother to give it all up," he explained as if he was reliving it all over again.

"By the time I finally said something it was too late. Your mother was in deep. She fell in love with the power and there was nothing left for me. She filed for divorce the day after I gave her an ultimatum. We didn't talk for several years. After about ten years we ran into each other and she just sucked me back in. I was married with kids and I didn't care. I've always wanted your mother, I still do. She has this hold on me like she has with everyone. She gets off on it." He paused to take a breath.

"I agreed to give her a child, praying, and hoping that it would somehow change her. That she would take one look at you and be the person that I once knew, but it backfired. She became worse. I swear to you that if I had known that this would have been your future…I would have never gone through with it."

He sighed. "She used me, Lilith, just like she uses everyone."

I stared at him, wanting to know more. I needed to know more.

"What kills me the most is that every time I see you, you look more and more like her. It breaks my heart and that's why I have stayed away from you these last few years. My worst nightmare is that you will become her spitting image, or worse. Power and control is a very fascinating concept, it changes people, and you're in the heart of it all. There's a very, very fine line and once you cross it, there's no turning back. Your mother tasted it and she wanted more, she still does. I have to live with the fact that I was a part of creating you, and now I just have to stand back and watch until you step into the very shoes that she did." He pulled out his wallet and slapped a few bills on the table.

"I love you. I wish I had done right by you. I can't change the past any more than I can the future." He sighed, kissed my forehead, and left.

"Oh, here, this is for you," said the waitress, pulling me from the twilight zone I was in. She handed me a photograph. I knew where it came from. There was only one person who would have had this, and it made my day so much brighter.

After my father dropped the fucking atomic bomb that destroyed Hiroshima in my lap, I went straight to the source. I ran on pure adrenaline and emotion. I didn't take five minutes to contemplate what I had just heard. I got in my car and drove to The Cathouse.

She looked up when I barged into her office.

"Let me call you back," she said into the phone. "Can I help you?"

"I had lunch with Dad today," I announced as I walked toward the window to look at the courtyard. I purposely kept my back to her, waiting for her response.

It was the same window that I had stood in numerous times as a child, waiting for my mother to pay attention to me; that was my life back then. My how things have changed.

"Oh really, it's baffling that he would take time out of his busy schedule to see you. How is good ole Charles?" she inquired, feigning interest.

"Happy...married...in love...you know, how you use to be." I turned to look at her face that didn't show any emotion what so ever.

"You know, *Madam,* you should practice what you preach sometime. It might make you a better person, because from what I hear, you're one selfish bitch. You should probably work on that unless you'd like to have a seat next to Satan. For some reason I think he probably already has it reserved for you," I announced.

"Wow, nothing to say. No quick clever rebuttal? Is your mind slowing down in your old age, or is it that you don't remember the lies that you feed me. Or wait, is it that you never planned on fucking telling me that you were once married!"

She remained speechless.

"And it's not even the marriage that gets to me, Madam! It's the fact that you were IN LOVE! The one thing that you have told me all these years is to never fall in love, to never give myself to someone. Love is weakness and I. Do. Not. Show. Weakness! Isn't that it? I'm supposed to be your motherfucking prodigy and here I find out that my Madam is just another goddamn statistic!" I screamed.

"The big, almighty, powerful, bow down to me Madam is a fake, a phony."

She crossed her arms and slowly cracked her neck. "Believe it or not, Lilith, I don't have to explain myself to you or anyone else, and that is the beauty of being in charge. I sit at the throne, people answer to me, I am the one, and until I say so you have nothing to do but to wait in line," she calmly spewed.

I grabbed the picture and placed it on her desk right in front of her.

"Was it a beautiful wedding? Was it everything you ever dreamt of and wished for? Did you get his and her towels, Madam?"

She picked up the photograph of their wedding day as if it was a disease-infested object and ripped it in half; not giving it one second of recognition, and threw it in the garbage.

"You still don't get it, Lilith. I don't give one flying fuck what you think of me. It doesn't faze me, it doesn't hurt me, and it most definitely doesn't change the fact that I own you." She stood up, grabbed her suit jacket and purse, and walked over to me.

"I have some business that needs my immediate attention. Go home and clean yourself up, you look like shit. You have a date tonight," she said before kissing the tip of my nose and leaving.

I don't know how long I stood there contemplating everything that had happened in the last few hours. I should have known that my mother wouldn't answer or explain anything. That's not who she was. All my life I wanted to be just like her, I wanted everything that she was, everything that she stood for. It took me almost a quarter of my life to realize that she was a fraud.

I would let her train me, mold me, and teach me everything I needed to know.

But...I would never be like her.

I would be better.

I walked over to the garbage and pulled out the torn photograph. I taped it up, looked at it one more time, and placed it in my back pocket.

My father was right about one thing, power and control does change people, he just forgot to include greed.

In greed we trust.

I proceeded to sit in Madam's chair, and from that moment, I knew what I wanted.

There is a fine line between loving life and being greedy for it, and I just crossed that line. I would take VIP when I wanted to, not when I was told.

I conquered myself that day, and it was only a matter of time until I would preside over VIP.

CHAPTER 12

The eighties were some of the best times of my life; I was in my twenties, able, free, rich, and fucking fabulous. I enjoyed all VIP had to offer, private planes, five-star hotels, endless amounts of jewelry, countless amounts of adoration and attention. Alcohol and drugs flowed loosely everywhere I went. I didn't know anyone who didn't have a party favor on them at any point in time. During the mid-eighties, there was a little blue and red pill that hit the scene. Ecstasy became the miracle drug to make it all go away; problems, drama, hatred, stress…all of it gone with the swallow of one tiny pill.

There was peace, tranquility, love, unity, and sex…lots and lots of sex.

The year was 1984; I was 24 years old, and on a date with James Jones. JJ was a bit of a wild card, though that's what I liked about him. Why be boring? It's my worst fucking nightmare to fade into the crowd. JJ and I seemed to have that in common. He requested my presence for the entire weekend, stating he wanted to party. Like I needed a warning label, I am always down for whatever. As a VIP, we were made like that.

We were in New York City, the island of plenty.

"I have a few friends that we're meeting up with at The Underground, is that all right?" JJ asked with excitement in his eyes.

"Of course, the more the merrier."

We made it to The Underground club a little after midnight and the place was already packed. There were people everywhere, both men and women. Now, I had been around my fair share of fucked up people, but this crowd took the cake. I made my way to the bar and I was about to get my drink when someone tapped on my shoulder from behind.

I turned and smirked.

"Well, well, well, lookie who I found. Isn't this place a little out of your scene, Angel?" Mika questioned with a sexy as hell smile that made me want to sit on his face.

"And what exactly is my scene? The dungeon?" I teased.

He grabbed the back of my head moving me toward his body.

"Don't say things like that when I feel like this, Lilith. I'm hard just thinking about it," he whispered seductively in my ear. He wasn't lying, I could feel his erection on my leg, but that's not what I wanted to feel. At least not yet...

I didn't hesitate. "What are you on?"

"Ecstasy."

"What's that?"

He licked his lips. "It's anything you want it to be. Looks like I'll be taking away those wings again tonight." He pulled out a circular blue pill that had a pinup girl stamped on it.

He brought it up to my mouth and I gladly opened, he stopped right before he placed it on my tongue.

"Remember, Angel, if you ever get asked to choose between the red pill and the blue one," he paused, placing it on my tongue, "always take the motherfucking blue one." I swallowed it with no hesitation.

It took exactly thirty minutes to hit my system and it was like a tsunami of emotions, sensations, thoughts, and feelings. I had never experienced anything even remotely close to what I was feeling.

JJ stared into my eyes. "What did you take?"

"What makes you think I'm on something?" I babbled teasingly.

He shook his head laughing, which made me laugh. "Only you would get ecstasy before I had a chance to offer it. Is there anything you can't do on your own?"

I put my finger up to my lips in a thinking motion. "No."

He laughed again. "At least we're both on the same page. Have you ever done this before?"

I shook my head and it made my whole body feel amazing, so I kept doing it until JJ grabbed my head.

"You are so fucked up."

"Guilty." I smiled enticingly.

The night progressed with dancing and talking. I don't think I had ever talked that much in my life, but even that felt amazing. JJ would rub my shoulders and neck and it was as if I was having an out of body experience. Every part of my body had tingles and was screamingly alive. Everything around me shimmered; it was surreal. When his hands would rub the nook of my neck, I swear I felt it everywhere. Prickles and shivers down my arms, my back, and my legs.

I heard Mika's voice from beside me as he put his arm around my body, bringing me close to him. I involuntarily put my head on his shoulder. Just the feel of his body touching mine was incredible. I didn't care that JJ was right beside me, and I could feel all that negative energy radiating off of him.

"Who the fuck are you?" JJ shouted over the music in the club.

"Her prince charming. Who's asking?" Mika calmly replied.

"Her date."

"You're dating now, Angel? Here I thought you were a bad girl. Didn't think you'd ever go vanilla on me," he said into my ear.

I laughed. "Boys…there's plenty of me to go around."

"So, JJ, you could either join, watch, or get the fuck out of the way. The choice is yours." I watched his eyes widen at the proposition.

"Your place or mine, Mika?" he asked without hesitation.

"Most definitely mine," he replied with the same enthusiasm.

Once we arrived at our after-hours festivities at Mika's, things took an unexpected turn. I undressed myself slowly and provocatively before lying in the middle of the bed with my legs spread.

They both were grinning from ear to ear, Mika whispered something in JJ's ear that I couldn't hear, and it made him smile wider.

They both took their clothes off leaving only their boxers on. "You coming down, Angel?"

I nodded, pouting like a child. I knew how to get what I wanted.

Mika crawled over to me and kissed me from my ankle to my mouth, leaving a trail of desire and willingness in his wake. He got close to my face. I perched myself forward to try to kiss him, but he teasingly moved his head away. He grabbed the back of my thighs and roughly flipped me over, making me yelp. I was now laying on my front. He grabbed my hips and made my ass stick up in the air.

"I do believe I made you a promise, little girl, and I always keep my promises," he threatened in a domineering, yet sexy voice that sent shivers down my spine.

JJ came up from behind him and it looked like he handed him something.

"Do you trust me?" Mika inquired with lust and determination in is voice.

"Mmm hmm," I moaned, closing my eyes.

I felt someone bite my ass cheek and then lick toward the pucker of my anus. They pushed their tongue into my pucker and I stretched my arms out in front of me to enjoy the sensations that were to come.

"You smell like you want to be fucked, Lilith, do you want us to fuck you?" I heard JJ's sinful tone behind me.

"Badly," I shamelessly replied.

"We will make you feel so goddamn good, Angel. You won't want us to stop." Mika spread lotion on my anus and I wiggled my hips. He pushed his finger in and out, stretching me, filling me, making me feel whole.

"You will keep coming and begging for more. Every fucking part of you will be touched in more ways than one." I whimpered at the loss of his finger, but it was replaced with two fingers pushing into my sex right toward my g-spot. I wiggled, trying to relive the ache that they were creating. I felt something being pushed into my anus. I opened my eyes and turned my head to see what was going on.

"What are you doing?" I asked with some hesitation.

"Making you a very happy girl. Ecstasy up the ass is like taking three of them orally, and it will hit your bloodstream in fifteen minutes. You're in for a wild night, little girl." The pill burned for a few seconds; nothing uncomfortable, just a stinging sensation. I let Mika's words sink in, it hit the bottom of my core and I shivered in expectancy of the sensations that I was about to feel. Mika and JJ took two more each and it didn't take the full fifteen minutes for me to be knocked on my ass.

The first pill crept slowly, this one decided to detour and went full fucking force. My whole body from the tips of my toes to my hair follicles felt tingles, like raindrops were falling on every part of me. I had intense rushing sensations and it was exhilarating. It was euphoric and I was having a full-blown body orgasm and no one was even touching me.

As I lay there, looking at the ceiling, I had full mental clarity. I had insight, a bursting holistic high; my vision was blurry, but heightened along with my tactile senses. My perception of everything around me would shift from second to second, and out of nowhere, I wanted to love and be loved. I looked over at the men whose eyes were black irises; there were no color in them. They were dilated, pulsating, and beautiful.

I smiled high from ear to ear.

"Angel, you are rolling your balls off. You have no idea what you just signed on for, little girl." Mika's voice intensified the tingles throughout my body, especially throughout my pussy, as I watched him leave the room.

"You ever done a Nuru massage?" JJ whispered in my ear, bringing my thoughts back to what they had in store for me.

Mika entered the bedroom with a blow up mattress and placed it on the floor next to the bed, and then placed a large bowl that looked like it had oil in it next to it.

JJ grabbed my hand and escorted me to the mattress where he laid me down in the center, my head on a makeshift pillow of a towel.

"You want us to fuck that beautiful glistening cunt, don't you, Lilith; you're dripping wet just waiting for it. You want us so deep in your pussy and ass that you won't be able to walk for days, and every time you do you can still feel us there. That's what you want…isn't it, dirty girl?" JJ expressed to me, making me crave exactly what he was saying.

They both dipped their hands in the bowl and brought it to their bodies, slathering and smearing it all over their chests. The substance was thick, and honey-like.

"What is that?" I questioned as I admired their glistening, toned bodies and their rock hard cocks standing at attention.

"It's Nuru gel, you're next," JJ responded.

They continued to gel every inch of their bodies until I couldn't take it anymore and started to crawl over to them. The gel had fallen onto the mattress and it made crawling over to them a little difficult. Once I reached the edge of the mattress, I cupped my hands into the bowl and proceeded to do exactly what I just saw them do. I provocatively began at my neck and worked my way down to my breasts, making sure to caress and entice my body as I went. My eyes closed with a flutter and my hands took on a life of their own.

CHAPTER 13

I was in my own little world where all my senses were active and aching around me. I didn't have to open my eyes to know that JJ and Mika were staring and stroking themselves to the vision of me applying the gel over my breasts, stomach, legs; purposely making them wait to see me touch myself where they wanted me the most. I didn't give them what they wanted, what I wanted, I teased my lower abdomen and my inner thighs just inches away from my sex, making the build up for all of us more explosive.

I opened my eyes and it was exactly how I pictured it in my mind, they were both on their knees, stroking their cocks with excitement in their dark dilated eyes.

I grinned at them, watching the way their hands glided along their glorious cocks.

"Put on a show for me. Let me see you guys touch and kiss each other," I requested, using the same tone that Mika had once used for Nakita and I.

"Not going to happen, Angel, but we will play with you," he asserted, making me whimper in disappointment.

I would make them do what I wanted; it was only a matter of time.

I eased my way back down, lying on my back and spreading my legs as wide as they would go as an open invitation for them to do what they pleased. They both started to massage my feet, which made me gasp and arch my back. I was not expecting to feel that much intensity from them touching me. My own hands did wonders, but theirs was a feeling like no other, leaving a trail of heat in the awakening of my body to their movements. The want, lust, and passion for me was burning off of them and radiating into my soul.

They moved simultaneously together, it was if they didn't need to communicate any words between each other to know what we all wanted; moving in sync up my thighs to my calves kneading and rubbing their way toward my happy ending.

I silently repeated "please don't stop" in my head over and over again, afraid that if I said it out loud they would stop just to torture me. The touch of their hands continued to caress my limbs and it ignited my nerve endings to a smoldering fire.

JJ moved in between my legs and Mika came to my side. He began to caress my breasts in soft, but demanding touches, the gel making it effortlessly easy for him to slide up and down from my breasts to the sides of my stomach.

"Your cunt wants to be touched doesn't it, Lilith; I can see your clit just poking its nub out, wanting to be touched and licked," JJ huskily taunted.

"I want my cock in the back of your throat, Angel." Mika moved on top of me in the sixty-nine position holding himself up and roughly pushed his dick right to the back of my throat and I greedily took every last inch of it. He pushed in and out, pumping in fast, hard strokes, and I kept up the pace as firm as I could, making my mouth a vice for him.

Mika lowered himself on to his elbows, never letting up thrusting himself into my mouth. I moaned at what I assumed he was about to do, it caught me off guard when I felt him lean his weight toward his left side and what I assumed to be his right palm push down on my lower abdomen.

"I'm going to fuck your pussy with my hand, Lilith, and you are going to come all over it. You're going to come so hard that your body is going to shake and I'm not going to let up. I am going to keep fucking you," JJ groaned as two of his fingers readily eased into me. I felt his index and pinky finger on my ass in a rock-star gesture; Mika pushed my lower abdomen harder and JJ started to pump his fingers up and down.

I moaned as loud and blatant as I possibly could with a dick in my mouth and it vibrated Mika's shaft. I had never been finger fucked like that before. Mika continued to push on my lower abdomen as JJ rapidly moved his fingers in an up and down motion keeping his fingers inside the entire time.

It was only a matter of minutes before my body was convulsing, contracting, and shaking, which made Mika thrust in and out of my mouth even harder and faster. It was an overload of emotions and sensations. I could physically feel my pussy pushing JJ's fingers out, Mika pushed a little deeper and JJ went firmer and quicker. Until he finally removed his fingers on his own and I came with such force that my entire body quivered and trembled.

I had no control over it, I shuddered and shook and JJ pushed his fingers back in and they repeated the process. I continued to suck Mika's dick as best as I could, but it got to the point where he just had to remove himself from my mouth and sit beside me to hold my body down as I writhed and moaned. They repetitively assaulted my g-spot, never changing their techniques.

"Jesus, Angel, the mattress is soaked. You're such a dirty girl. Get on your knees, put that beautiful ass in the air, and lick all your juices off the bed." I stood on wobbly knees and seductively brought my face to the mattress and licked as much of myself as I could, enjoying the taste and flavor that was uniquely mine.

I glided toward JJ and slid my way up his body, the gel making it naturally easy. Mika came up from behind and pushed my breasts into his dick, cupping them and making JJ jerk forward and backward in between them. I lavished in the feel of his cock between my cleavage. JJ lay down, taking me with him and I pursued my mission of sliding up and down his body, while Mika rubbed up and down my body with his hands. I got to JJ's mouth and fervently kissed him, making sure that he could taste me with every stroke of my tongue. He groaned.

Mika kissed his way up my back while he began playing with the pucker of my ass making slow tortuous circles. I grabbed the back of Mika's head and hastily pulled him toward JJ's face. I moved fast knowing that if I didn't, they would both resist. The second Mika's mouth touched ours we all groaned in unison. I was the first to make my tongue available and they quickly followed. We all kissed with hunger and craving for more. The feeling of having all lips tangled within each other enhanced every single response from my sex. I wanted and needed more.

I slowly and determinedly moved my face away to watch the naughtiness before me. JJ and Mika did not stop passionately kissing each other. It only added to my yearning. I watched as they roughly shoved their tongues in each other's mouths, not caring about the taboo of it all. I know it was the ecstasy that had worked its magic and they were so caught up in the tangle of the drug that they weren't aware that I wasn't a part of their three-way at the moment. The visual and the aroma of them captivated me, I hadn't realized that I was finger fucking myself until an unexpected orgasm crept its way from my body and I brazenly moaned.

The sound broke the zealous fervor of them kissing and they opened their eyes to watch me come apart.

"Angel, no one said you could come yet, little girl," Mika growled.

"Well…you also said you wouldn't touch JJ and look how that turned out," I taunted, slightly panting.

They shook their heads, silently agreeing with what I had just reminded them. "Come here, Lilith," JJ urgently demanded.

I made my way over to JJ and straddled his thighs, as Mika came up from behind me to play with the pucker of my anus. I bent forward to lavishly kiss JJ, and stroke his cock with my hand in a twirling motion. He grunted and began to make torturous circles around my clit, making the nub peak out once again. Mika's tongue licked my anus with abandonment and the purpose of creating lubrication for what was to come.

I had three-ways before, but this was the first time that I would take both men in each hole. Mika pushed two fingers into the dampness of my pussy, going straight for my g-spot, while his other hand pushed two fingers into my anus. JJ never let up on baiting my clit. The raw uninhibited craving to want to come again hit me like a ton of bricks, and before my core contracted, JJ and Mika both shoved their cocks into each hole making me scream out in nirvana.

Both men grunted "fuck" at the same time and I inaudibly agreed. We were quiet and still, relinquishing our bodies to the poetry we had created in our movements. I felt full, whole, and complete, as if my body was made for this. I was put on earth for this reason and this reason alone, to experience all the carnality that I could gather in one lifetime. JJ slowly but purposely moved my hips, and Mika gently guided himself out and back in.

"Jesus…I promised you that I would fuck your ass, Angel, but never in my wildest dreams did I think you would feel like this. Tell me, tell me how much you love my cock in your ass," he lured; his voice full of lust and want.

"Oh God, please don't stop. I want it harder. I want you and JJ to fuck me harder and faster. Please…ahhh…yes…yes…just like that," I praised as they both fucked me at the same time and pace.

They both moved in and out of me, and I exalted in being the center of attention, they were rough but I wanted it rough. I wanted them to brand me, to make me theirs even if it was just for the night. I craved being owned, for someone to etch their way into my skin, through my bloodstream, and leave nothing more than destruction in its wake.

"You love it don't you, Lilith; you love having your ass and your cunt fucked at the same time," JJ grunted.

"You will never be the same after this…every time you touch yourself or you're with another person you will come thinking about this exact moment. Where you felt completely satisfied."

They continued their assault on my most sacred parts until I could feel their cocks getting thicker and harder, and it made my pussy pulsate and grip even tighter. Mika caressed my breasts and pinched my nipples and JJ began teasing my clit. My head fell back on Mika's shoulder and he nipped and sucked my neck, while saying dirty and lascivious things that pushed me closer to the edge.

I don't know how long we fucked each other with a relinquishment of everything around us. The room smelled of sex and lust. The familiar response of wanting to come made its way down to my pussy and I began to completely come apart. I couldn't believe how many times I had already come, but my body still wanted more. All of our breathing and panting correlated. We were moments away from coming apart together, as one. It took a few more thrusts, grunts, and groans, and we all came at the exact same time and my body greedily accepted all of their juices.

We fell on top of each other's sweaty, slicked bodies.

All it took was one look from each of us and we did it all over again.

❊VIP❊

The next morning, or should I say afternoon, I was the first to wake up. I was pleased to see that both men were lying toward the end of the bed and we weren't in some pathetic cuddling position. My body was sticky and felt nasty so I decided to take a shower before hightailing it the hell out of there. I changed into a white button down shirt from Mika's closet and a pair of his boxers. I had a cab waiting for me downstairs. I tiptoed out into the bedroom, and to my surprise, they weren't where I left them. I made my way toward the living room and they were both sitting out on the balcony, drinking what looked like coffee.

Mika caught my stare. "Nice shirt," he stated, pointing to it.

"I guess you just decided that you were going to leave without so much as a goodbye, huh. Were you at least going to leave a thank you note, Angel? Should we be hurt?"

"I don't do mornings, Mika, I think you would be aware of that. It's too cutesy for me. I'm more of a hit it and quit it kind of a girl," I goaded, walking out toward them.

"Care to enlighten me on when you guys became so chummy?" I announced.

"It could have been last night when we fucked you…or maybe a few years ago when we went to college together, or maybe before that when we grew up together," JJ responded, making Mika laugh.

"You guys played me," I exclaimed, trying to control the anger that suddenly flooded me.

"Not exactly, I told you we were meeting a friend. Meet my friend Mika," he answered with a smirk that I immediately wanted to slap off his face.

"Oh come on, Angel…don't be upset. It's not like you didn't give it up to us over and over and over again," he taunted with a sexy smile.

"Fuck you."

He placed his hand on his chest, feigning hurt and pulled a check out of his pocket. "I guess you don't want this then," he said, placing it on the table.

I hadn't ever seen so many zeros follow the number one before.

It was that second that I realized I didn't have to share what I just made.

It was all mine.

I grinned, grabbed the check, and got the fuck out of there.

CHAPTER 14

A few months later, Madam and I sat at lunch.

"Darling, I will be canceling all dates and appointments until further notice."

"What, why?" I questioned.

"Have you not seen the news or heard about the epidemic of AIDS and HIV? I need to get all the VIPs tested, along with the clients. I'm also adding mandatory testing to the new clients. It's going to take a while considering the test has just now hit the market, but I'm sure I'll be able to get a hold of it before the public. I have people on it right now," she explained as she drank her $2,000 champagne.

"I have listened to the news and it's affecting drug addicts and homosexuals. I highly doubt our society of clients will be affected. What if I don't want to stop?" I argued, refusing to take my eyes off hers.

She turned to look behind her and then turned back to face me. "Excuse me? I'm sorry, were you just talking to me like that or is there someone behind me that I am not aware of?"

I rolled my eyes at her dramatics. "I think this idea is absolutely ridiculous. What you're saying is that I will not be making money and neither will the other girls. Don't you think it's about time that you let us control what we do with our pussies? It would give you the time to do whatever the fuck you do."

She looked at her nail polish and then at her nails, I could sense that she was considering what she was about to say.

She smirked. "Go home and get dressed, wear your Valentino mid knee length black dress, and red heels. I will pick you up at nine," she asserted, leaving cash on the table and walking away.

The Madam

I showered and got dressed in a dark maroon, tight silk blouse, with a low lying v-cut neckline; a black pencil skirt that had a slit up my right thigh, and black knee high boots. I kept myself busy doing a few lines of cocaine as I waited for Madam to arrive. Concierge rang, informing me that a white stretch limo was waiting for me downstairs. I was greeted with a glass of champagne from the driver that I gladly accepted. Madam was on the phone when I entered the limo and she raised an eyebrow, questioning my outfit when she saw me; I smiled in return.

"Ciao, bella," she said into the phone as she hung up.

"The boots are a little much, don't you think?" She examined my wardrobe, tilting her head to the side.

"Not at all," I replied with a satisfied grin. "Where are we going?"

She smirked and before she could answer, the limo phone rang and she remained on it for the duration of our ride. Twenty-five minutes later, we arrived at our location. I enjoyed almost a half of bottle of champagne on my own, the cocaine allowing the leniency to do so. The car came to a complete stop and Madam opened the door.

"Get out," she hissed.

I looked at her confused and stepped out of the vehicle expecting her to follow me as I got out, but the limo left as soon as I closed the door.

"What the fuck?" I whispered to myself.

I took in my surroundings and the street signs indicated that I was on 79th and Biscayne Blvd. It was dark, dingy, and dirty. I started to feel anxious and nervous; I had never been to that part of town. Women, from what I could only assume were hookers, were everywhere. They were on the street corners and by the intersection. Some were in groups and others were completely alone. They were dressed in trashy lingerie that left very little to the imagination.

I gradually felt the panic that started to arise from the pit of my stomach. I didn't have a dollar on me and from what I gathered standing there for the last ten minutes; cabs didn't bother to come to this part of town. I took a deep breath and started to walk my happy ass toward the next gas station, which seemed to be miles away, and my poor choice of five-inch stilettos weren't exactly accommodating. I could see him from the corner of my eye; a man had been eyeing me since the second I got out of the limo. I was tired of this cat and mouse game he appeared to be playing and I spun quickly around to face him, catching him off guard.

"What?" I shouted, annoyed at his blatant gawking.

He cocked his head to the side. "You lost, Little Red Riding Hood? Off to grandma's you go?" he mocked in a suggestive tone that disgusted me.

"What the fuck is it to you what I'm doing? Mind your own goddamn business, unless asked for an opinion, asshole! Women don't like men who talk," I stated, turning around, but he caught my arm before I could take the next step.

"Who the fuck do you think you are, little girl? I own this corner and since you're standing on it, guess what, princess? I own you too," he seethed in my ear.

"Fuck. You!" I shouted spitting in his face.

"You little cunt!" he sneered as he pulled my hair back to expose my neck, he slowly took his tongue and licked from my collarbone to my chin and all I wanted to do was throw up in my mouth. "You're mine now."

He started to drag me toward a dark alley, covering my mouth so I wasn't able to scream. A strange and unfamiliar feeling coursed through my body. I knew it couldn't have been fear- I don't fear anything- but it was something similar to it.

A car approached us and I silently prayed that it was a police officer.

"Miguel!" a man shouted from the driver's side of the vehicle.

He completely stopped and I could feel his elaborate heartbeat on my back.

The man got out of the vehicle and Miguel released me. I was about to take off running but watched as he right hooked Miguel in the face, making him fall to the ground and groan.

"I have told you time and time again to keep your fucking dick in your pants. Get yourself cleaned up and go home. You're done for the night," he growled through gritted teeth.

"Get in," he demanded once he turned to face me.

I didn't have much of a choice at that point, so I got in the car.

I put my seatbelt on as I waited for him to do the same and then we drove off.

"Ocean Drive please," I requested, thankful for the rescue.

He nodded. "What are you doing in this part of town?"

"Being punished," I blatantly said, knowing it was the truth.

We rode in silence for the next ten minutes and when he didn't take the turn needed to get to South Beach, I realized that my punishment wasn't over.

I hesitated. "Where are we going?"

He smiled but didn't answer. We came to a red light and I quickly tried to open the door to get out and it wouldn't budge. The fucking door was on child lock. I screamed in frustration.

"Please...don't do this. I have money; I have lots of money. If you take me home, I will give it all to you," I unashamedly begged.

"I have money, I don't need any more."

"Really?! Because judging by this piece of shit car it doesn't seem that way," I aggressively shouted, angry over the turn of events.

His hand reached over to graze my cheek and I closed my eyes in disgust.

"I'm not going to hurt you, calm down," he coolly stated.

I wasn't stupid, I knew whatever he had planned it wasn't anything that I wanted to be a part of.

He parked his car in an alley that I had never seen before in my life.

I glared at the darkness before me, not wanting to face him in any way. I heard him take his seat belt off and then he did the same to mine. I stood my ground; I didn't want to give him the satisfaction of making me feel weak.

He started stroking my arm with his fingertips in an up and down motion.

"Oh come on...this isn't so bad. I saved you back there and I think I should get something of a reward. Don't you think?"

I didn't respond.

"All I want is to finger fuck you, gorgeous. You come, and I drive you home. It's as easy as that," he suggested.

"It's still rape," I retorted, still not looking at him.

"Geez, you women nowadays, so quick to throw out the rape card. The thing is you're going to enjoy it and you're going to tell me exactly how you love it." He got close to my ear. "Exactly...how you want me to touch you...the faster you come, the faster you get to go home. Simple as that." He crudely grabbed my chin. "Look at me."

I did. It was the first time I looked at him, and he was actually a handsome looking guy and if he wasn't about to violate me and make me enjoy it, I probably would have liked him. He had piercing green eyes and slick black hair that was tied in a ponytail; his facial features were rough but strong.

He rubbed his nose on mine and then brought his thumb to my mouth tracing my bottom lip.

"Get it nice and wet for me," he said.

My tongue sought out his finger and I licked it just how he wanted me too, he groaned in appreciation.

"I know what kind of girl you are. What makes you think what we're doing is any different than what you will do with other clients, huh? Consider me driving you home as payment. Just because I don't drive a Bentley doesn't mean I don't have money." His voice was deep and raspy, causing the air inside the car to feel thick and warm.

Did I believe him? Who the fuck knows…Miami is full of all kinds of people. Did that change the fact that I didn't want him to do and get what he was going to take? Absolutely not. The ending was going to be the same, regardless if I wanted it or not.

He pulled his thumb out of my mouth and went right for the edge of my panties, moving them to the side to rub my clit with his thumb in a circular motion.

I wanted to cry, and if I thought for one second that I could overpower the son of a bitch I would have. Though, that would only leave me more broken and bruised. I hated that this fucker had the control, I hated that I wasn't getting paid, but most of all, I hated that my body was betraying me and my pussy was getting wet. He knew what he was doing. I didn't have to tell him shit. All he wanted was to belittle me, and make me feel like the piece of shit that he was.

The way his lust-filled eyes stared at me made me want to turn away. I wanted nothing more than to close my eyes and make it all go away. The way he manipulated my sex reminded me of Anderson and how he used my body to do exactly the same thing. Even though he was handling me with more attentiveness and care, it didn't matter; it made me feel cheap and used, like I could be easily discarded, like some drug addict sucking cock. In that instant I didn't feel like a VIP, I felt like a toy, like a fucking puppet that was not only being controlled by this man, but also by my mother.

"It's show time," he reminded me, bringing my thoughts back to the present. "Tell me…let me hear you say the words to make you come."

I slightly panted, "Keep moving your thumb like that. Push a little firmer on my clit...yes like that. Take your index and middle finger and push them inside me."

He did as he was told and my breathing accelerated along with his. I could smell the vodka and tobacco on his breath.

He eased his fingers into me, my dampness making it easy for him.

"Hmmm...your cunt feels tight. I can't wait to taste you on my fingers," he huskily stated. Normally these words would have affected me and I would have been agreeably willing to give him whatever he wanted. But I didn't want to, I felt like a slut, a hooker, a prostitute. Everything I was told that I would never be. I wanted to get this over as fast as possible. I wanted to shower and crawl into my bed, wishing this whole ordeal never happened.

I played my part. "Curl your fingers in an upward motion. Ahhh...yes...you feel that rigid end?" I heard him groan.

"Yeah...right there...fuck me there...move your fingers in and out... faster... harder..." I whimpered, trying to control the tears that were stabbing the backs of my eyes, begging to be released. I was in this fucked up limbo of wanting to get off and wanting to crawl into a hole. My emotions were all over the place.

"Your pussy is gripping my fingers, you love this you dirty whore, don't you? You want to be used...want to be fucked and put in your place. Rich bitches like you always want to be abused." I tried to block out his words, refusing to let them sink into my mind. There was no aiding it, his cruel and vicious statements sunk into the bottom of my being and I shut my eyes, hoping that it would take away the pain. The anguish and discomfort that I felt couldn't be controlled. He fucked my g-spot over and over again until my mind went blank and I came.

I didn't open my eyes to watch the satisfied glow in his smile and demeanor, I knew the second his fingers left my sex they were going straight to his mouth. I turned back around, pulling down my skirt and hanging my head in shame.

I gave him the directions to my condo and we didn't talk the entire time. We made it to my front entrance and I waited for him to get out of the car to open my door.

"You enjoyed it, princess; don't act as if you're high and mighty now. It's a little late for that."

I didn't say anything to him, wanting him to leave so I could be alone.

"You're welcome. Come on...let me hear you say it and you can go."

I bit my lip and tasted blood. "Thank you," I whispered, hoping that he heard it, so that I didn't have to repeat it again.

"Thank you for what, again?" he continued to taunt me.

"Thank you for driving me home."

"And..." Once again, he grabbed my chin to make me look at him. It took everything I had not to smack that smug look off his face.

"Thank you...for making me come," I stated through clenched teeth.

He smiled wide and I jerked my chin away, huffing in disgust.

I walked into my condo in a trance. I stood there with the door open, looking at all the extravagant beauty before me. My stomach churned and I ran to the sink, throwing up every last substance that was left. I rinsed my mouth out and I turned off the sink. I went to the fridge and grabbed the Pellegrino and poured myself a glass, I took two sips and hurled it across the room. I watched as it shattered against the wall, falling into shards on the ground.

My body moved fast and I started to push over everything that was in my immediate eyesight. I threw, flung, and swung at anything I could find. I screamed at the top of my lungs over and over again, until my throat burned raw. Minutes later, and I just stood there, panting and heaving; my chest propelling itself upward with every few hyper-vented breaths. I walked toward the trash and immediately removed all of my clothing, throwing away every article I was wearing in the receptacle.

I walked into the bathroom, never once looking in the mirror and turned on the shower. I stood under the running water for what seemed like hours, longing for the water to wash away my thoughts, my memory. Finally, my body and mind couldn't take it anymore and I fell to the floor crying.

The moment of a realization is a brutal and an ugly bitch.

I was a pawn, and my mother just checkmated me.

CHAPTER 15

The next morning I awoke with the memory of the night before still fresh in my mind. I heard noises coming from my kitchen and I didn't have to wonder who it was. I grabbed my black silk robe and took care of my morning routine before making my way into the kitchen. I could smell the delicacy before stepping into the foyer. There was a huge spread of breakfast laid out on my island, you name it, and it was there. My condo was also spotless, and I had nothing to do with that. I rolled my eyes and grabbed some coffee.

I walked into the adjoining living room and saw that Madam was on the phone on my balcony. I opened my liquor cabinet and poured some Kahlua in my coffee, and she walked in mid pour.

"Isn't it a little early for that?" she interrogated me in a calm tone.

I poured more. "You tell me," I disputed as I turned to face her.

She smiled coldly. "You should eat some breakfast."

"I should do a lot of things," I quickly countered.

I stepped toward her. "Tell me, Madam," another step, "if I cut you," one last step, "will you even bleed?" I mercilessly questioned.

She raised an eyebrow and grinned. "How was night last night? You still think you can control your own pussy? Learn from your mistakes, darling. That's what happens to VIPs who don't listen and follow direction. They end up on the street like some common whore; anyone can sell what's in between their legs, Lilith. It just comes down to how you sell it. My VIPs sell their pussies and see the world. Understood?" She arched an eyebrow and I scarcely nodded.

She kissed my forehead. "Great. Now…since you have been such a good girl, I have a present for you. Let's eat some breakfast, and then you can get ready, and I will show you."

An hour later and we were with the chauffeur in the Bentley. To say that I wasn't a little nervous to be in a car with her again would have been an understatement. Though I played it off well, it was what she wanted. We pulled up to the University of Miami and then took a detour toward the sorority houses. Once we reached the Alpha Delta Phi house, the car came to a complete stop. I watched Madam check her watch and then roll down my window half way.

Just like clockwork, a girl came out of the house with books in her arms. She must have been about nineteen, maybe twenty. She looked like a California native, with curly blonde hair, tan skin, and bright green eyes. She wore very little makeup, and her clothing accentuated her figure. She exuded beauty and confidence as she walked down the steps.

"I want her," I heard Madam say from behind me. "And you're going to make it happen. You have one week," she announced; and with that, the car drove off.

❊VIP❊

Money will always get you whatever you want. It didn't take long for me to have the girl's entire school schedule and daily itinerary in my hands, along with her name, age, and social security number. Taylor Vaughn was twenty years old, a Sagittarius, born and raised in California, studying marketing with a minor in business and was the secretary of her sorority.

Cute, isn't it?

Luck was on my side, it was Friday and the sorority was putting on their annual Hawaiian hula beach party. I dressed in the tiniest red bikini I had, with a see through, wrap around black skirt, and heels, of course.

I arrived at the party by midnight and the place was packed. I grabbed a couple shots at the bar and coincidently found Taylor with her friend in the corner, they were whispering in each other's ears, giggling and staring at someone. My eyes went in the direction of theirs and that's when I saw him.

Bingo!

He was chatting with what I could only assume to be his fraternity brothers. He was handsome in a boyish sort of way, not that I hate young guys or anything, but I prefer men. Boys are a lot like toys, they are great to play with, and this one wouldn't be any different. He had spiked, blonde hair, brown eyes, plump lips, and the v-shaped fuck me muscles that made me want to ride him all the way home. I grabbed two beers and made my way over to him.

There were five of them in a circle talking. I wedged my way right in the middle and their faces said it all.

Approval. Appreciation. Lust. Want.

All in that order.

I licked my lips in a seductive way before biting my bottom lip, and flipping my hair.

"Hi, my name is Lilith. I brought you a beer," I said, looking only at him as I handed him the cold bottle.

He cleared his throat. "Ahem, Ken."

I smiled and traced the lining of my bikini by my cleavage with my index finger. "Want to dance?" He quickly nodded and I saw his Adams apple move from swallowing.

I grabbed his hand and escorted him over to the dance floor, making sure we were in perfect view of Taylor. I took one look at her and got the exact reaction that I wanted.

Jealously.

With my back to Ken, I crept closer, so that my ass was right on his groin. I slowly and provocatively moved my hips downward and then back up again, I did it a few times until his hands found their way to my hips. And I hummed in appreciation, making sure he could hear me, his breath gasped in response. I put my hands over his and guided them to caress me from my lower abdomen to my inner thighs. I never once let up on swaying my body in the movement of the music.

His hips and body finally caught on and we began moving together, his dick got hard, and I laid my head on his shoulder turning my face to breathe on him. I repositioned my right hand behind his neck, bringing him closer to me. His movements started to get more demanding along with his hands, and I rotated my hips to move even harder and faster on his dick. The music started to slow down to let everyone know that the song would be changing, and I unexpectedly turned around, catching him off guard. I placed my hands on his chest and pressed my lips close to his, close enough to lick his top lip. He shuddered.

"So, Ken...you got a Barbie?"

"No," he answered without hesitation.

"You want one?" I roused as my hand made its way to the top of his board shorts. I let my fingers tease the skin right below his waistline and I felt his goose bumps become alert.

"Who are you?" he requested in a desired plea.

"Anything you want. What do you want, Ken?"

"You."

"How much do you want me?"

"So fucking much," he distressingly answered.

I looked up at his eyes and saw the want and lust shining brightly back at me. "Thanks for the dance," I stated and smiled as I began backing away. I watched his torn face turn three shades of red before I turned to walk toward the courtyard. It took maybe a minute for me to hear the clicking of heels behind me.

Hook, line, and sinker.

I entered the secluded courtyard with Taylor not far behind me.

"I'm not much for cat fights, Taylor," I announced, facing her.

"That's what you're doing out here, right? You've come to confront the girl who dry humped your...whatever he is...on the dance floor?" I assertively stated.

"How do you know my name?" she immediately responded.

I cocked my head to the side. "That's what you ask? Really? Oh, come on, Taylor! Don't let me down. I have such high hopes for you. Let's try that again."

She hesitated, only for a moment. "Who are you?"

I laughed. "Much better." I walked closer and moved the hair that had fallen over her face behind her ear. "I am your future. Do you see what happened in there? I know you did. Did you see how easy it was to make him want me? If I would have gotten on my knees and blew him in front of the entire room, he would have happily let me. It didn't matter that he knew you were in the room." I paused to let my words sink in.

"Do you want to know what it feels like to have men groveling at your feet? To have so much money that you could literally wipe your pussy with a hundred dollar bill every time you go to the bathroom and not think twice about it? How about seeing the world? Huh? To feel like you are number one at every moment of every day," I enticed, watching her eyes fill with wonder.

"You would be taken care of, wined and dined. They will give you everything you have ever wanted and then some. You check all of your inhibitions, judgments, assumptions, values, and beliefs at the door, Taylor," I blatantly declared.

"I can see it in your eyes, you want it. Right or wrong, yes or no, devil or angel…they're all just words, nothing more, nothing less. All you have to do is say yes and I will take you to the Promised Land. And I can guarantee you that you will never look back." I watched her smile and I knew I had gotten to her.

I watched as her tongue slowly but purposely moved out of her mouth to lick her lips. The tables turned fast. Little Miss Taylor was provoking me.

"Would you like to know how to please a woman, Taylor?" I whispered on the edge of her mouth, my lips softly kissed the corner of hers, and I continued to peck kisses till her mouth moved in unison with mine.

In an instant, her tongue found mine.

I took Taylor's first virgin girl card that night. It only took fourteen hours of Madam introducing me to her to make her come in my mouth. I couldn't believe how much that girl wanted it. Just goes to show that women do it better and blondes will always have more fun.

I sat in my car, reeking of cheap perfume and sex. I dialed Madam from my car phone the second I put it in drive.

She answered on the second ring, "Madam."

"It's done. She will be at The Cathouse at noon."

Silence.

I could hear her breathing through the phone, so I knew she hadn't hung up.

"Goodnight," I said, breaking the silence and hanging up.

CHAPTER 16

I arrived in Madam's office at 11:30 the next morning. She was looking through some files and put them away as I walked toward her.

"What are you doing here?" she asked with an annoyed tone.

"I've come to train my new recruit. She is mine, isn't she? I mean, I have already been between her legs and now I would like to see her in between someone else's." I satisfyingly smiled while I sat on the corner of her desk leaning my body on my hands.

"Oh come on, Madam Dearest, are you pissed off because it only took me a few hours to get her here or did someone come on your face this morning and ruin your mascara?" I said with raised eyebrows.

She crossed her arms and leaned back in her chair. "You think you can handle the training of a new VIP? Just because you got her here, doesn't mean she will stay. Thus, get off your high horse. It's far from a done deal, Lilith," she snubbed.

"You wouldn't say that if you saw how much I made her scream my name last night. We can reenact it if you wish. I could eat, I'm sort of getting hungry," I snickered.

She shook her head. "You think you can handle this…then by all means." She handed me a business card. "I want both of you there by ten." I put the card in my cleavage.

The door opened and Taylor was escorted in. She blushed the moment she saw me and I winked at her. I crossed my legs on the desk and put my hands on my knees, like a lady.

"Taylor Vaughn, I presume," Madam said, looking the epitome of the hierarchy she presumed she was. Taylor nodded.

"Darling, I don't bite. Please have a seat."

Taylor sat mimicking the exact same position I was in. This was going to be way too easy…

"Before we talk about anything else, let's talk about the logistics. By you coming here today, you have agreed to move forward with Lilith's proposition, I assume?" She nodded again.

I watched carefully as Madam moved from her seat to go sit by her, she grabbed her hands in a comforting, almost motherly, gesture. This was the first time I had ever seen Madam with a new VIP, I quickly realized how different our introductions to the lifestyle were.

"I am a Madam. Do you know what that is, Taylor?" she asked and Taylor shook her head no.

"Well…it's a French word for a lady. It could also mean queen, or a mistress, or it could mean a woman who owns a brothel. Do you know what that is?"

She looked down at her lap. "Something to do with prostitution, right?"

Madam smiled sincerely and grazed the side of her cheek. "Tsk, tsk, tsk, prostitution is such an ugly word, and it's highly illegal," she said in a high pitched voice.

She carefully grabbed her chin. "What I run here is very much a legitimate business. I pay my taxes like any other American citizen. Nevertheless, I'd like you to call this home a The Cathouse; I have some very important high society sets of clientele, who are looking for only the best. My little black book is filled with names from all around the world; politicians, celebrities, sheiks, princes, kings, doctors, men, and women, all looking for the same thing." She cocked her head to side. "You name it and I probably have it. My place of business provides services of all kinds, Taylor, not just sexual. We provide companionship, you *escort* a client for a duration of time and they pay."

"Ok…and this is where I come in. I would be with them?" she asked. I could see how much her interest had piqued since she sat down.

"Absolutely. You are what makes me so successful. You could be powerful! Do you know what kind of power you hold with that tight little thing between your legs?"

It was amazing how easy it was to get inside her head, to know her thoughts before she did. I knew her mind was racing. She couldn't take in everything that was happening around her. I could see her having some sort of out of body experience. Her brain wasn't processing what she heard as fast as she would have liked. She stood up and walked over to the fireplace. She stood there, thinking to herself for a few seconds in wonderment of what Madam was implying. I turned when I heard the clicks of heels. Madam was coming up behind her. She froze when she felt the tips of her fingers stroll up and down her spine.

I swallowed the saliva that was building in my mouth. This was completely different from how I approached her. I was arrogant about it. Madam was smooth and charismatic; she knew she was holding all of the power, but made Taylor believe otherwise. I was watching her mind fuck the hell out of her, just waiting for her to take the bait.

"Do you understand what I am telling you? I want you. I want you more than I have ever wanted any other woman."

She was too frightened to turn around; I could sense it all the way from where I was sitting. The saliva that had been building in my mouth was now a lump in my throat.

"You want to fuck me?" she asked, nervously.

"Yes I do, but not for the reasons that you think," she continued; while still rubbing her back, she kissed the left side of her neck. "I want to fuck you in order to teach you." She kissed the center of her neck. "I want to fuck you to please you." She kissed the right side. "I want to fuck you to taste you." She whispered in her ear loud enough for me to hear, "More than anything, I want to fuck you…to make you."

She closed her eyes, trying to soak in her words.

"Make me what?" she managed to say.

Moving her fingers from Taylor's back, she cupped her chin, beckoning her to turn toward her. She did. Madam looked deep her eyes and spoke with more conviction than I had ever witnessed.

"I want to make you a VIP."

She proceeded to tell her all about the business and how everything worked. It was as if I was watching a movie. Madam had a way with words, even her demeanor was different, and I quickly recognized how threatened she felt by me. My father was right, Madam got off on controlling people and with that came power. She couldn't do that with me, she knew that VIP would be mine, and there was nothing she could do about it. The only thing she did have control over was *when* it would be mine.

I learned a lot that afternoon. Madam was like a mother to her VIPs. She was captivating and alluring, the way she related every single detail of what was to come was astonishing. She painted a picture of it all with such strength and tenacity; the determination in her voice and the eloquence of her very existence was incredible. I was already a VIP and I was ready to sign my soul away on the dotted line. Madam's charisma had a magnetic pull and Taylor was the iron.

Taylor was excused to take care of all the necessary details of being a VIP.

I removed the business card from my cleavage. "I thought we weren't going to be working for a while. Is this date going to be PG?" I sarcastically questioned.

"That gentlemen is good to go, Lilith. I would never put you in harm's way," she said moving the hair out of my face.

"Mmm hmm…" I cautiously responded.

She smiled victoriously. "The limo will pick you up first and then it will go get her, all right?" I nodded.

"You're so beautiful, darling. I'm proud to have you as my daughter," she softly spoke.

"Mmm hmm…" I cautiously smiled back at her, wondering what game she was playing.

Madam was the queen of manipulation. She would take, take, and take, until she could feel you on the verge of the landing, and only then would she give.

But actions will *always* speak louder than words.

I dressed in a tight blue strapless corset dress with lace up heels. The limo arrived at 9:15 pm and I was once again greeted with a glass of champagne. It didn't take long for us to get to her new condo and I watched as she exited her building, her new makeover full in effect. She was glowing. It made me contemplate the awakening of one's persona…

Haven't you ever felt like that?

Primal, hungry, a thirst, an itch, an ache for the unknown?

That was VIP.

She was handed champagne and I could tell she was caught off guard when she saw me sitting in the limo, though she politely smiled with a hint of bashfulness behind it. She sat across from me and within minutes, she was fidgeting with her hands in her lap.

I grabbed the vile that I had in my purse for just this reason. I could sense she was watching my every move playing the fiddle of the innocent girl card very well.

"Are you ready?"

She took a deep breath but nodded.

"Taylor, we are way past playing coy, aren't we? I've already seen your landing strip," I declared, bringing my pinky up to my nose and sniffing.

"You want? I share," I stated in a teasing voice.

"I don't do drugs," she responded in a serious tone.

I chuckled. "I don't either."

"I've never done anything like that before."

"Never say never," I encouraged, handing her the vile.

She grabbed it, like I knew she would, and repeated the same process I just did. "It burns."

"Give it a minute to work its magic. She moves quickly."

The limo stopped and she handed me the vile with a satisfied smile on her face. I stepped out and grabbed her hand and we rode the elevator to the penthouse suite. The doors opened to the suite and Madam and a gentleman I had never seen met us.

"Girls," Madam said, "this is Luke. Luke, this is Lilith and Taylor."

He leaned in and kissed each of our cheeks and guided us toward the living room. The camera setup that was in the corner caught Taylor's and my attention immediately. Madam sensed it like she does everything and grabbed Taylor's hand from Luke to sit next to her on the couch. Luke handed each of us a glass of champagne.

"Luke is aware that this is your first time with a client. You're nervous, darling. I can feel it all the way over here. Please, don't be nervous, nothing is going to happen that you don't want to happen. You need to remember, that you run the show, Taylor. I am a mere spectator." She downed her glass of champagne in one gulp.

"Why is there a camera set up?" she blurted out. Madam cocked a smile at her.

"You are an eager little thing, aren't you? Before we talk about that, let's talk about the logistics. By you coming here today, you have agreed to move forward with my proposition, I assume?"

"Yes," she replied.

"The most important thing that you need to remember is that you never discuss anything about being a VIP to anyone. This is a legal business; I require the utmost discretion from my girls." She nodded.

"Since we established a comradery earlier today, how about I answer your question," she suggested.

"This camera is for you, darling." She smiled. "Well...not just for you, it's for you, and Luke." Taylor looked between it and Luke with excitement and trepidation.

"He is going to teach you how to please your clients. The camera is going to record this scene in order for you to watch what you look like when you're with a client. It will be sort of a tutorial that you can study and grow from. Luke is very good at what he does. He is actually one of my top clients." She turned to me.

"Lilith, baby, will you go get that robe." I slid from the couch to retrieve it.

"This career will let you embrace all of life's pleasures, the pleasure of pleasing your clients, and most importantly...the pleasure of pleasing yourself," she said.

Madam moved to sit on the opposite side of the couch, and I handed Taylor the robe while she sat beside me. I glanced at the camera that was now pointed directly at us and noticed a little green light blinking. I hadn't realized my role in all of this, but I moved when Luke made his way toward Taylor.

CHAPTER 17

My attention went back to the scene before me, and all I could see was the trepidation all over her face when he whispered something into her ear. He started to caress the side of her neck with his hand, and on the other side, he laid soft tender kisses. He continued his journey of touching and trying to seduce her, Taylor had her eyes closed the entire time. Her movements, demeanor, attitude, and appearance were all wrong. This wasn't the same woman that I had been with the night before, her confidence and allure was gone.

I turned to see if Madam caught on and if she was going to put a stop to it and assist the girl. What startled me was that she was on her phone; she wasn't paying any attention to what was happening in front of her.

VIP isn't ever about our clients, it's not about giving, it's about taking.

We take it all and it's handed to us on a silver-fucking platter with a bright red bow.

We run the goddamn show.

The sound of my heels brought Madam's attention to me. Taylor hadn't noticed that I moved to sit next to her, but her eyes were still closed. I grabbed her by her chin bringing her attention to me. Luke noticed and cocked his head to the side in confusion.

I ignored him and looked right into Taylor's eyes.

"Don't worry about the camera, Taylor...don't worry about Luke, just focus on me, okay?" I said in a sultry tone and she nodded.

"Sweet and innocent, Taylor." My voice was low pitched; it was soothing and intoxicating. I kissed her lips lightly enjoying the savor of strawberry from her lip-gloss.

"I can tell already that you and I are going to be amazing friends. I started off a little like you. You remind me a lot of myself," I lied, continuing to praise her as I pulled both straps of her dress down to expose her breasts. Her demeanor had slightly changed, her white skin started to get rosy, and her nipples were hard.

I knew what I had to do; I had to make her feel comfortable. I had to make her feel like I knew what she was thinking, feeling, wanting. I did know all of those things, but not from my own experience. I knew all of that because I was that fucking good at what I do.

I've said it before, and I'll say it again; I was made for this.

And soon, Madam would see it all too clearly.

"I knew I wanted more out of life, I couldn't quite put my finger on it," I explained, moving to crouch on the floor. Never taking my eyes from hers, I tugged on the hem of her dress, beckoning her to shimmy out of it. I slid the dress over her ankles and placed it on the table. She sat there in just her panties and heels, not really knowing what to think. The hesitation was still written on her face, but now there was also temptation. I glanced over at Madam, noticing the look of satisfaction on her face. I wanted to make her happy. For whatever reason, I still wanted to please her. I also wanted to show her that I could do it better.

I knew what the fuck I was doing.

Taylor needed to be cherished; she needed to feel enticed, as if she was being provoked and tempted. Some women can't be thrown into the wild and survive; it takes a very special breed to be able to find their way out without a guidebook. I was Taylor's guidebook. I would mold her to what I wanted her to be.

Always lead by example.

I turned my attention back to Taylor. "Phew…you are going to make clients very happy…your body is a paradise," I admired. "Isn't she perfect, Luke?" He nodded with a huge grin on his face. He expected what was to come.

I rose, resting my weight on my knees and etching my lips on her collarbone, I blew soft breaths on her skin. I felt her breath catch, as I lightly caressed the sides of her breasts. She was awakened, and her nervousness was vaguely perceptible.

"Your breasts are round, plump, and perky."

My tantalizing breaths progressed to the middle of her breasts. Which caused another hidden gasp to be released.

"Your nipples are just the right size."

I looked up at her face, and continued caressing the sides of her breasts.

"I know you don't see it, but you're radiating sexuality; you were made for this. There are very few women in this world who are made for pleasure, for giving and receiving such pleasure, and you are one of them. We are few and far between, Taylor."

My hands skimmed the sides of her body until I stopped at the edges of her panties. With my index fingers, I began to slide them down. She slipped out one leg at a time. My nails lightly skimmed the sides of her legs leaving a trail of warmth behind her.

"The shoes stay on," I asserted.

I grabbed the robe and she extended her arm while I slid it on; I left it open in the front. I moved to sit down next to her and I could sense her disappointment that she was clothed again. She was riding the thrill, this was all new to her, it was a high that she couldn't even begin to explain. I knew this because I felt that same high once; and I continued to look for something, anything that matched that feeling. This, training Taylor, was a high unlike any other. I knew this was the kind of high that would never go away, and I was going to make sure of that.

She had a gleam in her eyes, one that I recognized because I was damn sure I was born with it there; the one that always kept them coming back for more.

It was working. I found even myself wanting more as I knelt down in front of her. "Spread your legs, Taylor," I demanded, in a soft tone. She did as she was told and the excitement on her face was informative. She could feel all our gazes on every inch of her body. I could feel the yearning and hunger in the room.

We were the predators and she was our prey.

"Your pussy is sweeter than I thought it would be, you're just the right shade of pink. That pleases me," Madam stated while inspecting her pussy. I wanted to be the one doing the praising, but as much as I didn't want to hear Madam, I knew there were still things she could teach me. Although I'm sure there was more that I could teach her.

Taylor's eyes said everything that we wanted to know.

She was adored. She was wanted. She was loved.

Her nerves had subsided and she felt aroused. I could see that her core was throbbing and all she craved was relief. She suppressed the urge to touch herself; I could see her dainty fingers twitching at the seams. I turned to her and twirled her hair, as I had seen Madam do earlier. I moved her hair to my nose and inhaled. She didn't seem surprised by my forwardness.

"Do you know that you have a deep erotic smell about you? It's addicting," I whispered on her neck, feeling the small bumps rise on her skin beneath my lips.

I grabbed the back of her hair and pulled, she moaned. I kissed lightly at her jaw line. I knew she had forgotten about everything in that moment and all she wanted to do was please us, I was making sure of that. I no longer cared that Madam was in the room, or that there was a camera filming us. Taylor thought this was about her, but it never fucking was, not for one second. This was about me, like everything had been in my life, this was another test.

One that I passed with flying colors.

I turned to look at Madam and her face said it all. Amazed...her face was full of amazement. Amazed at my achievement, and amazed that I didn't fail. Intimidation flared through her eyes. I felt the satisfaction in the depths of my being.

I engaged my attention back to Taylor, I desired her, I wanted to touch and taste her, again. I wanted to feel every inch of her body and have her do the same to me. I brought my lips to hers and traced her bottom lip with the tip of my tongue, and then did the same with the top. I softly pecked her lips to provoke a reaction. She understood and opened her mouth as I plunged my tongue in and she sought it out. Our tongues twirled around and we tasted each other, we were both moaning at this dance. We breathed each other in, like it was our last breath, inhaling the invigorating scent of arousal and lust.

"I knew you would be like this, Taylor. I knew, once given the chance, you would surpass any thought I would have imagined," I proclaimed.

She didn't pay any attention to what I was saying. She couldn't. She wanted me, just like she wanted me the night of the party. I tugged the edges of her robe and slipped it down, never breaking our kiss, our connection. I removed my dress over my head quickly and went right back for her lips. I could tell that she wanted to look at me. I removed my lips from hers and looked at her eyes, her pupils were dilated and her eyes appeared dark. I knew mine looked the same. She took that time to really look at me. Her eyes scanned my entire body in seconds, and I took the opportunity to glance over at Luke who was now stroking his cock.

"You're a vision, Lilith," she said, bringing my attention right back to her.

I needed to make the transition slow for her, but this twosome, had now become a threesome.

My eyes moved from her face to her throat and I saw her pulse at the base of her neck. I blinked and moved my eyes to her breasts, she was breathing heavily, causing her breasts to move upward every few seconds. They were calling to me. I put her left pink, perfect nipple on my tongue and licked; she moaned again and grabbed the back of my neck, urging me to do more. With my teeth, I pulled on it at first and then sucked, gently, and then firmer. Once it was a hard pebble, I moved to her other breast and did the same. I peeked my eyes up at Luke as I sucked on her nipple; he was biting his bottom lip.

I moved forward, causing her to move backward until she was lying on her back. I spread her legs, placing one leg between mine and then straddled the other. It was then that I felt the moisture of her pussy on my leg, it made me wet and I knew she could feel my moisture on hers. She loudly gasped the second I lightly moved my thigh forward and then backward on her clit. I did it a few times, getting rougher with the movement each time. She was getting close to orgasm; I suddenly stopped and lowered my mouth to her neck.

She was panting so hard she could barely talk.

"What are you doing?" It came out in some sort of frantic pant that made my clit throb with anticipation.

I moved from her neck to her left nipple, licked and sucked it until it was hard, and did the same to the other.

"Shhh..." I breathed on her nipple giving her goose bumps.

"I'm going to take care of you...just lay back and enjoy it." I demanded.

I trailed my tongue from her nipple to her bellybutton. She knew what I was going to do. She was anxious and eager for me to move faster. She gyrated her hips forward, hoping I would understand her silent plea. I looked up and smiled at her.

"Taylor...you impatient little thing, don't you know that good things come to those who wait, huh? I want to lick your pussy as much as you want me to. Here's the catch though, Luke gets to fuck your mouth. You stop sucking and I stop eating...deal?" She looked back at

Luke, and then her eyes went straight to Madam. I didn't need to look at Madam to know that she approved. She was confused by my next move. I repositioned my body to the floor and sat on my knees.

"Sit up, and spread your legs on the sides of my body, put the ends of your heels to the edge of the couch."

The tone of my voice was demanding and captivating; she did as she was told, she couldn't help it. She had become my puppet. She looked so exposed and bare in that position. It was eroticism at its finest. Her clit was throbbing just wanting to be caressed. I wanted to play with her some more. She needed to learn now that I set the rules, and that if given the power exchange she would always need to be the leader. I leaned over and she thought she was finally getting what she wanted. She saw me inhale her scent.

"Hmmmm…Taylor, you smell heavenly. I love the sweet smell of a woman, and nothing compares to a woman's scent."

I nudged her clit with my nose and then casually kissed it. She moaned loudly, not taking her eyes from me. I licked her from her opening to the top of her clit. She moaned so loud that it made her head fall back to the couch. I nodded over to Luke who placed his cock at the entrance of her mouth. She didn't even open her eyes; she moaned and let him slip right in. I watched as he slowly pushed in and out of her mouth with a gentle, yet, firm rhythm.

I started licking her clit back and forth, back and forth. I brought my lips to an O shape and began to suck lightly in a teasing manner. She moaned and it only enticed Luke to go harder and deeper, making her gag along the way. Pre-come started to fall at the corner of her lips, and I brought my tongue up to the edge and licked it off while staring into Luke's eyes.

My fingers found her pussy and I circled around her clit as Luke removed his cock and had Taylor and I licking all down his shaft. He roughly thrust back into Taylor's mouth. I moved right back to sucking on her clit with more force as I manipulated the edge of my tongue to be in sync with my lips. I sucked on her until she was moaning senselessly. Which, once again, had Luke's approval.

I moved my tongue from her clit to her opening and pushed my tongue into her pussy as deep as it would go. She was going to come, I stopped and she made a disgruntled sound. I licked the palm of my hand and place it on her pussy as I began rubbing it up and down. She moaned again.

"Does that feel good? Do you want to come?" I asked, toying with her.

"Yes...I want to come so bad...please, Lilith, please make me come..."

I smiled and laid her on the couch, I winked at Luke and he moved to sit in between her legs. He shoved his hard cock in before she even knew what was going on. Her back immediately arched off the couch. I started to rub on her breasts, and repositioned myself to face Luke and straddle her face. Without me having to coax her into anything, she grabbed my thighs for me to sit on her face.

I moaned the second I felt her tongue on me. The night before was all about Taylor, she hadn't done one damn thing to me. I could tell her inexperience, but she was a quick learner and proceeded to do the same things that I had done to her. I rocked my hips on her face to make it easier it for her.

Luke grabbed the back of my head and kissed me, he wasn't gentle like he had been with her. He knew what I wanted; he was a pro. I sucked on his tongue and he groaned. He moved away from me and I spread Taylor's legs a little more, giving him the opportunity to lean his upper body away from her, so that I could move forward and suck on her clit while he continued to fuck her.

I moved my mouth to her clit and resumed my sucking torture. This time it was more immediate and urgent. She whimpered from all the sensations that were occurring simultaneously. I proceeded to ride her face and I was on the edge of coming undone. My body was tight, my legs were shaking, and my stomach was quivering.

Taylor's body mimicked mine.

"Oh...fuck...I'm gonna come...Jesus Christ you guys are a fucking sight," Luke huskily groaned.

Before I knew it my eyes rolled to the back of my head and Taylor's body convulsed for what felt like minutes, my brain was so foggy that I saw light flicker behind my closed eyes. I didn't stop until her breathing had slowed and I had rode out my orgasm on her face.

CHAPTER 18

I think this could go unsaid but the rich- people who truly have money, not the people who say they do- never want to be revealed. It's much easier to play dirty when no one is looking, or when no one expects it. Of course, you have your celebrities and high profile individuals that are "obviously wealthy", but what I am talking about is money of a different kind. Money that can truly take someone down; you have no idea where the hundred-dollar bill has been when it's in your wallet.

Two words; blood money.

Madam's and my dynamic changed after the evening with Taylor and Luke. I know she thinks she can read me like a book, but the feeling is very much mutual. I had learned a lot along the way, and the apple truly doesn't fall far from the tree. I am Madam's daughter.

It had been four months and I had trained and been responsible for Taylor's initiation after that night. She really was a sweet girl and fit in perfectly as a VIP. The men were taken with her and she strived on that admiration. At the end of the day, all women want is attention. If they are given that then they will give you the world in a hand basket.

I walked into my condo at 7 am from spending the night with Mika. I know…believe it or not, but Mika had become somewhat of a confidant to me, I would go as far as to say that he became a friend. We will get to more of him, later. I walked in to find Madam there, drinking coffee with my luggage at her feet.

She grumbled and shook her head. "Good morning. Get showered and dressed, the plane is waiting," she said before answering her phone.

I went right for the shower. I cleared off the fog from the mirror and inspected the damage of my appearance. My pupils were still dilated, and I had dark circles under my eyes. My lips were still swollen and my ass and the backs of my thighs were marked with welts. I rolled my eyes at my disheveled appearance and went to get dressed.

We were on the plane an hour later; I tried to drink some juice and eat some breakfast but the drugs that were still in my system did not like that idea. I felt like throwing up every time I swallowed a piece of food.

"Too much partying, Lilith?" she questioned with amusement.

I yawned, ignoring her, "I'm going to try to take a nap."

"You don't have time for that. The destination is three and a half hours away, and you already look like shit. Plus, I highly doubt you will be able to sleep."

"Where are we going?"

"Colombia, Medellin to be exact." I didn't ask any more, if she wanted me to know, she would tell me.

I didn't listen to her and took a nap anyway, going in and out of sleep. I felt like somewhat of a human being by the time we landed. There was a limo waiting for us as we stepped off the plane. We passed the slums with their colorful bright stack homes everywhere, buildings upon buildings, and natives walking in every direction. The unmanaged dirt roads made for an unpleasant ride. We turned down a secluded road, with palm trees on either side, and drove on it for about ten minutes. I began to see an infinite amount of water all around me before we reached golden gates. They let us right through, obviously expecting our arrival. The driveway was about a hundred yards and it led to a roundabout where the driver parked the car. We stepped onto limestone pavers that led all around the property. The mansion was breathtakingly beautiful, a tan waterfront estate with a terracotta tiled roof. It resembled a villa. There was a walkway in between the ten cathedral arches on each side, which held one vehicle in each port. The live-in part of the estate was further back.

I could smell the breeze coming off the water as we were escorted into the home. Grand angled stairs, led to ten foot high, custom made iron doors with intricate lattice work covering all the windows. They opened to a wide foyer with marble floors and walls as far as the eye could see. The sun shining over the clear ocean reflected onto the rear of the home. I noticed that the ceilings were covered in elaborate woodwork that I had never seen before. We walked into a cascading sunroom with windows on every inch of space that led to the veranda. It had the same limestone pavers that were in the front, and lush gardens surrounding the open waterfront estate. Beautiful fountains were all around the property, each intricately placed, although the olympic size swimming pool was the centerpiece. The patio furniture displayed an endless amount of food. The butler handed me a mimosa, and I greedily took it down.

I needed something to take the edge off from the previous night. I could see Madam looking at me from the corner of my eye and I didn't pay her any mind. I took in the scenery of my surroundings.

I heard someone speaking in Spanish and turned around to see a man with three bodyguards surrounding him. They were strapped, and by that, I mean they had more guns than the Russian Mafia. He was approaching us in a respectable demeanor, the power and control radiating off of him with every step that he would take. He looked like your standard Colombian hell raiser; devastatingly handsome with chocolate brown eyes, strong accentuated facial structure, and black shoulder length hair that was tied in a ponytail. His facial hair had some grey in it, but it only made him look more dangerous. He was probably around his mid thirties.

This man had an endless amount of pussy and never even had to try.

The moment he reached us our eyes locked, just for a moment, before he went to Madam and kissed her cheek.

"Buenos dias, Madam. ¿Cómo fue tu vuelo?" he asked how her flight was.

"Pablo, mi vuelo estaba bien, no turbulencia," she dismissively told him about our lack of turbulence.

"Inglés por favor. There are ears everywhere. Including the woman you decided to bring without invitation," he stated with an unpleasant edge to his voice. His accent was thick, but it was sexy as sin.

"You offend me, since when do you not trust me?" she countered in a neutral tone.

He smiled and turned to me, extending out his right hand. "Pablo."

I cocked my head to the side and grinned. "No kiss on the cheek? What do I have to do to deserve that kind of welcoming?" I held his hand lightly and moved closer to him.

"Lilith," I answered, leaning in to kiss the corner of his mouth. I felt him harden from my forwardness, but it was quickly replaced.

He gestured toward the table of food. "Please, let's eat before we talk business. It's not so good to do on an empty stomach."

We ate in silence for the most part. I was the last to finish my meal and our plates were immediately taken away and replaced with coffee. I took a sip and inadvertently groaned.

"That's 100% pure Colombian coffee. Good, eh?" he questioned.

"Extremely."

"Now enough of this chit chat, Pablo. We have places to be and people to see."

"Madam, all work and no play makes Madam a dull girl."

"Woman, Pablo. Lilith is a girl...see the difference?" I wanted to say something but I bit my tongue.

"Now, the farmers, is the shipment ready to be transported?" she asked.

I paid close attention to what she was talking about; I had no idea what they were discussing, but I knew it wouldn't take me long to figure it out.

"You know that I have my people working day and night to get the demand ready. Who isn't trusting whom, now?" he inquired with irritation dripping from his words.

"It's business...two hundred and fifty kilos isn't something I want to fuck around with. It will be the largest shipment we have transported," she reminded him, speaking to him like he was some child instead of the Colombian drug lord that he was.

"I'm aware of the facts and as always, nothing will be traced back to you. You really have nothing to worry about. It's a win, win for both of us," he promoted.

I had so many questions that I wanted to ask, but I made sure to keep my mouth shut. Anticipation of what was to come filled me, rejuvenated me, and set my senses on fire.

"I have paid off everyone that needs to keep their mouth shut and the remaining were laid to rest. I think this transfer will be the easiest one yet." Between his accent and his demeanor, I found myself physically turned on when he spoke.

"You think?"

"I know."

She nodded. "We will keep that number on a monthly basis."

He raised his left eyebrow. "You're joking? Two hundred and fifty kilos a month is nothing. We could be transporting four hundred kilos a week with how much we are producing. We are losing a lot of time and money by not taking advantage and shipping as much as possible."

"I don't need the money. I want the best; for myself, and for my clients. I have distributors everywhere and that amount is enough for me. The end."

"You're passing an opportunity of a lifetime," he declared.

"I'm not a stupid woman, I know the limits. If you have a problem with that then I will find someone else."

He slammed his closed fist on the table making me jump. "I am the best. How dare you?"

She smiled mockingly at him. "This is your third world county. I run Miami. I know people who can make your life easier, or they can make it more difficult. I can slam my fists on tables too; want to see who can make it move more?" She sighed. "However, if you could so kindly remove the guns that are pointing at me and Lilith from under the table, I would appreciate it."

I saw the men retrieve their weapons and place them on the table. I don't think my heart had ever beaten as fast as it did that day. I felt it in my chest, the pit of my stomach, and especially my throat.

He cleared his throat, bringing my attention back to him. "The limo is waiting; let me show you the warehouse."

Again, we rode in silence while we drove on a dirt path through the slums. These roads were much worse than what I had seen before. Madam didn't bat an eye. We pulled up to a compound that had a gated fence and at least thirty guards that were holding machine guns; they were also covered with other weapons around their bodies.

We walked up to a warehouse that looked to be about 2,000 square feet, and the doors were immediately opened. To this day, I will never forget what I saw. My mouth dropped open and my eyes widened. There were rows beyond rows of kilos of cocaine, all perfectly placed and packaged from floor to ceiling.

Madam walked away from me to discuss business and I stood there by myself, not sure what to do. Was I supposed to move or stand still? I watched as Madam conducted business, her mannerisms, demeanor, and especially her tone of voice. They spoke Spanish to each other back and forth and I paid close attention to what they were discussing, taking in each and every word. Having the ability to read people was my sixth sense. I learned how important it was to be able to interpret all of your surroundings at a very young age.

That day changed my life.

It leveled the playing field.

The ball was in my court.

If I was seriously going to do what I was thinking, then I needed to move fast. I always knew that I would take over VIP one day, and this was Madam's way of showing me how powerful she was, and how much I should fear her.

The Almighty Madam.

It backfired on her.

It only made me want it more.

CHAPTER 19

Are you surprised? Have you not learned a damn thing about me, yet? I take what's mine...when and how I want to. I make my own decisions; NO ONE makes them for me. The Colombians hated her, every last one of them. Now, here is the beauty about being me, I am whatever you want me to be. I can do whatever I put my mind to.

"Penny for your thoughts," Pablo whispered in my ear from behind me. He kept walking and motioned with his index finger to follow.

I followed him to the back of the warehouse where it was private and we were alone. My fingers caressed along the sides of the bags of kilos as we walked by them.

"What are you to her?" he questioned, making me turn to look at him.

"Excuse me?"

"To Madam, why did she bring you?" I could hear the curiosity and interest in his tone.

"I'm a VIP," I paused, "I am also her daughter."

He was taken aback by my answer, it was written all over his handsomely distressed face.

"But don't worry we have a love/hate relationship." It made him laugh.

"Is she always that much of a cunt?"

I giggled. "It's part of her appeal. I think it's actually in her DNA."

He stared me straight in the eyes and said, "Is it in yours?"

I slanted my head to the side and peeked at him through my eyelashes, biting the corner of my bottom lip. "Want to find out?"

"I can only deal with one Madam."

I placed my hand on my chest. "You offend me."

He moved closer to me. "I find that hard to believe. You mean you aren't made of stone?"

"Among other things. So how about a taste?"

His eyes wandered from my face to my breasts, to my pussy, and then he started to unbuckle his belt. I raised an eyebrow and put my hand on his chest. "For your coke, not your cock." He smiled, grinned, and gestured for me to once again follow him. I did. We walked into a secluded back room that needed a key to get in.

He quickly turned on the lights. It was an average size room with a desk in the middle and bags of kilos of cocaine on each of the four walls from floor to ceiling. He grabbed a bag, placed it on the desk and ripped it open with a key. He scooped the key into the bag and brought some white dust up to my nose, I inhaled.

It burned the entire way down, making me grab my nostrils in surprise.

"That's the real motherfucking shit right there, it's not broken, it's pure," he said.

As soon as he finished the sentence, I felt my heart start to race. The cocaine was so unbelievably strong that it made me nauseous. I lunged for the trash can by the desk and dry heaved. I heard him laughing from behind me.

"Awe, you gringas don't know how to have a good time. You're completely used to your broken down white. That is the Black Widow, nasty isn't she? You get use to her, I probably should have warned you," he mocked.

I looked up at him through dilated black eyes. I watched as he snorted some off the key and his reaction was completely different from mine.

My heart was racing, my palms were sweaty, and if I hadn't just seen him take a bump off the same batch, I would have thought he laced it with something toxic. I sat down in one of the chairs trying to catch my breath and he handed me a glass of water. I took the entire drink down in one gulp.

"Better?" I nodded.

"She's a cunt isn't she? Sort of reminds me of your Madam." he chuckled to himself.

I started to feel it.

The beauty of cocaine.

Invincible.

I smiled at him. "You know, Pablo, the day God established the seven deadly sins, he created women."

He grinned. "How much?"

"That's not very nice, Pablo. If you play with me, you're not allowed to hit below the belt."

"What if the only thing I want is what is below your belt?"

"The feelings not mutual. I want you for a lot more than just your cock. I think you and I should become friends. I have a proposition that may make you and I very pleased, although I don't mind mixing a little business with pleasure," I teased as I stood up to walk closer to him.

"Who do you think you are, Pablo? You know you're only Madam's errand boy, don't you? She doesn't believe that you can do anything on your own. I have seen her destroy people by just blinking, are you intimidated by her? Do you know the power I hold for us both. The things we could do together? I am your inside woman, use me." I perched myself on the edge of the table in front of him, enticing him with every word.

He lowered his eyebrows. "What are you talking about?"

I set my feet on either side of him, resting the soles of my heels on the chair beside his thighs. I made sure to leave my legs wide open for him; I was wearing a skirt with no panties. I know where his eyes and mind wandered. I knew that would work to my benefit.

Money and sex always go hand in hand.

"I am talking about taking what's mine." I motioned with my palm at him. "With your help, of course. I am not looking to be top dog, Pablo. All I am looking for is my piece of the slice. I want nothing more or nothing less than to take down Madam as much as you do. I wouldn't have approached you if I didn't think that you could get the job done. You seem like a man that finishes what he starts and I am looking for someone like that on my side." I informed, leaning back on the table to let him have a better view.

"And what exactly do you have in mind?" The anticipation and want in his voice is something I still remember to this day. He wanted it and he wanted it bad. He was like a dog drooling at the bone, and I was his master dangling it in front of his face.

My bite is much bigger than my fucking bark. Too bad he didn't know it, yet.

"I believe we may have the beginning of a beautiful friendship, Pablo. You scratch my back and I will rub your balls." I moved the toe of my shoe to his groin, rubbing it gently. "Madam doesn't need this, you are aware of that, aren't you? She doesn't give a rat's ass about this transaction; she's just trying to get a piece of the action, that's all. None of this is her concern and because she knows all the right people, she has you on your knees, just waiting for you to get her off. What if I can change that for you? What if I can give you everything you want and more and all you have to do is say please." I was pissing him off; I could tell he wanted to tell me where to go and how to get there. But he was silently biting his tongue, waiting for me to say the magic words.

To show him the way.

"I know the same, if not more people than Madam does. We can do whatever you want, all of it. Just to add some frosting on the cake, I will throw in some of the VIPs on the side. They will take care of any and all important people needed. Madam doesn't ever have to be the wiser." His cock was hard, for me, for the cocaine, and for the endless possibilities for the future.

"How are you going to make any of this possible?"

I immediately closed my legs and hopped off the table to stand in front of him. The shear disappointment was prominent across his face.

"Don't fucking worry about that part. You just worry about getting it over to the United States of America," I said in an exaggerated tone.

I hiked up my skirt, exposing the sides of my thighs and lightly ran my hand up and down. I looked down at him through my eyelashes. "Let me make you a very rich and powerful man, huh? You have nothing to lose and everything to gain." I baited.

I opened my blouse and began to swipe my finger along my cleavage. "Let's jump off the cliff together, Pablo. I know you know how to swim."

He didn't have to say a damn thing. He would have done anything for me at that moment if I had asked him. He slowly and determinedly stood up, getting mere inches away from my face and waited. He wanted me to make the first move, and I gave him exactly what he wanted.

It's give and take. Except…when you're dealing with me. He may think that he was the one in control, but it was the exact opposite. I was driving the car and I let him believe that he also had his hands on the wheel, when in reality he was in the fucking trunk.

The second my lips touched his mouth he growled and opened them. His tongue plunged deep into my mouth and I moaned. His hands were all over me, he couldn't decide where he wanted to touch me the most and I leaned into every touch and sensation. Enjoying the thrill of what was to come.

I reached for his belt and he eagerly moved his hips into my hands. I couldn't get them off fast enough. I pulled out his long, thick cock and aggressively stroked it back and forth. He picked me up under my arms and I wrapped my legs around him as he spun me around. My back hit the door so fast that it should have surprised me, but it didn't.

I vaguely felt him sheath his cock with a condom before he slammed into my wet cunt and it had me scratching at his back. He roughly pushed in and out of me, hitting my g-spot with every push and pull. It wasn't nice or soft. It was pure, unadulterated abandonment. We were fucking. I was close to release within minutes. He thrust deep into the back of my pussy and just started to move his hips; his lower abdomen glided on my clit and I threw my head back against the wall matching his hip movement.

I came hard.

His hips jerked forward and his hand covered my overly enthused mouth, making me whimper.

"Pablo, Lilith!" I heard Madam say from behind the door.

We placed our foreheads on each other, trying to come down from the intense orgasms we had just shared and remain quiet at the same time. We finally heard Madam's heels clicking toward the opposite direction before he slowly placed me on the ground. At first, it was hard to find my balance on my heels. His strong arms held me up.

I could smell the perspiration on his neck and it was all man. When he realized that I could hold myself up, he removed the condom from his cock and disposed of it in the trash can. It was the first time I had ever used a condom with a man before. I briefly contemplated what it would feel like to have him bare inside of me, and it made me anticipate the feel of him between my thighs, again.

I watched as he buckled his pants and composed himself, it took me out of my daze to do the same.

"I will be in touch," I said, breaking the silence.

He nodded and I moved away from the door as he opened it. He glanced out, and when he knew we were safe to exit, he gestured for me to quietly follow.

We made it outside without being discovered and Madam was talking to the same people she was when we arrived.

I waited until she realized I was near her. "Where did you go?"

"I needed to use the restroom," I calmly responded.

"That's what you get for being such a lush. I can only hope that you squatted, darling."

I had my eyes closed the entire plane ride home, feigning sleep. We landed and there were two chauffeur's waiting for us. Madam kissed my cheek and went on her way.

Later that night I lay in bed, unable to sleep.

The time had come.

VIP would be mine.

CHAPTER 20

The next several months weren't as bad as I had expected them to be. Everything went rather smoothly. We were transporting hundreds and hundreds of kilos per week and I had five VIP girls working the clients whenever they needed it. I was giving them 75% of their cut from every date. They were ecstatic and it assured they kept their mouths shut. It just further ingrained in my mind that you can't trust anyone in this world other than yourself.

I didn't care that I was only getting 25% of the dates because it was never about the money. It was beyond that. I was still making millions off the cocaine. Everything continued as it should be.

I was a VIP and Madam still ran the show.

✻VIP✻

As I was saying before, Mika and I became friends, but it was more like partners. He jumped at the chance when I told him about what I was doing. He always marched to the beat of his own drum, which is one of the reasons I enjoyed his company. Mika was a trust fund baby. He had all the money in the world and didn't care one bit about it. He wanted to live in the fast lane. His motto was "you only live once", and he made sure to make every minute count.

It also didn't hurt that he looked like a badass and fucked like a God. It wasn't all about sex with us; it was more than that. He was real. I know that doesn't really make any sense, but let me try to explain it. Mika didn't pretend. He was what he was and if you didn't like it then you could go fuck yourself, and he would tell you that to your face. He often put me in my place and as much as I hated it, I also needed it. I didn't threaten him, there was no competition there, and I know that I met my match when I met Mika.

Now, don't let your mind wander. This isn't a love story. Mika and I didn't ride off into the sunset together. He was my means to an end.

A year went by and several disturbing things started happening in Miami. It had been the drug trafficking capitol of the world for many years. Everyone, and I do mean everyone, was involved. If you had money or status, you were doing something dirty. Over the last few years or so, people started getting murdered left and right, fighting for greed and power. It got so bad that tourists weren't traveling as much as they were before, and Miami went from becoming the "Magic City" to the "Blanca Cuidad", meaning "the white city". Time magazine had also put out an article slaughtering the reputation of the city, calling it the "most dangerous place in the world". It was bullshit, but at least it didn't affect me.

But…there was money. It was everywhere. I couldn't keep up, no one could. Corruption led the city; even cops were in on it. Top dogs were going down daily; attorneys, celebrities, politicians, CEOs, et cetera. Madam started to get worried; I could see it every time something hit the news or the papers. Sometimes I wondered if she knew it was coming, if she could sense it somehow. I knew she protected herself; I didn't know to what means, but I knew that she had to have something in place if someone were to rat her out. Whatever it was, it wasn't good enough to protect her from me.

However, it only made what I was doing that much easier.

The sad thing is, some VIPs started going down. I personally watched their demise as they let the white takeover. Some overdosed, and two died. I've told you time and time again; that I don't do weakness and neither does Madam. To her, it was like she was weaning out the weak and only the strong survive. She got more girls, better ones.

✻VIP✻

I lay out naked on Mika's lanai furniture as I watched him swim laps in the pool. I moved my position on the chase lounger from my back to my front.

"I liked the position you were sitting in before, Angel. Your pussy was like the end goal of the lap," he said as he started to do the back stroke.

"I needed to turn over. You don't want me to look uneven, do you?"

"I suppose not. I'm surprised you're still here, you usually fuck and run."

I laughed at his depiction of me, mostly because it was true. "That's completely not true, sometimes it's just foreplay or a good ass beating."

"Oh, how you love the belt on your ass, Lilith."

He continued to swim laps and I hungrily took him in. Mika was a fine specimen of male. He knew I was gawking and lavished in the attention. I watched as he got out of the pool and shook the water out of his hair. The water dripped off his body with every step that he took and his cock just hung free in between his legs.

I could see it coming before it happened. He jumped on the back of my body, soaking me completely with his. I squirmed, trying to get loose.

"You know you love it. Stop moving, I'm trying to get comfortable," he demanded as he placed his body on top of mine.

"I can't breathe," I mumbled into the cushion below me.

"Shut up. You just don't like cuddling."

"Oh, is this what this is? Here I thought you were just trying to get me wet."

He cocked an eyebrow. "Angel, you're always wet. It's one of the reasons I like you around."

"Really? Because the only reason I have you around is because you're nice to look at. You make for better scenery in my life. I don't care too much about you talking as much as you do, though. Which is why I always like to sit on your face. It's the only way I can shut you the fuck up," I teasingly provoked.

135

"Do you kiss your Madam with that mouth?"

"No, I kiss her ass with it."

He slid to lie on the right side of me and we faced each other. He pulled my wet hair out of my face.

His hand lingered on my cheek. "Don't change once you take over, Angel."

"I wouldn't dream of it."

"I'm serious. I've known Madam for a very long time. I know what it takes to run that empire. Power changes people. I see it happen every day. Don't let it take over you. Do you hear me?" he demanded in a tone I didn't appreciate.

"Why, Mika? I thought you liked it when I was a bad girl."

"I'm serious."

"So am I."

He shook his head. "Listen you stubborn ass woman, people respect and admire kindness, even though you are a bitch most of the time. There is still kindness in your eyes. Don't let them grow cold. Don't become jaded. VIP can do that to you, fair warning." I leaned into his hand that was still resting in the same spot.

"Everything happens for a reason, Mika."

I quickly removed myself from him and went to find a shower. I could not allow myself to get attached to Mika. I had other plans, plans that I had been working on since I was a child. It was my destiny. I couldn't let feelings control me. It wasn't the way I operated. I wasn't made like that. I noticed the more time I spent with him, the deeper our connection became. I didn't know what to do about it.

I couldn't walk away from him; he was helping me in more ways than one. But my thoughts began to wander to him sometimes, whether it was something that reminded me of him, or if it was a memory. It was fucking with me. As I showered, I wanted to remove him from my skin and my mind. But I couldn't, I wanted to go back out there and say something. To see if he was feeling the same way I was.

I was scared, what if he was? What would happen?

I wouldn't know how to handle it and that's what terrified me the most. I had finally gotten to a point in my life where I didn't know how to control something. It pissed me off, but it also reminded me that I was human. Maybe I did have a heart. I continued my mind fuck as I showered and prepared myself mentally for the possibility of something happening with Mika and me.

I turned off the shower and heard something that sounded like moaning coming from the bedroom. I wrapped the towel around my body and opened the door to find Mika's face in between some chick's thighs.

I laughed. But on the inside, I was seething. He looked up at me while he continued to devour her pussy; she hadn't even opened her eyes to see that I was in the room. She moaned and grabbed the sheets above her head, kneading them in her hands. He licked and sucked her, never taking his eyes off mine. I could see the moisture on his mouth as he manipulated her body to give him what he wanted. Her body started to tremble and we both knew she was close to orgasm. When she called out his name in ecstasy, he let her ride out her orgasm on his lips. He moved up and wiped off her come from his mouth.

I shook my head.

He grinned seductively at me. "I got her for you, Angel."

"Oh really? Seems to me that you couldn't wait to get her open. You may have ruined my gift, Mika," I stated as I grabbed my clothes. I didn't even bother changing; I wanted to get the fuck out of there.

I got to the door and slightly opened it before it was pushed closed from behind me. He grabbed my upper arm, turning me around to face him.

"What the fuck was that?" he questioned with anger and confusion in his eyes.

"Nothing. I need to go," I stated, trying to remove myself from him; it only made him hold me harder.

"Are you jealous?"

"Fuck you," I said through gritted teeth. I could still see the moisture around his mouth and smell her on him and it made me sick to my stomach.

"Jesus, Angel. What the fuck? When the hell did this happen?"

"I have no fucking clue what you're talking about. How about you take down your over inflated ego for one second and let me go," I demanded, trying to push him away from me. He aggressively pushed me up against the door and grabbed my chin.

"We have made no goddamn promises to each other. We are birds of a feather that flock together. I don't do commitments or relationships and neither do you. That's the beauty about us, Angel.

We are two of the same kind. Now get your ass back in the room and have a good fucking time with me," he insisted, letting me go.

I pushed him, catching him off guard. "Don't tell me what to do. If I wanted to have a party I would have invited the guests. Go fuck yourself. I'm not jealous. You are nothing to me. Do you understand that, Mika? I use you. And the feeling is mutual. That's the beauty of us," I responded and could see the hurt look in his eyes. And it made me feel better.

He put me in my place and I returned the favor.

CHAPTER 21

In October of 1986, President Reagan signed the Anti Drug Act and things moved quickly, as did I. I waited and watched how members of the high society started to crumble, each hitting their own demise, one right after the other. I personally got to witness the rise and demise of it all, and I'm not just talking about "La Blanca Cuidad".

It was New Years Eve and Madam had a huge celebration at The Cathouse; she invited over five hundred people. It was the who's who of Miami socialites. It wasn't her normal VIP party, although that was happening behind closed doors, it was more like a gala type event. I wore a black fitted gown that exposed my cleavage and had a low back neckline. I mingled and played nice until the clock struck 10:00 pm.

I grabbed everything that I needed and made my way upstairs to her office. I precisely placed every document on her desk, making sure that every last one was as visible as it could be. I sat in her chair and waited.

At 10:15 pm, Madam walked in, followed by Mika.

I smiled because I could see the confusion all over her face. "What are you doing in my office?" she asked in a seething tone.

"Correction…what are you doing in MY office," I replied in the same manner.

"Excuse me?"

"You heard me. Things are going to start changing, *Mother*." I hadn't called her mother since I was seventeen years old; she was my Madam, but not anymore. She looked like I had slapped her across the face.

"Get the fuck out of my office before I have you escorted out, and don't you dare refer to me as anything other than your Madam. I will wipe that sorry ass smirk from your face if it ever falls from your mouth again. Do you understand me?" she roared. I set the line and she bit the hook. Now it was just time to reel her in.

I sat in the oversized chair, leaning forward with my elbows on the desk. My shoulders were squared to let her know I meant business. I stared at her while I held my hands together in front of me. It may have looked like I was saying a prayer, but in reality, she's the one that needed it.

"I believe I have something that may interest you, better yet, I know it will. You see these documents that are so perfectly organized? All of them have your name and signature on them. You see, Mother Dearest, for the last two years Pablo, Mika, and I have been transporting enormous amounts of cocaine to the states. We have dealt to thousands of distributors all around the world; but here's the catch, it is all tied back to you." I smiled like a Cheshire cat.

"All it takes is for me to send these documents to the DEA, and not only will your ass fry in federal prison for this lifetime, it may go on to other lifetimes as well…just saying." I mocked in an exaggerated tone.

"Who the fuck do you think you are, Lilith?"

"I'm your daughter. The seed of your spawn. Apple of your eye," I said.

"I honestly don't want to turn you in. I really don't. I love you in my own fucked up way; you gave me life and showed me the way. I appreciate everything you have ever done for me. I promise. However, the time has come for you to step down. You have all the money in the world. You could travel and you know, enjoy the fruits of your labor."

She slowly walked over to me. "You think you can intimidate me? Scare me away? You're swimming in the big girl pond, don't make me drown you."

"From where I am standing I'm not the one that's choking. The tables have turned. I am no longer the little girl standing outside the window looking in. I hold all the power. All of these documents are ready to be mailed. Just say the word and we will all remain silent. One big happy family," I explained in a singing voice.

"I've created a monster," she announced.

"No, Mother. You've created a Madam. All's fair in business and money. Take the gavel and pass it the fuck on."

She folded her arms and sat in the chair in front of *my* desk. Mika sat in the other. She looked over at him.

"You fucking moron. How many times have I bailed your ass out of jail! And you do this to me? You think you can get away with this?" she yelled.

"I already have! Cut the shit, Mother. Just bow down. It would all go so much smoother if you would tuck your goddamn tail between your legs and just accept it. I could do things that you've only dreamed of; I'm the fresh fucking face of VIP. I'm young, vibrant, and eager. You should be proud. This has been very thought out. There is nothing you can do to change the fact that when you walk out of this office, you are no longer in charge. Happy fucking New Year."

"You think I'm going to walk away that easy, Lilith. VIP is MINE! And until I say so, it's not leaving my hands, don't for one second think I won't take you the fuck out for this."

I laughed and cocked my head to the side. "What makes YOU think that there aren't guns pointing at you this very second? I'm not scared of you. That is a gun in my pocket and it is very happy to see you."

"Fuck you!" she shouted, lunging over the table to come at me.

My chair fell back from the force of her impact. I knew she would go down fighting. I was expecting it.

I grabbed the gun and pointed it directly at her forehead. I would never pull the trigger and it wasn't loaded. But she didn't have to know that.

"This feels a little familiar, doesn't it, Mother? In this office with a gun in my hand. You told me you were glad to see I had it in me to pull the trigger...still proud? It's game over, Mother...I WON! I am the Queen Bee...I don't take shit from anyone. That's what you taught me, isn't it? I am every fucking thing you ever wanted me to be. Back. The. Fuck. Up." She removed herself from me and got up. I grabbed Mika's hand that he held out to help me up.

I composed myself as I watched my mother from the corner of my eye. She turned to face me with a huge smile on her face, which caught me off guard.

"Touché," she said as she clapped her hands. "There comes a time where everything must come to an end, my time has come. You want to be in my red soles, darling, then you wear them to sleep. Don't ever take them off, you trust no one, even me," she declared. She took one last look at her surroundings and walked out.

I sighed. "Well, that went better than I was expecting."

Mika smiled, "Is it fucked up that I have a massive hard-on for you right now?"

I grinned. "I have a present."

He turned when he heard the door open from behind him and in walked Layla. She had been with VIP for almost a year. She was a Miami native with brown curly hair, bright hazel doll-eyes, and lips that were made to suck cock. I hadn't gotten the opportunity to play with her yet. She was wearing a black bra with matching panties and garter set. She looked tasty.

She strolled over to Mika and began unbuttoning his shirt. His eyes went to Layla's face, which was looking back at me.

"It's my party and I can come if I want to," I vowed and unzipped the side of my dress, making it fall to the floor. I was wearing red panties, a garter belt holding up thigh high stockings, heels, and no bra.

I observed as Layla completely undressed Mika, leaving him naked and hard. She never took her eyes away from me; she knew who controlled the room and scene. I sat at the edge of my desk and crossed my legs.

"Get on your knees, Layla." I demanded. She did as she was told and sat on the heels of her feet; Mika grinned and grabbed the back of her neck.

"Eh, eh, eh, did I say you could touch her? I don't think so. Play by my rules or get the fuck out." He laughed and removed his hands, placing them on his sides.

"Grab your cock, Mika. Show Layla how you love to stroke it and tell her what you want her to do to it."

He grabbed his dick from the base and held it at attention. Layla greedily took it all in, his smell, stance, and demeanor. His hand moved possessively and with purpose from the base to the tip, never letting up on the twist and turn motion.

"I want you to open your beautiful, wet, tight mouth and take me deep in the back of your throat until you gag. I want to fuck your face, while you tug and caress my balls. Let me feel the graze of your teeth as you take me in and out, and then I want you to suck on the head of my cock and swallow all of the pre-come that oozes out of my dick. You think you can handle that?" he added.

"Do as he says, Layla. I want to watch you salivate down the sides of your face." She opened her mouth wide and Mika forcefully plunged in, making her gag and moan. His hips thrust deep, hard, and fast. She could barely keep up, but that didn't mean she didn't try. Layla sucked his cock like her life depended on it. She indeed had all his pre-come dripping from her mouth. It only stimulated Mika more by having the wet suction of it all.

I let it carry on for a few minutes and strode my happy and eager ass over there. I fervently kissed Mika, savoring each and every feel of his wet demanding mouth. My body pushed Layla's face harder and it restricted her movement into Mika's groan as he pumped firmer and with more urgency. He wanted to come and I wasn't going to let him.

I pulled her head back and Mika groaned. I bit his lip before moving away from him to look down at Layla, who was politely but willingly waiting for my next command. I got down on my knees next to her and grazed my hand on the side of her face and she leaned into my embrace. I placed two fingers into her mouth and told her to suck. She repeated the same process on my fingers as she did to Mika's dick mere seconds before.

Mika crouched down to our level to get a better view of her sucking my fingers with the same tentativeness she just portrayed for his cock.

"Remove her panties and bra." He removed the panties first and then her bra, never once stopping to touch one ounce of her body that she so desperately craved. I slowly removed my fingers from her mouth and worked my way down her body, stopping on her pubic bone. I traced the outer lips of her pussy, deliberately gentle and soft; she panted in appreciation. I let my index finger swipe her opening, never parting her lips to give her what she wanted.

I licked my lips and watched her mimic the seductiveness of my tongue. I grabbed her by her neck and laid her down. I spread her legs wide open.

"Mika, do you want to play with the pretty pussy?" He nodded.

"Beg me," I asserted.

"Angel," he stated in a serious tone.

"Madam," I reminded him with authority.

He lowered and shook his head; the disappointment was seething off him. I could sense that his mind was spinning trying to process everything; that one word changed everything for us, especially for me. He couldn't possibly believe that I wouldn't change, or maybe he did. Either way I didn't need his opinion or approval.

CHAPTER 22

"Madam got your tongue?" I taunted. "I have something to make it better." I repositioned Layla on her front, making her ass lift slightly higher. I poured some cocaine that I had in a vile on Layla's ass cheek. I snorted half of it, and Mika followed suit.

"Are we friends now?" I provoked.

"*Angel*...we never stopped being friends." I narrowed my eyes at him and placed my attention back to Layla. My face went to the back of her neck, breathing her in. She smelled like sex and lust, my two favorite combinations. I lightly blew air and trailed soft kisses to her shoulder blades, leaving her skin aroused and alarmed.

"Layla, since Mika isn't playing nice how about we play without him." I said, staring only into Mika's eyes.

I continued to make my way down until I got to the crevice of her ass. I licked her pucker and she hummed. Mika's cock bounced, I smiled and licked her again. I seductively walked my fingers down her spine and to the curve of her ass. I spanked her hard. She yelped and moaned at the same time, which only made me do it again. I spanked her until her ass was red and my hand hurt.

See, sex got Mika off but not as much as S&M. He liked pain, he loved to watch it, feel it, and do it. I never played fair. I knew how to get what I wanted, even if I had to play dirty.

"What do you want me to do?" he pleaded.

"I want you to spit on your hand and push your finger in to the second knuckle."

"Where?"

I spanked her ass. "Anywhere you want." I spanked her again and her whole body vibrated.

He leaned into her ear, "Huh, you dirty girl? You like that don't you. You want me to stick my fingers in your cunt or your ass? Tell me, baby…where do you want it?" he dominated.

She panted, "I want it wherever Madam wants me to have it."

I spanked her again. "Good girl. Stick them in her ass." She swayed her hips back and forth, in a silent plea of asking for it. Mika did exactly what I told him to do and eased his fingers into her pucker. She cried out in desperation, her entire body quivered, from her fingertips to her toes. She pushed back onto his fingers, making him go deeper and harder. He obliged but just for a minute.

I told you he was sadist. He spit in his other hand and wrapped that one around his cock, he stroked up and down making it wet. He aimed it at her ass and hit her with it.

"You want his cock, Layla?"

"Mmmm…I want what Madam wants," she repeated.

I pulled her hair at the nook of her neck. "You're such a good girl." I pulled her hair harder with every accented word I praised. I motioned with a nod for Mika to thrust his cock where I knew he wanted it. He nudged at her anus and I watched as he filled her completely; her insatiable body took him in.

He grunted, "Fuck…you're tight." He licked his hand and smacked her ass. I reached for his pants and grabbed his belt. It made it swoosh sound as I roughly pulled it from the belt loops. Once it was free, I snapped it on the ground, Mika's eyes averted back to me and he groaned. I snapped it again and that time it got Layla's attention.

The trepidation was engraved all over her beautiful face.

"Do you trust me?" I questioned with a certain edge to my tone.

"Yes, Madam," she immediately responded, not giving it a second thought.

I gripped her wrists together above her head and looped the belt around them, tying it as tight at it would go. Her breathing escalated and I held her forward to hold her still; Mika began to slide in and out of her. At first, he was gentle, the louder her moans grew the harder he fucked her.

I repositioned myself to the side of her body, laying the length of her. I slipped the toe of my shoe beneath the belt between her wrists, and straightened my leg to keep her body stiff. I put my fingers in Mika's mouth and then lowered them to her clit. I manipulated her body and when she'd start to spasm, I pushed my leg further, stretching her body and stopping the shaking of her impending orgasm.

I was an asshole.

Her legs started to tremble; she was close. I looked up at Mika as I used my other hand to push two fingers into her pussy.

"How do you like being fucked in every hole, Layla?" he antagonized.

"Awww! Oh fuck, please don't stop, please don't stop," she repeated, over and over again.

She was soaking wet and seconds later, she came with such force that she pushed my fingers out of her. Mika let her ride out her orgasm and then pulled out of her. He removed the belt and dismissed her. She happily obliged.

I looked him square in the face. "Who the fuck do you think you are breaking up my good time? I wasn't done with her. You need to realize where your place is, Mika. I don't need to keep reminding you."

"No, Angel…you need to realize that all this bullshit of Madam isn't going to work with me. Now bend over the desk and stick out your ass. You have been a very bad girl. You know what happens to bad girls, I have always shown you. I think you are the one that needs to be reminded," he stated, walking toward me. He grabbed the belt from the floor and whipped it for effect.

I didn't move an inch and with the belt in his hand, he lashed it at my thigh. "Move!" He shouted. I cringed having to follow orders, but I knew Mika and the look in his eyes meant business. He had this ability to change into someone I didn't recognize, especially when he was in scene mode. I begrudgingly moved one foot in front of the other and perched my hands on the corner of the desk, sticking my ass in the air.

This is where the tables turned. As much as I wanted to be in control, my body had other desires; it wanted to be controlled. I wanted to feel the pain, the burn, the sting. I wanted to feel the fire of the only man that I ever allowed to get close to me.

I heard the belt before I ever felt it and my fingernails dug beneath the desk. He made me count every last blow and by the time he was at twenty, I was sweating, panting, wet, and horny as fuck.

He rubbed at the skin that was already developing welts; playing me like a fiddle to lean into him and lavish everything he had to offer.

"Where is the big bad Madam, huh?" He breathed into my neck, leaving a trail of his moist tongue behind.

"You love it, Angel. Just fucking admit it. You love what only I can offer you...we both get off on it. I could have come with that VIP, but I didn't. I wanted to come with the one and only. There is no pussy like yours, I always come back for more and you always willingly spread your legs. It pisses you off as much as it turns you on."

His hands continued their assault on my ass. I wanted to push him away, I wanted to yell at him and tell him to get the fuck out and never come back, but I couldn't. It fucked with my mind as much as it did my heart. I had to shake the thoughts that consumed my very being. Mika had made it very clear where we stood, and I couldn't let my guard down. I wouldn't show him any sort of weakness and that's what love was to me. It was something that people use against you. It's the very tool that can control and finish you off.

I would never let that happen to me.

Not then, not now, not ever.

I pushed all those thoughts to where I kept all of my feelings, deep within my core. Where only I would ever allow them to be seen or heard.

He smacked my ass, bringing me back to the present, to the moment where I lived and needed to be.

"Where did you go, Angel?" he whispered, kissing his way to my ass.

"Nowhere. Just fuck me."

"Not until I take what I want." I watched his mouth move to my pussy from behind and I fell forward on the desk and spread my legs wider. My elbows held me up, and my face fell in between my forearms. He spread my ass cheeks and licked me from my anus to my opening and pushed his tongue as deep as it would go. I bit my bottom lip, trying to relieve the pressure that was building in the pit of my stomach.

He slid in between my legs and was now facing my pussy; he grabbed my left leg and laid it on his shoulder. He licked all around my outer lips; I gyrated my hips forward and back, trying to entice him to lick my nub. He wouldn't have it. I knew what he wanted. He wanted to hear me say the words. Mika was a sadist bastard; as much as he didn't want a commitment with me, he still wanted to bring me to my knees. He always wanted to feel like he could do whatever he wanted with me.

It didn't matter how many clients and scenes I had done, it was all for show, it was all part of the fantasy, the rouge. Mika knew when it was me and him, there were no such things. We had this connection that only we understood. I hated it as much as I loved it. Anything I spoke, I meant, and he knew that.

He kissed the top of my mound. "Say it," he demanded, making me whimper.

"Ugh…" I groaned.

"Say it or I will fucking leave you like this. Tell me what I need to hear."

I hesitated. "Please…" I whispered, loud enough for him to hear.

The second the word left my lips, he devoured my clit. He sucked on my nub making my nerve ending come alive, his hands reached around and he slapped on the welts of my ass, making me feel the pleasure and pain that I craved. The softness and warmth of his tongue had me needing and pleading to come. He moved his head up and down, left and right, and in circles, driving me closer to the brink.

He aggressively rocked my hips into his face and I moved in sync with him.

"God, yes, please don't stop…that feels so fucking good," I shamelessly pleaded.

He shoved his thumb into my pussy and pressed down, over and over again.

"Mika…" I screamed out in ecstasy. I could feel the fucker smiling under me as he licked me clean.

I barely had time to catch my breath before he pushed my entire body forward; making me lay flat on the desk.

"Grab onto the sides of the desk." I did.

"I'm going to fuck you hard. I want to have your cunt gripping me so fucking tight that I can barely move in and out of you. Every time you sit tomorrow you are going to feel the burn of my belt and when you walk, you're going to know whose dick was inside you." He plunged in with so much force that I moved forward and my hands hurt from the impact.

The angle of my body made it precise for him to hit my g-spot every time. It didn't take long for my pussy to throb and my body to start to tremble. The desk pressed into my lower abdomen and the sensation made it all the more inviting for my orgasm.

"I'm close," I revealed as I moved my thigh to lie on the desk.

"Fuck...you're wet. You know what your wet pussy does to me." He moved faster, quicker, and with more determination.

I started to play with my clit and my pussy clenched and clamped down on his cock. He thrust in one last time before he came deep inside me. His forehead dropped to my back and we both panted and breathed each other in for I don't know how long. He removed himself from me and held me up until I regained my balance and equilibrium.

We both redressed quietly, neither one of us wanting to break the silence. When we were both dressed, he came over to me and kissed the inside of my wrist and left.

That night changed a lot of things for me and we both knew it.

I sat in the office chair overlooking the entire office. It was mine. I was twenty-six years old and I had the world at my fingertips, and by that I mean VIP. I held the key to the city.

Take it or leave it, I was in charge now, and nothing or no one was going to change that. Winner takes all.

There is no fiction here.
It was fact.
I was no longer Lilith.
I was The Madam.

150

CHAPTER 23

The days turned into weeks and the weeks turned into months rather quickly. Six months came and went at rapid speed. I enjoyed every fucking second of it; I'm not going to lie and say taking over didn't come with some confusion or hit and misses, I experienced it all. My mother left that night and I had barely heard from her since, last we talked she was taking a sabbatical through Europe.

Trust me, I didn't for one second think or imagine my mother would hold my hand through the process of me taking over. It was sink or swim with her, it always had been. The most time consuming part that I never got to witness was how much paperwork and organizational skills I had to have to make sure that I crossed all my Ts and dotted my Is. I learned quickly that my mother ran a very successful business, but I will toot my own goddamn horn and say that I found mistakes and corrected them immediately.

For one, I made sure that everyone loved me, and by everyone, I mean all the people I paid off with pussy and money to keep their mouths shut; especially the Chief of Police, Governor, and the DEA. They were my new best friends. I also made all old and new clients sign release forms; not just with a black pen, but also with blood. If I went down, they were coming with me, and they knew it when they signed on the dotted line. It was a win/win for everyone involved.

I hired some new girls and got rid of some others. I made it perfectly clear that there was no bullshitting around. One thing I never received from my mother was affection, I knew she loved me, but there wasn't a time I could think of that I received an embrace just because. I wasn't very good at expressing myself because of it and it made me want to be different. I wanted to show the VIPs that I would be there for them, in any way, shape, or form. It was important to me for them to see me as their Madam, but it had to have a much further in depth definition than what my mother implied.

It had to be all or nothing.

They needed to trust me, love me, and die for me. Just like any family member would do for you. I made sure that I established a different kind of relationship than my mother had with them. It wasn't all about money and they needed to be certain of that. It came down to respect, admiration, and loyalty. It required me to be their one and only. I learned from my mother's mistakes like most children do. Although my upbringing was much different than the norm, I still learned to take the bad with the good.

My mother wasn't a bad woman by any means, there are far worse out there. She did things in the way she thought she should. I never met my grandmother or grandfather; now that I think about it, I never met anyone in my family outside of my parents. I never asked about them and they were never discussed with me. I'm not quite sure if it was hush-hush for a reason, but I never looked into it. The day I took over was the day that I realized that I had a family, I had a responsibility to my girls. They were mine to look after and to love and cherish.

That is one thing that I changed immediately. My heart opened in an unexpected way. It came the minute I sat in the office chair, and I glorified in the supremacy that I held. It wasn't just about my life anymore. I had VIPs that I needed to look after. It was beyond any commitment I had ever willingly placed myself in. It scared me as much as it intrigued me; like I have said throughout this entire story, I don't do love. I don't know how to handle it, but it changed the day I took over. I love VIP. It was the first time that I ever felt something for someone else. It wasn't just about me anymore; it was about everything and anything it encompassed.

My life had always been about VIP.

It was my one true love.

VIP was my beginning, my middle, and my end.

I showed, taught, and explained to all the VIPs how things were going to proceed and they all accepted it with open arms. These women weren't lost children who needed or wanted a mother. They weren't broken. It wasn't about me fixing them. It was a mutual two way street where we each got to drive a car. It was a partnership; 50/50. They made decisions as much as I did. From my experiences, people will do something ten times more when they are told they can't, it's human nature. You want what you can't have.

Well...I allowed them to have it all. The human mind is a beautiful thing if appreciated; you give them a taste, they will always come back for more. You give them an inch and they will take a mile. I wanted them to have that mentality, it made them better and I wanted the best. Only the strong survive and that was VIP. The elite. I choose you, and if I did, there was a motherfucking reason for it.

Now...don't get confused and interpret my honesty for weakness. I was still very much a hardcore bitch; you don't run an empire by being nice. I still needed to instill fear and curiosity; it was a necessity to understand that I was always going to be a wildcard. You bark at me and I bite back. I was a double-edged sword and you didn't fuck with me. They knew not to mistake my kindness for weakness; I didn't have to explain it. It was an entitlement for me. I was one lucky bitch to get the cards that I was dealt and I wasn't stupid enough to take that for granted.

From the second I was born I was handed a silver spoon and I made sure that my VIPs felt precisely the same way. They were treasured jewels. The clients were aware of this as much as the girls were; becoming a client of VIP was like trying to join the CIA. There were certain characteristics and charisma you needed to carry in order to have one of my girls. I made sure that they were wined and dined before any sexual act were to occur. It was essential that VIP stood for something other than Very Important Pussy. The principle behind it was indispensible.

❊VIP❊

My father still stayed in and out of my life, but like I said before, I always made time for him when he wanted to see me. I sat in my office waiting for him to arrive one afternoon. The door opened and I didn't have to look up to know that he was disappointed. The atmosphere of the room dropped significantly from light to dark; he was coming in to battle. I should have expected it.

He walked over to me and sat on the chair and I didn't bother to look up.

"Tell me it's not true," he pleaded. It was the first time I had heard desperation in my father's voice. I braced myself before I looked up, and when I finally did his eyes were glossy. We stayed silent, just staring at each other for a few seconds; I didn't have to answer for him to know the truth. He knew it the minute he walked into the office, maybe even before that.

"Lilith," he tested.

I cocked my head to the side and corrected him, "Madam." His head fell down in shame.

"What do you want from me? What did you expect? I'm not here to point fingers or anything, but fathers who live in glass houses shouldn't throw stones."

"I didn't want this for you," he said barely above a whisper.

"We don't always get what we want, now do we? I don't know why you're so concerned; it never stopped you before. Don't cause yourself more grey hair, I am sitting pretty," I reminded.

"I hate this. You have no idea what life awaits you. You're already changing. I noticed it the minute I walked into the room. VIP will consume you. You will never have a real life. It will eat you up and spit you right back out."

"Who the hell do you think you are? You have no right to come in here and judge me for my choices and decisions, not one goddamn right…you need to remember that you may be my father by blood, but that's all we share. There is no father-daughter bonding between us. I see you because I choose to, not because I have to. If you'd like me to change that, then I gladly will. But don't come in here and pretend we are anything more than blood," I scorned.

He looked up and there were tears falling from his eyes. "I failed you."

I laughed. "You failed me from the day I was born. Let's not pretend to play house, it's not a good look for you," I tormented.

"I can't see you like this. I won't. I watched VIP destroy your mother, I can't go through that again."

I shook my head and sighed. "The door is right behind you; don't let it hit you on the way out."

"I love you, Lilith. I never thought it would come to this. I never imagined that you would actually take over. I thought you would find love, a nice man to give you a family. Something, anything other than this," he suggested.

"You have no idea who I am, you never have. I was made to do this! It's my fucking destiny. I will never be like my mother; I will be so much better. VIP is my legacy. If you can't stand to watch me succeed then you need to get the fuck out. I have never needed you in my life. I didn't ask you for anything, ever! If you want to pretend like we are more than what we are to each other and you want to win the father of the year award, then you need to call your other children for that. This one has no idea who you are other than someone who comes around when it's convenient for him." I took a deep breath and stood up to walk around the desk.

"I don't need you in my life. If you want to continue to see me then I will make time for you, like I always have. You want to leave and never come back, then that's your choice. Decisions are a very personal thing. You made your bed, now it's time to lie in it," I spewed.

"You want to know what the most frightening thing is, it's change. Even though it happens every single fucking day, it still scares the shit out of us. That's the difference between you and I. I look for change in my life, I am not scared of anything and I didn't inherit that from you, Daddy. Call my mother whatever you want, but at the end of the day, I am The Madam," I reminded.

He looked up at me. "I won't be around for this. If you continue, I won't see you again."

"Is that supposed to stop me?" I laughed. "You haven't been around my entire life; your threats don't mean shit to me. Do you understand? You gave me life and that's as far as it goes," I stated.

The worst part of this whole conversation is that I didn't mean one fucking word I was saying. As much as my father hadn't been in my life, I still wanted the bits and pieces that I did have. He was the only family I had.

But...I don't do ultimatums for anyone. I don't care who you are.

He stood up, walked over to me, and pulled me into a hug.

"I can't do it again. It's like I am staring into the face of your mother. I have always been a selfish man and I never did right by you. I am fully aware of that, but I just can't do it. You will always be the best thing I created. I have no one to blame but myself for the outcome of your life. I cannot stand around and watch it go down...I just can't. My only hope is that one day you will understand and you will forgive me, Lilith," he whispered in my ear.

I awkwardly wrapped my arms around him and he squeezed me harder. I could feel the tears coming down his face. We broke away from each other and he kissed my forehead, both cheeks, and the tip of my nose before he turned and walked out of my life.

I sat back in my office chair and overlooked my empire.

I had the world at my disposal. Absolutely anything I ever wanted I could have. Except love…

I was alone.

I shed one lonely tear and swore to myself that I would never cry for another man again.

CHAPTER 24

The year was 1992 and I was thirty-two years old. It had been five and a half years since I had taken over. The last five were probably the most pivotal in my growth as The Madam. I built a solid foundation for VIP with the clients, the city, and of course the girls. Miami changed in more ways than one. On August 24th of that year, hurricane Andrew made his appearance known to all of Florida, especially Miami, causing over twenty-five billion dollars in damage alone. It was the strongest hurricane to hit Florida in thirty years. The downfall was severe.

Miami was completely unprepared for a hurricane of that measure, during and after its effect. The city was in debt and it took a really long time for it to get back on its feet; slowly but surely it did. However, just because the city was in debt didn't mean people weren't spending money. The rich always get richer; it's a well-known fact, the reality of life, my friends.

The nineties were also the time of mainstream sex. The seventies and eighties did everything behind closed doors. The nineties said "fuck that". Women wore bikinis that showed off everything, thongs became a thing of the norm, including women walking around topless on South Beach. Playboy took over the world; it was everywhere. Hugh Hefner was the man of the hour, his empire was everywhere and it did wonders for VIP.

The nineties were also the time for blondes to have more fun, they were everywhere and men were crazy about them! They all wanted the California girl, and the face of beauty was a needle and a scalpel away from being you. Plastic surgeons were all over South Beach. Everyone wanted a quick fix. It started the era of instant gratification; from cell phones, to the internet. VIP became much more accessible to old and new clients. I had all black business cards made up with silver VIP lettering on the front and the number and address on the back. It gave clients the liberty to market for me without me having to lift a finger.

It was genius.

I spent most of my time in my office believe it or not. VIP almost ran itself…almost.

The door opened and Mika walked in with coffee in one hand and a box of donuts in the other.

"Get that shit out of my office, Mika. You know I can't eat that, but I will take the coffee." He sat down in the chair and opened the box; I could smell the calories from behind the desk.

"You never fucking eat, Angel. A donut isn't going to kill you and you're gorgeous, so shut it," he said.

I rolled my eyes. "What are you doing here?"

"I came to see you and to bring you breakfast. You're welcome." He grinned.

I rolled my eyes again. "Seriously…what are you doing here?"

"I came to ask you something."

"You could have picked up the phone."

"I wanted to see your face. I miss it." He smiled at me again.

"Sweet talking me isn't going to get you what you want. Just come out with it. I don't have time to fuck around today. I have a plane to catch in a few hours," I announced, trying to make sure I had all the paperwork I needed.

"Where are you going?" he asked.

"Switzerland," I responded.

"Want some company?"

"No," I said without hesitation. "It's not that kind of trip."

"All the more reason for me to come. Literally."

I laughed, "Oh my God! What do you want?"

"Fine. There's a gala in a few months; I want you to go with me."

I raised an eyebrow. "That's what you came over here to ask me?"

"Mmm hmm, Scouts Honor," he said, raising three fingers together in the air.

"I have to check my schedule but some of the girls are going, I can set you up with one of them," I stated, trying to dismiss him.

"Angel," he said in the tone that made my panties wet. "If I wanted one of the girls I would have asked for one. I didn't. I want you."

I sighed. "Mika, I don't have time for your shit today. I told you that I would see if I could; if I can't, then you're out of luck."

"Then make time," he demanded.

This was Mika to a T. You would think that over the years, I would have gotten used to him playing games with me, but it was quite the opposite. He didn't pussy foot around. The more I ran and pushed him away the harder he pursued, that's definitely one thing I learned about him. It was just easier to give him what he wanted and I got used to digging myself deeper into a hole with him.

I was already ten feet under, how much further could I possibly go?

"I told you. I will see." I smiled and my phone rang. I quickly answered it, trying to get Mika out of my office. The fucker leaned further back in his chair, folded his arms, and put his legs up on my desk. My eyes widened as I continued my phone conversation and all he displayed was a smug look on his face. I flicked him off and he laughed. I grabbed a piece of paper and wrote on it.

L: Get your feet off my desk.
M: Make me.
L: You are incorrigible. Fine. I'll go.
He grinned and left my office.

✵VIP✵

Two months came and went and The Gala was upon us. It was a fundraiser for Hurricane Andrew and the wealthy of Miami came out to share their support, and by that, I mean their checkbooks. I dressed in a strapless lavender fitted gown that was low cut, and my hair flowed loosely in large curls. Mika dressed in a black tux with his hair tied back in a ponytail. He looked good enough to eat.

I had several girls working the event and they were all dressed to the nines. My girls were dime pieces, every last one of them. The night started off with its usual antics, mingling like you pretended to care what they were saying. I had that down to an art, as did Mika. We worked the room ridiculously well together and I always had men eating out of the palm of my hand.

We were about midway through the night when I felt something shift. Call it a sixth sense, woman's intuition, or just basic instinct. Someone tapped on my shoulder and Mika and I turned. I recognized the man immediately; he was high profile in Miami and one of VIP's regular clients. I smiled when he leaned in to give me a kiss on both cheeks.

When we pulled away from our embrace, my eyes caught something from across the room and I couldn't turn away. I watched the next few seconds of my life happen in slow motion. He was speaking to me, but I didn't hear a word that came out of his mouth. All I could hear was the sound of my heart beating its way out of my chest. My ears were ringing from the palpitations and I could feel my mouth hang open. It was the first time that I wanted the earth to literally open up beneath me and swallow me whole.

We stared into each other's eyes as the whole room seemed to disappear in the background.

We knew who we were to each other.

All the memories came tumbling down on me and I couldn't breathe. I felt like I was suffocating from the emotions that I felt in a split second, all of them hitting me at once, one right after the other. I hadn't felt any of it in almost two decades. I didn't think it was possible to feel so much and not physically die.

I told you I never saw him again.
I wasn't lying.
Lilith didn't ever see him again.
The Madam did.

Julian...

CHAPTER 25

We continued to stare at each other from across the room, and our connection was strong and evident. We couldn't take our eyes away from each other. There was this imaginary line that was pulling deep within my bones. I felt it in every part of me. It was flashes of a life that wasn't mine anymore. I wasn't that person. I hadn't been that person in a very long time. It didn't change the fact that he was there and so was I.

I could hear Mika saying my name in the back of my mind, it was like I was at the end of a tunnel and he was trying to pull me back in. I was terrified that if I looked away he would disappear, and a huge part of me didn't want him to leave. I knew that if he left so did everything else, the feelings, and emotions, the physical need to feel something for someone else. The truth that I had been hiding for so long. The fact that I given her up, and that I had no idea if she was dead or alive. I had turned my back on something that I created, something that was mine, and a piece of me.

A part of me died that day and I had just realized it by looking across the room at the person who had helped me create it. I had given life and it was brutally taken away from me. I couldn't take it anymore and I ran. I ran on pure impulse to pull myself from a situation I didn't think I could survive. It was fight or flight mentality and I chose the latter. I ran as fast as my legs would allow me to go.

As soon as I felt the strong hand wrap around my arm, I turned around and I fought. I fought with everything I had in me. I pushed, slapped, and hit. I knew it was Julian and I just wanted to hurt him. I wanted him to feel like he was dying. I wanted him to think that I was fucking burying him in the ground, alive. I wanted to piss and spit on his grave. I punched him in the face with such force that he fell back and I thought I broke my hand. Mika's arms wrapped around from behind me and lifted me in the air.

"Angel, calm down," he repeated over and over again.

"You don't know! You don't fucking know what he put me through! You don't know what he did! I fucking HATE YOU! I wish you were fucking dead!" I screamed.

"I'm sorry, kitten. I'm so fucking sorry!" he said.

"Don't fucking call me that! I was sixteen! I was a fucking child. You could have done something; you could have done anything. You didn't do one goddamn thing but tuck your tail in between your legs and walk the fuck out. You gave her what she wanted! You let her fucking win! How can you look at yourself in the mirror?" I yelled.

"I have no idea where the fuck she is! I don't know what the hell happened to her and it's your fucking fault!" I tried with all the force I had to get Mika to release me, but he wouldn't. The more I tried, the harder he would hold me.

I hysterically cried big, fat, ugly tears. They poured out of my eyes and the pores of my skin. I was hyperventilating and my vocal cords felt like they were on fire.

"You didn't do anything, Julian. Nothing. I hate you. I hate you so fucking much because I didn't do anything either. I let all of it happen right before my very own eyes. I didn't even get to fucking hold her or say goodbye. I didn't get a fucking chance to do anything but cry. It was the only day my mother ever allowed me to shed one tear over my loss. I went through it all by myself. You're to blame for all of it! DO YOU HEAR ME! ALL OF IT!" I shouted. My body couldn't take it anymore and my legs finally gave out beneath me. I fell to the ground in Mika's arms.

I cried for it all.

"Her?" Julian said barely above a whisper. I looked up at him and he was crying. He was still one of the most gorgeous men I'd ever seen; he had aged but it only made him look better. I took in his disheveled appearance, he had scratches all over his face and his lip was bleeding. The bruising around his eye was becoming darker and it had a cut from one of my rings.

I slowly nodded. "Get the fuck out of my face."

"Kitten…"

I cocked my head to the side, "Madam, motherfucker, and if you don't get out of my face I will destroy you. Do you understand me? You will never be able to show your face in this city again."

"I'm so-"

"Listen, fucker, you heard her. If she has to say it again you will have to deal with me. Let me tell you a little something about me, I always let my hands to do the talking," Mika threatened.

Julian placed his hands in the air in a surrendering motion. He wanted to say more, but he succumbed. He took one last look at me before he stepped back and walked away.

I breathed a sigh of relief and Mika picked me up under my thighs and behind my back and carried me to the limo that awaited us. We were back at The Cathouse fifteen minutes later. He carried me inside the house and we went straight for my bathroom. He turned the shower on and undressed me slowly and carefully and then did the same to himself. He helped me into the shower and as the water dripped from my head to my body, I felt like it was washing away all my sins.

Mika washed my hair, face, and body with tender touches and caresses along the way. He kissed all over my face, my neck, and down my body. Anywhere he washed me he would kiss right after. I closed my eyes, taking in the feel of him. Mika and I weren't like this, we weren't sweet, caring...loving with each other. That's not who we were. He treated me like a doll that was going to break at any moment.

The truth was...I was broken.

I just never let myself admit it.

After he dried me and changed me into a silk robe, he put on a pair of boxers and I sat on my bed up against the headboard.

He got up off the bed; I panicked and grabbed his arm. "Don't leave."

He lightly smiled, knowing that must have been hard for me to say. "I'm not going anywhere. I was going to get you something to drink. What would you like?"

"Tequila." He was going to say no but he thought about it before he nodded. He brought back a glass with the bottle of Patrón and handed me both. I grabbed the bottle and he sighed. I took three huge gulps straight from the bottle, so lady-like. It burned the entire way down and after a few seconds, it warmed my insides. I repeated the process three more times.

Have you ever tried to get fucked up when you're upset? It doesn't fucking work. I did feel nothing though, and I guess that was something. We stayed silent for a while, just passing the bottle back and forth between each other.

"I've lived a really fucked up life, Mika, and at the same time a very privileged one. It's all I know," I said in a Tequila haze.

"Angel, no one is perfect and you pretend to be all the time. You are your own worst enemy," he declared. "What happened back there?" I took a deep breath.

I had never shared this with anyone before. I had never shared a lot of things with anyone before. I trusted Mika, and somewhere deep within my subconscious and heart, I probably loved him. My guard would never allow me to say that out loud. I wasn't made like that.

"You know my mother. I don't have to explain the infant, child, teenager, and adult I had to be. I hated being told what I was allowed to do. I am my mother's child, after all. When I found out about VIP and what my life would become, I wanted it then, right there at the ripe old age of sixteen. I had a very thought out plan, as best as any sixteen year old girl could have, I guess. I waited till my mother's eyes weren't on me for one fucking minute and I took what I wanted. Julian wasn't anybody to me other than someone who gave me attention. Our encounter was brief and he was the first man I ever had sex with." I took another gulp of Tequila not wanting to say the next words.

"I got pregnant." I nervously laughed. "What a cliché right? First time I have sex and I get knocked up. Make a very long story short I ended up in a facility where I became someone else's problem. I went into premature labor, there was a lot of bleeding, and they had to perform a hysterectomy." I took another two gulps of the Tequila. I really didn't want to say what was next.

"I can't have children, Mika. I have no one to leave this empire to. I watched my child through a window in an incubator on machines that helped her stay alive. I never got to touch or look at her face. You could put hundreds of baby pictures in front of me and I couldn't pick which one belonged to me." I bit my lip, trying to control the tears that were threatening to flow. I cried enough that night. I wouldn't allow for it to happen again.

"And Julian?" he questioned with some hesitation.

"He didn't do one fucking thing to stop my mother. He signed all the necessary paperwork to make the baby and I go away. Tonight was the first time I had seen him since the day he walked out on his mistake." I tried to take another gulp and Mika took the bottle away.

"That's enough, Angel."

"Fuck you," I stated, trying to get the bottle out of his hand. He quickly grabbed my wrist.

"You want to forget? Let me help you forget." He placed the bottle on the nightstand and stood up facing me. I looked up at his face, taking anything he had to offer. He untied my robe and slowly opened it, never taking his eyes off mine. His eyes were intense, they were blue, dark, and beautiful; they were Mika. I reached for his belt and he grabbed my hand.

"No, Angel. Let me take care of you," he said in a soft tone.

He slid my robe off my shoulders and kissed along my neck as it slid down. Mika has seen me naked hundreds of times, but it was the first time I felt like he was truly seeing me. I was in true form. The layers of all the bullshit were gone and all that was left was me. Mika had peeled away the mask that I wore and I had temporarily placed it in my back pocket.

His mouth grazed down my neck to my breasts where he licked and sucked at my nipples, making them hard stones. His path continued to my navel and my lower abdomen and he got down on his knees. I lay back staring at the ceiling. The foundation of a room…if it caved in, it could kill you. It would happen so fast and you would never see it coming.

The Madam was the ceiling to VIP.

"Angel," Mika murmured while his hands lightly touched up and down my thighs. "Stop. Don't think about anything other than how good I am going to make you feel."

His eyes were different; I had never seen them like that before. This wasn't the Mika that I was use to being intimate with. There was no darkness present in my bedroom that night. It was just me and Mika, two people coming together as one. I didn't need to feel the sting of anything.

We looked into each other's eyes as he kissed from my mound to the folds of my pussy. They were soft, tender strokes of his tongue, while he moved his way toward my opening. He started there; opening me tenderly and slowly, and then gently pushed his tongue in and out of me, making my breath catch. His warm, soft tongue licked all the way to my clit where he stroked his tongue back and forth and then in a circular motion. My breathing became labored and I waited for the words that never came. Mika loved to make me beg for it and I anxiously awaited to hear them.

When he took my nub and lightly sucked on it, I gasped. He went tortuously slow, lapping and manipulating my bundle of nerves. I had no control over my reaction, he did. I felt his thumb proceed to make circles around my opening and he eased it in. He pushed up, making sure to hit the upper walls of my pussy. It was rough but tender and I was close to release. Mika could sense it and his techniques continued to become more persistent and demanding. When he pushed what felt like his middle finger inside me, my legs started shaking.

My eyes closed and my head fell back. "Don't close your eyes," he ordered.

I moaned and watched as he sucked my clit and finger fucked my g-spot. When he started to hum, my vision blurred and my eyes rolled to the back of my head.

He licked all of my juices and then his fingers as he made his way up my body. I was all over his face and he leaned forward to kiss me. I tasted myself and the distinctive taste of him, and I sucked on his tongue enjoying the taste of us. The shaft of his cock slid up and down my slit and I came once again, lathering up our sacred parts with more of my moisture.

"Jesus, Mika. Just fuck me already," I begged, wanting to feel his hard cock deep within me. I couldn't take this dry fucking anymore.

"Angel, you're always so fucking wet. I have never felt a woman who can get as wet as you. Do you have any idea how much of a turn-on it is to a man like me?" he praised, never letting up from rocking on my clit.

"Ahhh…" he captured my mouth with his as he forcefully thrust into me. My back arched off the bed and he put his arms under mine, holding me close. My legs curled on top of his ass, waiting for him to move. He didn't. He stayed inside me, just holding me and kissing me. We had never been like this with each other. I knew we were crossing lines but we allowed it; even the feel of his skin felt different to me.

I rocked my hips, trying to get him to move because I was growing anxious and impatient with all the emotions and sensations he was causing. I couldn't handle it. This night had been an overload of it already and my mind and body needed to just be fucked. Mika wasn't having it; he knew what I wanted. I had no idea what game he was playing, but with each kiss and caress, he made his way deeper into my heart.

I wanted to hate him for it, but the heart wants what it wants. She's a brutal cunt like that.

He grabbed the sides of my face and looked deep into my eyes; he was searching for something, I didn't know if I had what he was looking for, but I didn't cower down. I kept his gaze as intently as he looked into mine. It was as if we were absorbing our way into each other's blood streams, where neither of us could function without the other.

Never taking his eyes off mine, he started to move; it was slow, loving, and passionate. I had never been with someone like that before and for some reason I believed that he hadn't either. His hand reached for my neck and he softy pressed down on it. It was the one Mika move that did seem familiar to me; he always wanted to feel like he could control me in any way, and what's more dominate than knowing you could stop someone's breathing. I leaned my head further back to expose more of my neck to him, and he pressed down further.

I moaned and my pussy pulsated. He started to pump faster into me and the nerves in my lower abdomen throbbed for release.

"Fuck, Angel...do you have any idea what you do to me? Your pussy is my kryptonite. You fucking devour me," he groaned. "Tell me...tell me what you're thinking. I want to know."

"I'm thinking how fucking amazing your cock feels and if you keep hitting my g-spot like that, I'm going to come," I muttered.

He kept hitting the same spot, more aggressively than before. "No...that's not what I want. Hmmm...give me what I want, Angel."

I knew what he was implying. "What do you want from me? Ahhhh...why are you doing this?" I pleaded in the middle of climaxing.

"Because I always give you what you need, not what you want," he simply stated as he angled my leg to hit my g-spot harder. "Tell me or I'll pull out."

"Fuck...I'm thinking...how much I need you..." I moaned, closing my eyes as I arched my back.

"Let me see your eyes, Angel." I opened my eyes and looked intently into his. I could feel he was close to losing it because his thrusts were becoming faster.

"I'm glad I have you in my life. You're not going anywhere," he groaned, taking me over the edge just as he was.

We lay like that for several minutes, just kissing and enjoying the feel of being connected. We passed out in each other's arms.

I knew things were going to be different in the morning, and for the first time, I would embrace it.

CHAPTER 26

I woke up the following morning, feeling full. My heart thundered in my chest at the thought of Mika. That had never happened before. I didn't know what was going on, but it put a smile on my face, a different kind of smile. One I hadn't worn a day in my life.

The smell of coffee flowed into my bedroom, lifting me from my blissful haze. I got up and put on a robe to join Mika in the kitchen.

He stood against the counter with his back toward me. He didn't hear me approach as I snuck up behind him, wrapping my arms around his muscular torso, feeling far more content than I had in a long time.

"Good morning, Angel," he rasped in his sexy morning voice. It was a voice I barely heard since we rarely made it to waking up together.

"Mmmm...good morning indeed."

"Feeling better?" he asked as he spun around to take a look at me.

"Yes...although I'm sure you could find a few more ways to make me feel even better." His eyebrows rose and a smile appeared on his handsome face.

"As amazing as it would be to bend you over my knee and make you feel all kinds of better, I have to get going. I have some business to take care of."

"Business? What kind of business?" I prodded.

The smile fell from his lips as he stared at me harshly. "Business."

"Oh, we're being secretive now?" I tried to make it sound like I was teasing him, but from the look on his face I knew I had failed.

"Angel, let's not get all clingy. I don't question you about what you do."

I have been called many things in my life, but clingy was never one of them. I was actually as far opposite from clingy as one could get. It enraged me.

"Clingy? Really, Mika? You didn't seem to mind my legs clinging to your body last night. Or my thighs clinging to your face as you fucked me with your tongue."

He let out a harsh breath. "Let's not get into this right now. Drink your coffee and I'll talk to you later." He handed me a mug and began to walk away.

I threw the ceramic mug against the wall beside him, barely missing the side of his head. "What the fuck!" he roared as he spun around with a crazed look in his eyes.

"What was last night, Mika? Huh?"

"That was me giving you what you needed! I told you that!" he screamed as he slowly walked back in my direction.

I didn't back up. I stood taller and glared right back at him. "And who the fuck are you to decide what I need? I don't recall telling you that I needed you to make love to me. I don't recall ever needing someone to make love to me."

"You were hurt and vulnerable. Don't deny it; I know you were. You were feeling the pain of losing your child all over again. You didn't need me to make you feel any more pain. You needed me to make you feel loved. And that's what I did."

"Well what is it then? Are you telling me you love me?"

"Don't do this. Don't fucking twist my words around. You know how I feel about you. We are the same. We are incapable of that kind of love. Do I love you as one of my closest friends? Yes. I love you in the only way I know how to. And you know that. You know that I'm not the kind to settle down and play house. You know it because you aren't either. That's not who we are." His voice had calmed down, but his words were still harsh, cutting into the heart I just discovered I had.

For months, I had tried to come to terms with my feelings for Mika, and I thought last night made it clear. But hearing him say those words cut me deeper than I knew possible.

My hurt came out as anger. Pure anger, as I fought with him. "What did you mean when you said you were glad you had me in your life? And that I wasn't going anywhere? What was that supposed to mean? Just something else you thought I needed to hear?"

"No, Angel. I am glad you are in my life. You're fun. And let's face it; you fuck better than anyone I've ever fucked. And you're not going anywhere. We're in this together; we're business partners and friends. What did you think I meant by it?"

I stared at him, feeling foolish. And I don't tolerate anyone making me feel that way. "Just go take care of your *business*, Mika. I don't want nor need you here anymore." Even the words came out sad and pathetic.

He tried to kiss me on my forehead but I backed away.

"You apparently seem to misunderstand what it is that I need," I said in a monotone. "I don't need your kisses or your pity. I need for you to get the fuck out of my house."

He shook his head, backed away, and left.

I felt broken. First, it was Julian last night. Now Mika this morning. Both men that I allowed myself to be vulnerable with cut my heart out of my chest. I was unlovable; my own father proved that when he turned his back on me in the prime of my life. I decided right then and there that I would also be incapable of love. No one will ever deserve that from me.

I didn't need to contemplate if I had a heart anymore. Because I didn't. It lay beaten and bruised on the floor in front of me. I grabbed the only thing that loved me, my vile of white powder, off the counter and breathed it in. Feeling the euphoria cloak me, I stood and watched what was left of my bleeding heart die.

I spent the next two months focusing on VIP. I hadn't talked to Mika since he walked out that fateful morning. He didn't reach out to me and I didn't bother to try to contact him. I knew he'd be coming back. He always did.

❖VIP❖

I sat at my desk, finishing paperwork for a new VIP, when the door burst open. There was only one person in this world that refused to knock before entering. I didn't even have to look up to know it was Mika. I heard him walk in and shut the door behind him. I waited for his next move. He sat down on the chair in front of my desk and cleared his throat.

I looked up. "Can I help you?" I questioned with a raised eyebrow.

"I missed you, Angel. I've missed you a lot."

"Mmm hmm…"

"Oh come on; don't be like that. I came here to play nice and make friends again. Don't you want to be my friend?" he provoked teasingly.

I sighed. "You look like shit."

"I feel like shit. How about you make me feel better? Come over here and sit on Mika's lap." I bit my lower lip.

I should have kicked him the fuck out, however I didn't. I walked over to his lap and hiked up my skirt to expose my creamy thighs and then he reached for his belt. We spent the next two hours getting reacquainted.

I buttoned my blouse as Mika sat on my desk.

"I've missed you. You know that, don't you?" he announced, making me look up at him.

I shook my head confused. "What are you talking about?"

"I fucked up, Angel. I fucked up real bad."

"Okay…you're being really vague. What's going on?" I asked, trying to sound casual and not show the emotions that were playing in my head.

He took a deep breath. "I'm getting married tomorrow."

They say that crimes of passion happen in a brief second. The human mind just twitches for a brief moment in time and you act on the pure impulse of someone crushing all your dreams and illusions right before you. I never understood that. I couldn't comprehend how a person couldn't have control of their actions, regardless the situation.

I understood it that day.

If I had a gun in my hand, I would have shot him and not thought twice about it.

I did the next best thing. I showed him indifference. The only way a person can hurt you, is if you let them.

I laughed, but inside I was dying. "Congratulations. Is that what you came to tell me?" He cocked his head to the side, expecting something different from me.

"Would you like to tell me where you're registered, I'll send a gift."

"She's pregnant. I'm marrying her because she's pregnant," he declared as if that made things better. I still had his come dripping down my leg, how about that for irony.

"Well then...I'll make sure to send two gifts."

"Come on, Angel. You know I didn't plan this; it was an accident. She was a random fuck and the condom broke. I don't go bare except with you," he agonized.

"Right...listen, I'm happy for you and other than the fact that you just fucked me, literally, I have high hopes for your marriage."

"I have to marry her, if I don't all my money is gone. It's the only way I can keep my trust fund. My father would never let a bastard of mine be on the streets. I have to take care of my obligations. I don't love her and she knows that. She wants to be taken care of, that's all." He pointed between him and I. "This. Is not over. I'm not going anywhere and neither are you."

I walked right over to him, barely a couple inches away from his face. "Who the fuck do you think you are? When have I ever been interested in coming in second place? You think you fucking know me because I let you call me Angel. Get one thing straight, Mika. I will never be the other woman and if you thought for one second that coming over here and saying this to me was going to have me waiting in line for you, then go fuck yourself. Do you understand? Now...if you would so kindly get the fuck out of my life."

He lunged at me and roughly grabbed the back of my hair. "Oh yeah...you think so, huh? If I were to put my fingers in your panties, I wouldn't find my come? It's not dripping down your leg right now?" He pulled my hair more, trying to make me yelp, but I was never one to cower down.

"You're mine, Angel, and possession is nine-tenths of the law. I don't give a fuck who The Madam is and don't think you can stay away from me. At the end of the day, I know whose pussy this belongs to. Do you understand?" He quickly let go of me and walked out of my office.

CHAPTER 27

After Mika walked out of my office, essentially my life, I had to do something. I decided to clean. I had all intentions of clearing out my mother's belongings that I had yet to get to, but I was not prepared for what I was about to find. It was as if God had made me his personal entertainment for the last few days.

I had removed all the files in the last drawer of my desk. The bottom of the drawer jiggled when I placed my hand on it. It took me a few minutes to figure out how to get it open and when I did, I found a single file named, "Elizabeth". I put it on my desk and opened it. There was a Polaroid of a newborn clipped on the back left side; on the right, there were documents. There, before my eyes, were all the documents of my daughter; the paperwork that Julian signed, the hospital documents, and the adoption papers.

The adoption was a closed case. There was no information given other than the parents' names, no leads. I grabbed the file, put it in my purse, and drove to where I needed to go without giving it a second thought. Gregory Switzer was the best private investigator in Miami and he had been working for VIP for years.

"With all due respect, Madam, I don't have much to go on here." His thick German accent wafted through the small office.

"Are you telling me that you can't do it?"

"That is not what I'm telling you. I just need some more information. Anything you can remember would be helpful."

"Then you're shit out of luck, Gregory…I don't remember anything."

"I can read the file, but how about you tell me what you know. Maybe there's something in your head that's not in here," he pressed. It only irritated me to have to think about it all over again.

I sat in a chair across from his desk and crossed my legs. I'm sure my attitude was blatant, but I didn't give a shit. He worked for me, not the other way around.

"I had a baby. She was adopted."

He stared at me, waiting for more. But he wasn't going to get more.

"The only thing you need to worry about, Gregory," I said his name with such distain it made him squirm in his chair, "is finding her. Is that clear?"

"Yes, Madam. But I hope you know it will take some time."

I stood up and pressed my hands to his desk, leaning over until we were face to face. "My mother had this information for a reason, and kept it from me for a reason. I'm assuming she had gotten it from somewhere. And since you are the one that worked for her, one could only assume where she got it from."

I straightened back up and fixed my blouse. "VIP is mine now. I had no problems cleaning house after I took over. Would you like me to add you to the donation pile as well?"

"N…no, Madam." He radiated with nervousness, and if I had a cock in my pants, it would have been standing at attention. Not because of the sweaty man in front of me, but because of my power.

"I was not involved in her finding any information, I swear it," he pleaded.

"Too bad. If you were, you would at least have a place to start looking. I suggest you halt any other projects you may be working on, now or in the future, until I have what I need." I turned to leave but he stood up.

He came around his desk and stopped me from leaving. For the first time since walking in, he seemed like a man. He wasn't shaking like he had been, nor was he acting nervous. It made me notice his muscular arms and reminded me of how attractive I used to think he was.

"I'm talking years here, Madam."

I grabbed his tie and pretended to straighten it. Instead of fixing it, I tightened it as hard as I could around his neck and used it to pull his face to mine.

"If you'd get out of my way and start working, I'm sure it'd take less time."

I licked his lips and then released him. He didn't move from where he stood.

I grabbed him by the balls, the only way to let a man know you mean business, and moved my lips to his ears. "Do this...and I'll let you do me. I know you've always wanted to, Gregory. I noticed how you used to look at me. And I see the way you look at me now." I backed away and released him. "Don't do it, and I'll make sure you never stick your dick in anything warm again."

Without a glance back, I walked out of his office and closed the door behind me. It had been a while since I felt that kind of power over someone. Sure, I had VIP and held all of the power over that, but to watch the pupils of a man change so drastically by one touch, or one word; it had been a while.

I could still feel his lips on my tongue, and I knew what I had to do.

I made my way to the bathroom and stood in front of the mirror. My girls were always busy with handsome, rich men, while I stood back and worked the business. I was over that. It was time for me to mix a little pleasure with my business. And I knew just where to go.

One of my girls was set up with a new client. I met him once when he came in to sign his paperwork. He was devilishly handsome for someone around my age. Maybe it was the slight salting of his hair on the sides that did it for me. Whatever it was, it was going to be his pleasure to stick his cock in me for the night.

I knew where they were meeting, where they were going to be, and I was going to make an appearance.

I went straight to the hotel room that had been booked and opened the door. These minimum wage hotel clerks would do anything for a tip; including giving a stranger a room key.

Cynthia was already on the bed, spread eagle, and her company was beginning to undress. They never even heard me come in. I walked up behind him and began to unzip his pants.

"Here, let me help you with that, darling."

He spun around, excited to see me. Cynthia on the other hand, looked a bit shocked but stayed where she was. She knew better than to move or cover up.

After helping the client out of his pants, I sank into the bed next to my VIP, smelling her body on my way to her face.

"As much fun as I could have with you right now, I think I'll have you go. I can handle Mr. Morisette from here." She looked shocked but didn't say anything as she removed herself from the bed and dressed.

I put my heels on the edge of the bed and opened my legs wide, showcasing the fact I was not wearing panties. "What do you think, hmmm? Think you can handle me?"

"Only one way to find out." He began to move over me, placing his body between my legs to move up.

"Tsk, tsk, tsk, Gabriel," I said as I placed my heel right in his chest. "Why don't we start here?" I insisted, pointing to my pussy. "And by that, I mean with your mouth." He grinned and dove right in.

Gabriel Morisette was a power player and he fucked the exact way that he did business; hard, rough, and dirty. The best kind of way. Leaving that room that afternoon made me feel like a weight had been lifted off my shoulders. My mother was wrong about a lot of things; who I was, who I'm supposed to be, and who I will become...

Moments of weakness build character and reinforce stability. You take the good from the bad and vice versa. We pick and choose our demons, just like we do our battles; it's the beauty about being human.

Everything happens for a reason...just remember that.

✳VIP✳

A year went by and it was December 16, 1994, I got the phone call that I had anxiously been waiting for.

"Madam," I answered.

"It's Gregory," he immediately replied.

I felt my heart speed up and all the blood from my face drained. "Yes..." was all I could say. It felt like an eternity for him to reply but I knew it was only seconds.

"She's gone," he stated those two words that could change my entire life.

"What do you mean?"

"She ran away from home in 1990 when she was thirteen, and no one can find her. She was adopted into a nice home with very comfortable surroundings. Nothing looked suspicious. Her parents tried all avenues to find her and ended up with nothing. No one has heard from her. I have used every resource I have to find her, and still nothing," he hesitated. "I'm sorry, Madam. She's gone."

"Thank you." I said and hung up.

There are some things in life that are better left unsaid, and at times we want answers to questions we don't even know. I had never run across a problem where throwing money at it didn't fix it. The fact that I had no control over finding something that belonged to me fucked me up in more ways than one. There was no bittersweet moment, no resolution, and no clear conscience on my part. I take care of what's mine and I wasn't even given the opportunity to make things right.

I finally felt what I was trying to hide all those years.

I hated my mother.

And I think she always wanted me to.

CHAPTER 28

Y2K…sound familiar?

January 1st, 2000, the arrival of the new millennium, December 31, the great Y2K scare and the horror that the end of the world was near.

I threw a costume, slash orgy, slash drug party.

I'll give you a quick recap of the last five years. I did a lot of drugs; I fucked a lot of men, and women. I lived, I laughed, and I loved…myself, VIP, and my girls. I call that era my careless time. I was really messed up after finding out about Elizabeth, Mika, and even Julian. I lost myself for a while; my dark period. The cliff notes version is that I did what the hell I wanted to do. I didn't once think about any of the consequences of the things that I did.

The Madam was powerful, envied, feared, and loved. I had anything at my disposal at any given time. No one said no to me, and if they did, they didn't live to do to it again. I could destroy by just looking at you. You may think that I grew cold or cruel, and you are entitled to your opinion, but the truth is people who make it to the top have to crush those below them.

I didn't make the rules for the first time in my life; I just followed them.

I invited anyone who was worth a damn for my New Year's Eve party. I figured if the world came to an end, at least I was in good company. I know what you're asking yourself as you read this…

Where's Mika?

Am I right?

Mika and I remained "close" throughout those five years. To put it as blunt as possible, we still fucked. How much of a hypocrite am I, you ask? I was the other woman and trust me; it wasn't by choice. As much as I wanted to walk away from him, I couldn't, and he wouldn't allow it. He was absolutely right about one thing, he always gave me what I needed, and it really was the beauty of us.

I never met his wife or his child and we never talked about it. Mika always lived multiple lives; it's who he was. He never made excuses or apologizes for the shit he did either. That's not to say I was the only other woman, I'm sure he had one everywhere he went, but I was his number one girl; at least that's what he loved to tell me. It also gave me the liberty to do whatever or whomever I wanted to. I was still The Madam, and I never let Mika forget that. In its own completely twisted way, our "relationship" worked for me, and I was aware that it was the only way that I was able to be with someone and not truly be with them; if that makes any sense at all.

Anyway, I had a special plan for New Year's Eve. One thing that I learned about high society people is how much they love their recreational drug use, the wealthy love to get fucked up. Think about, if you had all the money in the world and never once had to fear that you couldn't buy your way out of something, then there were no consequences. People need consequences for change. Thus, taking "recreational" drugs is like going on vacation. You do it because you can. Now their sex was a different story; they loved to do those things behind closed doors. It's so much easier to be who you are without anyone knowing it's you.

When the clock struck midnight, I had someone turn off all the lights, literally. One would think that my guests would experience paranoia and panic, quite the contrary...the music changed and so did the mood. There were candles spread out throughout the entire room and it gave it a soft glow. It had a translucent appearance, a certain je ne sais quoi quality about it. And then...the VIPs walked in. All dressed in nothing but heels. They took center stage in the middle of the room and swayed their hips to the music. I didn't have to see the guest's faces to know that they were aroused, which is exactly what I wanted.

They danced provocatively, provoking and seducing everyone in the room. Their movements were carnal and sinful. I watched as the women captivated the attention of every last person in the room and I was proud. My girls were made for sex; you could see it, you could taste it, and you could fucking feel it. No one took their eyes off of them. They hypnotized the room through their movements. The music changed to Beethoven's Moonlight Sonata and the girls glided their way toward their prey.

My guests didn't stand a chance.

Even I was being pulled toward the vitality of my girls. However, I was always a voyeur, as were some other guests. I surveyed the room, breathing in the smell of lust, abandonment, and pussy.

Some people need love...

I need sex, money, power, and control.

I stood in the corner of the room with my back against the wall and observed all the primal hunger around me. My hands eased their way up my thighs and I lavished in the velvetiness of my skin. My nails lightly skimmed the first layer of pores that left my hair standing up at attention. I caressed my thighs in an up and down motion as I looked everywhere around the room. The eroticism was a work of art that I created. I was living a piece of history and people would talk about this for years to come. The thrill of it all was enough to get me wet.

As I observed bodies being devoured and adored by one, two, three or more people. There was no judgment...this was not depravity...this was VIP.

I didn't have to look to know that he was there.

I didn't have to find him to know that he was watching me.

As Beethoven's melody continued to assault our senses, it illuminated the raw acts before us. The new millennium was welcomed with unadulterated passion.

My right hand found its way toward the lining of my panties and I touched the layer of silk right above the labia of my lips. The palm of my hand swayed back and forth on my pussy as I felt the moisture seeping through. My other hand slowly moved its way up my body and I began rubbing at the back of my neck while my fingers found the inside of my panties. I didn't touch where I wanted myself the most; instead, I teased my labia and spread around the wetness from my opening.

My hand made its way down to my breast and I massaged myself through my dress. I bit my bottom lip as I watched a client suck on a VIPs clit. Her head fell back, as did mine. I pushed two fingers inside of my heat and moaned. There I was, shamelessly fucking myself while everyone else was getting fucked. My eyes closed on their own as I pushed harder on my g-spot and moments later, I felt him.

His fingers lay on top of mine and he pushed me in deeper and firmer. He kissed and sucked on the side of my neck as he removed the straps of my dress and bra to expose my breasts. I whimpered when he bit me.

"You've been waiting for me, Angel?" he whispered in my ear as he sucked on my earlobe.

"Tell me...huh...tell me you've been waiting for me. I want to hear you say it."

"Mmmmm..." I groaned and he stopped my hand from moving. I griped at the loss of movement. I was so close to coming undone and he knew it.

"Tell me and you can come," he insisted.

"Fuck...Mika," I pleaded as I tried to move my hips, but he pushed all his body weight on me, caging me in.

"You want to come...then be a good girl..." I opened my eyes and stared into his dark, abandoned eyes. He was as fucked up as I was. We were both lost and used each other to find our way out of the solitude.

I leaned into his ear and blatantly admitted, "I've been waiting for you. I'm always waiting for you and I fucking hate you and love you for it."

"That's my Angel," he groaned as he manipulated my hand to fuck me harder. He roughly kissed his way to my nipple and took one in his mouth. I could feel his teeth as he nibbled, making me feel both pleasure and pain. I grabbed the back of his head, pushing him and molding him into me as his hand went into my panties to draw circles around my clit. I could hear panting all around me and the endless amounts of skin on skin contact.

Mika urgently kissed me and our tongues twirled and tasted each other. I sucked on his bottom lip as I removed my hand and found his belt. I freed his hard cock and soaked it with the juices that were on my hand. He grabbed under my thigh and pulled my leg up as he plunged deep into my wet core.

"Fuck...you feel good. I've been thinking about this pussy all day." We stayed like that for several seconds just enjoying the feel of one another. He wrapped his hand around my neck and squeezed lightly as he began to thrust in and out of me. All the sounds and smells added to the sensation of our joining bodies.

"Harder, Mika…fuck me harder," I begged as he grabbed my other leg to wrap around him. My back hit the wall with every give and take, and I knew I was going to bruise. I needed the pain and he knew it. The harder he fucked me the tighter I squeezed on his shaft. I could feel my juices dripping down my ass. I met him with every thrust until I couldn't take it anymore and came.

"Jesus…Angel…come on my cock…just like that…" he panted as he thrust into me one last time, his entire body shook along with mine.

The second he placed me on the floor, his phone rang.

He pulled me into an embrace. "Happy New Year, Angel," he said into the side of my neck.

"Happy New Year," I repeated.

He kissed me one last time and left. I didn't have to wonder where he was going. I laughed it off and enjoyed the rest of my night with my guests.

Happy fucking New Year!

CHAPTER 29

A year and a half is all it took for things to take a drastic turn; June 6, 2001 was my 41st birthday. I was never one to make a big deal out of my birthday, but you can imagine the attention that it brought. I didn't care about getting older, I never looked my age, and you are only as old as you feel. I did my normal routine early that morning until my phone rang; I was expecting it to be another celebratory phone call. Except…I was wrong.

"I found her," Gregory declared.

As soon as I heard the words, my knees gave out and I dropped into my office chair in shock. He explained everything to me carefully and precisely and I took in every syllable. A part of me didn't believe what I was hearing; so much so, that he had to repeat the address of where she was three times before I could write it without shaking.

The past always has its way of catching up to you, and mine crept in slowly. It took twenty-four years for me to get to that point and I had no idea what I was going to do with the information. Sometimes in life, you think you know the answers to questions that you constantly ask yourself, but when the moment truly comes to your front doorstep, you don't know whether to answer the door or slam it shut. I don't care who people think you are or the persona you have people believe is you, nobody knows what goes on in your mind when you lay your head to sleep at night.

And that is the reality of lies and secrets.

Defense mechanisms are a part of our everyday existence, and everyone engages in some sort of self-deception. My favorite would have to be denial; what is fact or fiction in one's mind. That day, my mind was racing with thoughts of the unknown and that is by far the scariest emotion one can feel, especially for someone like me. I shut out the world that day and it took me exactly three weeks before I was able to recognize that I knew where to go to find my daughter.

The real truth behind The Madam is that I needed a goddamn prodigy. Someone to take the reins when I was done and I wouldn't hand it down to anyone that didn't have my blood in them.

It took me another week before I made my way to where she was, to where I could find her. It was exactly one month after Gregory first told me. As I drove in a state of trance, I hadn't realized that I was heading toward the slums. At first, it was confusing because I couldn't picture my twenty-four year old daughter living in this hellhole that I was driving by. I was fucking disgusted and I hadn't even gotten out of the car yet. As I made my way toward the destination of the house, I couldn't believe what was happening. I thought Gregory must have given me the wrong address or I took down the wrong information.

But something inside me told me to get out of the car, and so I did. I carefully walked up to the house trying to avoid stepping on shit, cigarettes, or needles and ruining my $3,000 shoes, internally praying that this wasn't my daughter and this was some sort of mistake. The floor creaked below me as I stepped on the porch and I could smell the stench coming from inside the house, even with the door being closed. I knocked several times and there was no answer. I noticed a window on the side of the house and walked toward it. I didn't see anything at first and was about to turn around and that's when I saw her.

She was dressed in a tank top that barely covered her breasts and shorts that had filth all over them. I could see piles of garbage all over the house and liquor and beer cans everywhere. I watched and waited as she took a seat on the horrendous couch. Her face was red; I'm sure it was from massive doses of strong whiskey. Her hair was dirty, greasy, and straggly looking. I was positive she hadn't washed it in days. Her darkened eyes were tunneled by the puffiness around them. She was a fucking mess, but beautiful.

Had she had the opportunity to blossom the way I did, she would have no doubt been a beautiful VIP goddess. She was a VIP, behind the drugs, the alcohol and God knows what else, the dreadful creature before my eyes was a VIP. Any parent in their right mind would have felt guilt. I felt fury. That part of my feelings didn't exist. Not this time. All I kept thinking was, *how dare she? How dare she pop the cap of a needle right in front of me? Who the fuck did she think she was?*

She was a goddamn Stone and VIPs didn't look like this. VIPs didn't dress like some dumb cunt on a street corner. VIPs seeped poison from their pussies, not from their fucking veins. The stench, pouring from every crevice around me was revolting. The sight of that needle piercing the skin was disgusting as the blood trailed down her arm. The thought of this sickly little thing in front of me repulsed me. My daughter was a piece of shit, the bottom of the barrel, just another fucking junkie wasting her life away. I felt sick to my stomach; she was a weak, worthless nothing. I turned to leave immediately, not wanting to waste my time any more than I already had.

I got in my car and floored the gas pedal, wanting to get the hell out of the neighborhood. My fingers anxiously tapped on the steering wheel, trying to drown out the catastrophe that I had just witnessed and the awful taste it left in my mouth. I hadn't even noticed that I ran a stop sign until I had to slam on my breaks because a woman was crossing the street. My body jolted from the impact and it was like a sign from God himself as I stared into the greenest pair of eyes that I had ever seen in my entire life. The girl was a fucking vision, enough that it took my goddamn breath away.

She was perfect.

I knew it right then and there. Come hell or high water, I would have her by any means necessary. She shyly smiled as she walked away; she must have been around sixteen. I made sure to wait a few minutes before I trailed behind her, keeping enough distance to where she didn't see me but I wouldn't lose her. She crossed the street and I watched in horror as she walked toward a house to retrieve the mail and then yelled, "mom". I watched her mother walk out and it cemented my thoughts on needing to get her the fuck out of there.

She was mine she just didn't know it yet and that would change real soon.

❊VIP❊

I spent the next few days getting everything in order. I had a plan, and it didn't take me long to execute it. This will be the part of my story where you will think that I am fucking monster, you will turn the page and you will hate me. Like I've said from the beginning, there are always three sides to every story. Things don't always go according to plan, but know this...I have no regrets for the things I have done, because the bottom line is, I am The Madam and I will ensure my legacy by any means necessary.

Money can buy anything you have ever wanted and it doesn't matter if it's right or wrong, green is the most powerful color in the world. I waited in my office for my "guest" to arrive. The minute he walked in, I knew I had him, and it wasn't even going to cost me that much. I had no idea who he was or if I could even trust him, but it was a risk I was willing to take. He took a seat and crossed his leg; he looked about late thirties, stubble on his face, dressed decently, but nothing to brag about.

"Did I tell you could sit down?" I questioned with an arched eyebrow.

"You need me, princess, not the other way around," he replied with a condescending tone.

It made me chuckle. "Mika said you could get the job done, so let's get one thing straight, you work for me not the other way around. If you have a problem with that I will find someone who doesn't." He hesitated but nodded.

"I need you to scare someone for me and it will be the easiest ten grand you've ever made." He nodded again as I handed him a piece of paper with the address.

"She lives there and I will give you an extra grand to pay off the mom. I have no doubt that she will eagerly and gratefully accept it. You scare the girl and then you come back and I pay you. Understood?"

"Perfectly. Where do I meet the mom?"

"She hangs out at this dive bar in town and the address is also on that paper," I informed the piece of shit sitting in front of me.

"Can I fuck her?"

"You can stick it in whatever hole she lets you. As far as the girl goes, just spook her. Am I clear?"

"You honestly think the mother is going to go for this?"

"I have no doubt," I divulged.

✳VIP✳

Five days later, he was back in my office sitting in the same chair as I grabbed the envelope full of money.

"I fucked her," he beamed.

"Good for you, hope you didn't catch anything," I said, laughing as I handed him the envelope.

"I'm talking about the girl. You could have told me she was twelve." I quickly pulled back the envelope.

"What the fuck are you talking about?" I yelled.

"Listen…we smoked some crack and the mom pretty much threw her at me. What the fuck was I suppose to do?" he explained.

"What part of spook her did you not understand YOU FUCK! I wanted her out of the house not fucking traumatized," I screamed.

"I did what you told me to do! Blame the fucking mother; she didn't give a shit what I did as long as she was getting paid."

"So you decided to rape a FUCKING CHILD?!"

He stood up. "Fuck you, lady. Get off your goddamn high horse; you're the reason I was even there. Whatever happened to her, it's on you. I did my job because you put me there; let's get that fucking straight. You are no better than me. Just because you make your orders behind some fancy desk doesn't make you any less of a villain. Now give me my fucking money."

I grabbed the envelope and walked around my desk to stand in front of him. I shoved the envelope in his chest and then I spit in his face. "You have one minute to get the fuck out of my house or I'm calling the cops." He grinned, showing his disgusting yellowed teeth, and walked out of my office, not bothering to even wipe his face.

I stood there in shock not being able to move, I couldn't believe what I had done. I couldn't even argue with him because everything he said was true. Even if she had been sixteen like I had originally thought, it wouldn't have made it any better. But the fact that she was only twelve made it so much worse. She was just a baby, no matter what kind of life her mother put her through. Hearing that her mom was fine with what he had done, made me even angrier. I should have just taken her when I was there and she was in front of me.

The Madam

I felt violently sick. Over the years I had felt many emotions, most of them foreign to me...this one was no different. I had never felt so guilty or distraught before. And the feelings were quickly rising in my chest. I leaned over and emptied my stomach in the wastebasket next to my desk. I washed my mouth out with some Tequila I had in my office. I wanted to go get her, but I knew I couldn't. I just had to wait for her to come to me. And I was going to make sure that happened.

The days that followed left me feeling empty and soulless. Nothing I'd ever seen nor did, prepared me for the mental hell of what I was involved in with an innocent girl- an innocent twelve-year-old girl. What the fuck did I do? I should have gone after her. I could have paid the mother off. I could have taken her under my wing and taught her all that I'd been taught. It was all I could do not to do that. I had to wait. It was done, and there was nothing I could do about it but wait. I did something my mother would have despised. I wallowed in a drunken self-pity for days, feeling like a piece of shit. I was a piece of shit. I spent four days trying to drown myself in Tequila, hoping to relieve the scar from my brain and forget. After feigning an illness for four days, I picked myself up, and got back to my life.

I pushed back the emotions where I kept everything, deep inside me where no one could see it.

What's done is done and there's no going back.

Living in sin was the new thing.

CHAPTER 30

Two years passed like a breeze and it was June 2003; VIP had become a staple piece of Miami and my girls were everywhere. I lived in the lap of luxury. I would see my mother here and there, but we both kept to our sides of the fence. It was much easier that way.

My eyes stirred and I woke up to Mika staring at me. "What are you still doing here?" I yawned, still half asleep.

He grinned. "You kicking me out?"

"Would you leave if I was?" I laughed.

He trailed a single finger up and down my stomach. "Not a chance."

"Didn't think so," I quickly replied, trying to get up. But he grabbed me around the waist and pulled me back, nudging his hard cock on the crevice of my ass.

"I'm up." He nudged the side of my neck.

"I see that."

"Did I say I was done with you yet?" he whispered in my ear, molding my body to his.

"Hmmm…" I moaned.

"Relax," he coaxed, I knew what he wanted and it made me shiver with anticipation.

He lowered the front of my body onto the bed and straddled my lower torso. I felt his cock on my back as he started massaging my shoulders. "You're always tense, Angel. You need to learn how to relax and enjoy life. It's too short to not make the best of it." He reminded me of this often.

"Oh yeah…and how do you enjoy life, Mika?" I retorted as his callused hands dug into my shoulder blades.

I could feel him smiling. "With you."

"And…"

"You. Always you, Angel," he urged.

Those were the times where I would completely let my guard down, it was easier behind four walls where no one could see or judge me. I had done several fucked up things in my life, however, I never felt like that with Mika.

I should have.

His rough hands massaged down my back and he lowered himself down my legs as he penetrated my muscles with his touch. His body reached my calves and he leaned forward, placing kisses down the crevice of my ass as he kneaded my cheeks. He spread me open and I felt his tongue lightly lick my anus; I pushed myself up and he spanked my ass.

"Don't move," he demanded, holding my hips down where he wanted them. My ass was slightly angled in the air and he continued to lick from my anus to my opening. He started to rub my pussy with the palm of his hand and then placed it over my clit and slowly made delicious circles around my bundle of nerves. At first it was tender, and then it became rough and hard. Every time I tried to pump my hips into his hand, he slapped my ass and it only provoked me to do it again. He stuck his tongue in my opening, pushing in and out and he licked up all my come that squirted out.

He groaned and took his soaking wet hand to my anus and pushed in what felt like his middle and ring fingers. I bit my lower lip enjoying the pain and sting of him opening me up. His thumb played with the outside of my opening until he finally shoved it in. I could feel him everywhere inside my most scared parts and then I felt him sit up, which only made the angle of what he was doing to me more intense.

"You like that don't you?" Smack. "You love getting fucked in both holes," he grunted as he repeatedly smacked my ass. I was still sore from his belt from the night before and it added to my pleasure. I could feel the pressure once again building in my lower abdomen and my body was starting to sweat and shake all at the same time.

"Fuck, Angel…you have no idea how tight your cunt is squeezing my hand. You're so wet, get that asshole nice and wet for my cock." His dirty mouth did it to me every time and my face pressed into the mattress as I shook and went over the edge.

I didn't have any time to recover before he was in between my legs, spreading my ass cheeks as I felt him nudge the head of his cock into my anus.

"Easy…slow…slow…" I breathed into the mattress.

"Relax…let me in," he reassured. "I'm almost all the way in…just relax…"

My head turned to the side to watch his face as he entered me from behind.

"Argh…Mika…fuck…easy…go easy…" I repeated.

"You like it rough, Angel. Just relax so I can fuck this beautiful ass," he grunted as he spanked my ass, making me jolt.

He stopped when he was balls deep. "Jesus Christ you feel amazing; you're tight as shit. I am going to fuck you now, and it's going to be hard and rough. You are going to love every fucking second of it because it's me that's doing it to you." I recognized that tone and when he grabbed my hair by the nook of my neck and pulled back, I knew he meant every word.

I moaned as he pulled out and pushed back in and his balls slapped against the outer lips of my pussy. He went slowly for the first few times and then his thrusts became urgent and forceful as he gripped the lock of my hair tighter around his hand to keep me where he wanted me. His thumb found my opening and he eased it in, going straight for my g-spot.

"Ahhh…Mika….Mika…" I repeated over and over again.

He never let up, he fucked me with raw passion and no inhibitions whatsoever. I could feel my pussy clamping down on his thumb, and when I would clench he would push my head back more. I was soaking wet and it allowed him to be more aggressive with me.

"Fuck…please…please….Mika…let me come…please let me come…" I shamelessly begged.

"Angel, you didn't even make me ask for it, where's the fun in that if I don't make you beg."

He knew I couldn't come with his thumb pressed deep inside me when I was getting fucked in both holes and he needed to ease out some in order for me to be able to release. He pulled my hair firmer, making me yelp and then raised his right leg onto his foot to get in deeper. I started to push myself onto his cock and he slapped my ass.

"Angel…" I knew it was a warning, but I couldn't help myself; I wanted to come and so I did it again. He pulled out and flipped me over so fast that I didn't see it coming. My legs were on his shoulders and he shoved himself inside my ass, making me arch and scream before I even blinked. He was much deeper this way and he was now able to thrust two fingers inside me and play with my clit all at the same time. I didn't know if I could take all the stimulation.

"Now..." he panted as he finger fucked my g-spot and dove deeper into my ass. "Beg me to come. Let me hear you fucking scream."

"Ahhh...please let me come...I can't come with your fingers pushing into me like that...please, Mika. I want to come so bad..."

My whole body was shaking and I was moaning loudly enough to where the whole mansion could hear. I finally felt him remove his fingers and my head and back arched off the bed as my orgasm took over me. Mika pumped in a few more times and released all of his seed deep within me. We both experienced aftershocks from our orgasms and we lay there tangled among body parts, covered in perspiration and breathless.

✳VIP✳

I had a fourth of July party at The Cathouse a few weeks later. It was the usual festivities, although I hadn't expected what happened a few days after it.

The intercom buzzed in my office. "Madam."

I hit the button and replied, "Yes."

"You have a visitor."

I wasn't expecting anyone. "Who?"

"Someone by the name of Brooke."

"Brooke?" I questioned.

"Yes, Madam. Brooke Stevens."

"All right, send her up."

Minutes later, there was a knock at the door. "Come in," I announced and in walked a blonde bombshell. My breath actually caught a little bit, she was slender and curvy in all the right places. Her bright blue eyes radiated from across the room and her legs went for miles. She looked like she stepped out of a Vogue magazine, wearing a black petticoat and fuck me heels.

I cocked my head to the side. "Hello."

She smiled and walked over to have a seat in front of my desk.

"Can I help you?" I questioned, not taking my eyes away from her amazing face.

"Not as much as I can help you," she responded.

"And how pray tell can you help me?"

She unbuttoned her coat from top to bottom to expose her creamy naked white skin and then she spread her legs.

She licked her lips and said, "I want to be a VIP."

I chuckled, the girl had balls I'll give her that. That was the first time anyone had come in to offer themselves; VIP didn't work like that.

I placed my hands on the desk in a prayer motion. "I pick you, darling, not the other way around," I informed.

"I know," she pulled her bottom lip in her mouth. "Fuck me. If you don't like it I'll leave, but I guarantee you will."

I smiled. "Stand up." She did.

I did a twirling motion with my finger wanting her to turn around and she understood. I looked her over. "Stop," I said as her back was to me. "Bend over." She did and her perfect pink pussy and anus were in my face.

"Turn around." She turned and raised an eyebrow. "What makes you think that I would take someone throwing themselves at me? That's not an attractive quality, darling. VIPs aren't made…they're born. You just seem like a slutty girl wanting to make some money; I can give you the card of a very exclusive strip club. They will love you there."

"I want to work for you, no one else," she argued. "I'm a VIP." She reached for her jacket and pulled out a dildo, I tried to hide the fact that I was proud and intrigued.

How far was she going to take this?

She sat in the chair and placed both her heels on the sides, spreading her legs wide open. I felt my panties get wet with anticipation. Her eyes peeked up at me, asking for silent permission, and I instantly loved her. She knew who was in charge and I appreciated that. I nodded, allowing her to proceed.

She took the impressive size toy into her mouth and deep throated it all the way in and didn't even gag. I would have stood and applauded if I wasn't itching for her to continue. She sucked the cock like it was an actual man in front of her. Her hand and head did all the motions of actual oral sex, and I had to stop myself from putting my hand down my panties. After she got it nice and wet she slowly and seductively slid it down her body.

She stroked it against her clit until her pussy got wet and then she slid it in. Her other hand kneaded and caressed her breast as she fucked herself with the toy never taking her eyes off me. I couldn't take it anymore and moved out of my chair to bend in front of her.

"You want to be a VIP?" I asked and she eagerly nodded.

"First lesson you need to learn is I make the rules, not you." I placed the palm of my hand on her clit and pressed forward.

"I tell you when to come," I whispered in her ear as I worked her nub into a frenzy and assisted with her hand, working the dildo into her cunt. It didn't take long until she was withering and moaning to come. My tongue found its way into her mouth, and I sucked on her bottom lip as she came unglued on the seat.

Brooke was always one of my favorites and she was also the first one to disappoint me.

CHAPTER 31

A year went by and everything was perfect, which should have been my first suspicion. All of my girls were handpicked by me, other than my Brooke, but nothing could have prepared me for the indiscretion that was about to happen on her part as well as one of my loyal clients. Brooke quickly became like a daughter to me, there was something about her that just stood out and I admired that. Each of my VIPs had their own flavor to them, however when Brooke walked into a room, they always stared at her first. She knew it as well as I did.

Jaxon was one of my high profile clients and he had been with me for years. He worked in politics and was the epitome of a happily married man with children, in public. He had been with several of my girls more than once, but the moment he met Brooke he was struck. I allowed it because it wasn't unusual for one of my clients to fall for my girls; they were treasured jewels and any man was lucky to have an hour with them. He started to request only her and much more frequent than he ever asked for any of my ladies.

I trusted my girls to never fuck with their hearts.

Brooke and I were always close and I could read anyone like a goddamn book, so when she started to change I immediately noticed it. Although, Brooke wasn't the one to disclose her little secrets, Jaxon did all that on his own.

"Why did you want to meet with me?" I interrogated one afternoon when Jaxon showed up uninvited. The dark circles around his eyes made it evident that he hadn't slept in days.

His hands brushed back his hair in a repetitive movement that just added to his disheveled appearance.

"I fucked up, Madam. I royally fucked up," he wallowed.

"Stop being a pussy and start from the beginning."

He sighed, leaned over, and placed his hands on his head. "During the last business trip I took Brooke on, she forgot her birth control. I thought we were careful."

I cut him off not wanting him to say the words. "You thought? Please tell me you aren't about to say what I think you're implying."

"Yes..." he whispered.

"How far along?"

"Six weeks."

I shook my head in disbelief. "Let me get this straight! You take one of my girls on a business trip and you *think* you're careful and now I have a situation that I have to deal with, complimentary of you? Did I get it right? Please let me know if I carelessly missed something as important as not sticking my fucking cock into pussy that is unprotected!"

"Madam-"

I couldn't hear another excuse he had to share. "Take care of it," I roared without hesitation.

"What? How?"

"Don't make me spell it out for you! You work in politics, make it go away."

"I love her," he divulged, looking me straight in the eyes.

I crossed my arms. "Oh yeah. You *love* her? Well then excuse me, I had no idea that this child was made out of love. Please let me start over; when exactly did you get a divorce?"

"Don't patronize me. I am not a fucking child. I know the fucked up situation that we find ourselves in but that doesn't change the fact that I love her. I've never met anyone like her and if things were different, it would be her on my arm and not my wife. I married my wife because I work in politics and you more than anyone knows what is appropriate and what is not."

I laughed, "Right. Then let me make it crystal fucking clear for you Mr. Bureaucracy, how is it going to look when the tabloids get wind of your love child? Huh? Are they going to understand because you were in *love?* Does that make what you did anything other than adultery? I'm just an outsider looking in and from here, it looks like you got one past the goalie with your play toy. Congratulations, your boys can still swim," I mocked.

His head spun with all the truth that I spoke. I took the opportunity to keep going.

"This is how it's going to go. You are going to tell Brooke she needs to get an abortion as soon as possible. You are going to make her believe it's the right thing to do and that of course, you will be there for her every step of the way. When the time comes, you won't show up. I don't think it needs to be said that you are no longer a client of VIP."

"What?" he stated in shock.

I smiled. "If you would like to continue in your house of corruption then I highly suggest that you do exactly what I say or else I will take care of this." I kneeled down close to this face and looked him square in the eyes. "Trust me...you don't want that to happen."

"Madam..." he whimpered.

"Answer this, Jaxon. Are you going to leave your family for her? If you are, I will let her go." I waited for the response I already knew he was going to give. It was always the same fucking answer; it didn't change just because it was a different man in the situation.

He shook his head no. "Then you have your work cut out for you. Get the fuck out of my office and do what needs to be done." He nodded and walked out of VIP.

I know what you're thinking...you hate me don't you?

It's all right, I didn't write this for you to love me. I don't care if you love me. I don't care if you hate me. But before you judge me, take a second and look at how he jumped on the opportunity to make it all go away. See...that's the thing about love.

It fucks you.

There is never a happily ever after, that's only in books. You have to make your own fairy tale, you don't wait for someone to do it for you; and if you do, I suggest you sit down, your legs will ache by the time you realize that it's not coming.

Men think with their dicks and that's exactly why all the blood flows there when they are hard. They can't multitask to save their lives. I wasn't bluffing when I said I would have given her up, I would have done it in a heartbeat to have someone prove me wrong. Oh yes, the big bad Madam isn't as evil as you think she is, I do enjoy being right, don't doubt that, but that doesn't mean that I wouldn't enjoy to see this so-called *love* prevail.

I am a woman.

The Madam

✳VIP✳

Brooke called me three weeks later to have lunch on South Beach. I knew what was coming but she didn't have to know that, we ordered our food and I waited patiently for the bomb to drop.

"I can't work for a month, Madam. I need some time off," she finally revealed, it only took her ten minutes. It made me proud.

"Oh yeah, why is that?" I countered.

"I'm looking for some me time. I think I need a break for a bit; I'm getting burnt out," she stated, keeping my gaze.

"You know, Brooke, being Madam entails a lot of accuracy. I have my eyes and ears everywhere and I know when one of my girls is lying to me. Why don't you try that again, but this time be honest. I am here for you; I don't need to remind you of that." She bit her lower lip and burst into tears.

You gotta love hormones.

"I don't even know where to start. I got caught up in it all, Madam," she cried, wiping away her tears. "I swear to you I didn't mean for any of it to happen, but I believed him every time he told me he loved me. He seemed honest and sincere. I promise I would never be that girl. I don't know how he was able to fool me so well. I just got lost…I have never had someone treat me like he did. I swear, I swear I would never disrespect you and everything that you have done for me. I love you," she wailed uncontrollably.

I pulled her into a real and tight embrace. My heart did break for her, but she needed to learn now that she couldn't rely on anyone other than me. This was a punishment as much as a reassurance. I rubbed her back and let her cry on my shoulder for as long as she needed, her tears started to subside and I grabbed her face, wiped away the tears, and kissed her forehead.

"Start from the beginning. What happened?"

"Okay…" She sniffled while she grabbed a napkin to fix the running mascara down her face. "Jaxon and I got close," she admitted, trying to gauge my reaction.

"One thing led to another and I ended up pregnant." Her eyes glistened with new tears. "I had an abortion, Madam, and he didn't even show up for me, for us. I went through it all by myself and I can't even get a hold of him, he's changed his phone number and I have no idea where he lives," she bawled.

I should have felt remorse as I watched her fall apart, especially since I myself went through the same emotions that she was going through; however, I didn't. I did the right thing. You may not agree with me, but at the end of the day, all she needed was me and VIP. We were her fairy tale and now she would know it. There is a very fine line between love and hate, and once it's crossed you can't ever go back. I made sure that I was there for Brooke for the next few months, although she came out of her depression on her own. Brooke was a survivor and that's what makes her one of my favorites.

But it didn't stop me from being The Madam.

I am the puppet master.

CHAPTER 32

It was May 2005. I don't think I need to remind you that I always take care of what's mine. Ever since the day I found her, I had been watching her. I knew every step that she took without her knowing that I was even around. I never thought that she would become the little vixen that she was, however I was unbelievably proud that she took it upon herself to get whatever she wanted by using her body and looks. I guess you can say that what happened to her may have been a blessing in disguise; I told you everything happens for a reason.

To my surprise, I woke up one morning and good ole Mr. Pedophile was on the news, he was found brutally murdered and sodomized near an alley. I have no idea how that happened...cross my heart, and by heart, I mean my fingers.

I went to Tampa one afternoon and watched as my dear girl was on her knees with some pubescent boy. Now, clearly, the scenario wasn't my idea of ideal, but I will give credit where credit is due and she was sucking his cock like a fucking pro, and she also made him wear a condom. She got a bag of clothing and some food after she was done, I would have much rather preferred to see some money, though the girl was clearly in need of food and clothing. After he was done, they sat beside each other smoking a joint.

"I want out of this fucking town," she stated, breathing out the smoke from her nose. I could smell the shitty potency from the corner and it further pissed me off that she would let nothing but the goddamn best near her face. My mother's words quickly making their way into my thoughts.

And here is where the light bulb went off and it was so bright it hurt my eyes. I drove to her school and lingered around just waiting to find my bait. The second I saw the decent looking young man make his way to his disgusting old pickup truck, I followed him. I called Gregory.

"Madam," he said into the phone.

"H43 LMD."

"Excuse me?" he questioned.

"It's his license plate. I need all his information immediately. I want to know it all, including how many times a day he jerks off."

"Madam…"

"You have 72 hours." I informed and hung up.

⁂VIP⁂

Eric Johnson, senior, accepted into the University of Miami, comes from a middle class family, had one girlfriend who never gave it up, and he's a virgin.

B-I-N-G-O.

I waited till it was dark and he was leaving his movie theatre job. I leaned on his driver's side door, one leg crossing the other and smoking a joint. He saw me immediately and I smiled.

"Want to hit it?" I smirked as I blew the smoke from my mouth.

I saw his Adam's apple move and the mix of caution and intrigue all over his face. He took the joint from my fingers. "You a cop?" he asked.

"Do I look like a goddamn cop?"

He shook his head and brought the lit joint to his lips, inhaled, and immediately started coughing.

"That's some strong shit," he blurted as he coughed up a lung.

"I have an ounce of it in my car. Would you like it?"

His eyes narrowed down. "Ummm…sure. Who are you?"

I cocked my head to the side. "Your fairy Godmother, aren't you lucky."

He smiled and said, "Well…you're hot as fuck." He took another few hits, trying to look mature and grown. Men were too easy.

"I said I was your fairy Godmother, not your sugar mama, Eric."

He stepped back. "How do you know my name?"

"Marijuana causes paranoia. I'm not going to hurt you. You have something that I can use to get me what I want and I know a lot about you. It's the perk of being your fairy Godmother and all," I teased and he laughed. "I also have a great idea…want to hear it?" He nodded.

"See, I have this girl, she actually goes to your school, maybe you know her or maybe you don't. The point is she could help you."

"Okay...with what?" he questioned as he handed me the joint. I took another few hits, held it up to see if he wanted any more and he declined. I threw it in the bushes behind him.

"I assume you aren't hanging on to your v-card by choice? Right?" I sassed.

"What…I'm not-"

"Really? I can almost smell it on you. It's a shame, you are very good looking, and I can tell you from experience, girls aren't fond of men who don't know how to get it in," I ridiculed with a pleasant tone.

I moved away from the car and stepped closer to him, I grabbed the piece of his hair that had fallen out of place and put it behind his ear. He licked his lips and there was a tiny pink hue that came upon his cheeks.

"She can help you and all you have to do is bring her to Miami. It's very simple," I whispered close to his ear as his breathing elevated. I didn't have to look down to know he was hard.

"How?" he hinted with desire behind his words.

"You proposition her with taking her away from here and you also tell her that you will give her $100 if she will take your virginity."

His eyes narrowed in on me. "Are you crazy? That's just going to get me slapped across the face. What kind of joke are you trying to pull?"

"She's not that kind of girl. I can guaran-fucking-tee-you that she will not turn you down." I put my hand on top of his jeans over his hard cock and he jerked forward.

I moved my hand up and down. "And if she does, I'll fuck you."

"Who is she?" he groaned.

I didn't stop moving my hand. "Ysabelle. Ysabelle Telle." He nodded.

"Drop her off on South Beach." I grabbed the bill from my pocket and placed it in his as his hips moved frantically into my hand. I never let up on moving my hand up and down.

I wasn't a horrible person; I let him come.

❊VIP❊

Three months later and she showed up exactly as planned. It couldn't have been easier. I met Eric at the end of Collins Street and handed him his ounce. He was bright eyed and chipper.

I had gotten her where I wanted her. Now it was a waiting game.

❊VIP❊

I made it a point to stay away, I had come that far and I wasn't going to let anything fuck it up. For the next two years, I molded Brooke to train the girls; she became like my right hand woman. She assisted me with whatever I needed at the drop of a dime, and I honestly don't think she would have had it any other way. A lot of the girls were getting older and it was time for them to retire; I brought in new, fresh faces. I learned that it was much easier to start them young; they were easier to mold and train. Not only that, they were eager.

My clients appreciated the young blood.

I can't say that I didn't appreciate it too. There is something about surrounding yourself with women that are younger than you; it's as if it keeps you young. I have never felt old and I personally believe that I look better now than I did before. On my 46th birthday, I decided that I needed a change, so I gave myself a makeover. For the first time in my life, I cut my hair; I had always had long blonde luscious locks and I had it all cut off. It was styled in a short pixie cut and dyed platinum blonde; I also changed my wardrobe. I started wearing tight suits with corset tops, and I possibly went and had some Botox. I had always taken care of myself; it came with being The Madam.

I looked fucking amazing.

"Well, well, well, look at you…" Mika boasted as he came into my office. He sat down and folded his arms.

You want to know the real cruelty of the world…Men get better looking as they get older. While women are constantly trying to make themselves not look old, men fucking embrace it. Mika looked better now than he did when I first met him. He got rid of the long hair a few years prior but he styled it in a shaggy mess that always hung around his eyes. I couldn't see a gray hair on his head because it was that blonde. His physique was still toned and defined and the barely-there-wrinkles around his eyes made him look distinguished. He still drove a motorcycle and dressed like a bad boy; it still made my panties wet every time I was near him.

"What's with the makeover?" he addressed, pointing at me.

"You don't approve?" I smiled.

"Angel, you know that you're fucking gorgeous. I am enjoying the new hair and the outfit makes me want to see what's under it. It makes you look like you're trying to fit the part."

"Darling, I don't fit the part, the part fits me. I just wanted something fresh and so I made it happen," I reminded.

He put his index finger up to his lips. "Come sit on Mika's lap, I want to show you something."

I laughed, "I have somewhere I have to be. You'll have to show me another time."

He raised an eyebrow. "Where are you going?"

"None of your business."

"Do you think that is going to work with me, Angel? We both know I can keep you here," he proclaimed setting his elbows on my desk.

"Fine. I am going to a meeting and when the meeting is done, I plan to sit on his face. Better?" I badgered. "I can do what I want, any time, any place, anywhere."

His demeanor instantly changed and he was no longer the charismatic Mika that walked into my office. He was sad. There are times, few and far between, that I have witnessed Mika be anything other than demanding.

"I love you," he declared out of nowhere. It was the first time he had ever uttered those words to me. I tried to hide the yearning in my heart, but that didn't stop it from beating its way out of my chest.

"I love you, *Madam*, every last part of you."

We stared at each other and as much as I wanted to say it back, I couldn't.

I had seen too much, I had experienced too much.

My heart had grown hard and black.

I wasn't the same woman I had been years ago; too much had happened, to me, to us. Nothing would have changed if I had said it back that day…he wouldn't have left his wife, and he would have known that he had me. I couldn't show him any more weakness than I already had. Mika consumed me.

He knew it. But I didn't have to prove it.

"What about your wife? What about your kid? You know me, Mika, I don't play mommy to anyone but you," I teased. I knew what I was doing; I was about to catch a big fish.

He stood up and came closer to me. "You know I can't leave her, Angel. We don't have a relationship, but until my dad dies, I have to stay married to her."

"So where does that leave us?"

"I don't care how we do it, as long as I can be with you. I was so stupid before. I tried pretending that these feelings didn't exist. But they do. And I see them clearly now. We can have a life together. Just you and me."

"And your wife and your kid," I reminded him.

"As long as she has the big house and the fancy cars, and my child is taken care of, it doesn't matter. She knows about you, always has. I need you, Angel. And I know you need me too. We are made for each other."

He was getting deep with his professions. It felt like not so long ago I had wanted to hear him say these things. I practically begged to hear them. But instead, he shattered me. And then again, when he told me about knocking someone up and marrying her.

He had always come back to me, and I always welcomed him back. I loved hearing him tell me how he felt, but it didn't change anything. I was in the midst of all of my dreams falling at my feet. I wouldn't trade it for anyone, Mika included. But that didn't mean I wasn't entertaining the idea.

"Mika, I thought you said we weren't built for this."

"I didn't think we were. But the older I get, the more things make sense. And you and I make sense. We always have. From that very first night when I tied you up and watched as the VIP devoured you. From the first time I shared you with someone. Remember that, Angel? Remember how well we work together, in and out of the bedroom? We belong together. Tell me you feel the same way," he begged. I had never heard him beg before, and I've got to say, the sound of it made me wet.

I touched his face with the tips of my fingers. "Oh, Mika, I don't know what to say."

"Tell me you love me too."

I didn't hesitate. "I do." It was the closest I could get to saying it. I knew I would never be able to turn back once those words left my lips. It was a hard fight, but I won and kept those three sacred words inside.

"Tell me you want to be with me. Tell me you want me to bend you over my knee right now."

"You can bend me over your knee another day, I have an appointment that I am eager to attend. You should go home to your wife maybe she will play with you." My tone immediately changed as soon as my hand dropped and I backed away.

I wanted to see his face. I wanted to see how he felt when the tables were turned.

His eyes grew wide with shock. "Angel," he said in his dominant tone. "Don't do this."

He stepped toward me, caging me in between his hard body and my desk.

"Don't be so clingy." I had wanted to say that to him for fourteen years. And damn did it feel good.

I watched his eyes grow cold and fill with anger. "You're a day late and a dollar short. What we have is amazing the way it is, why fix something that's not broken."

He grabbed my neck pushing me back against the wall. "You don't mean it. I know you, Angel, and you don't mean one fucking word you're saying. Stop. For one second just live in the moment and say what we both need to hear," he urged, tightening his hold to prove his power over me.

"I have always lived in the moment with you. That's the fucking problem."

"Please…"

And that's when it all shattered, every last bit of me. "I love you, but I'm not going to play house. Take us as we are or nothing at all. I'm not that woman, Mika. I will never be that woman, and fuck you for trying to make me become her." he placed his forehead on mine and moved his hand to the side of my face.

"I have an appointment," I reminded. "I'll see you later." I stepped beside him and he let me.

I walked away from the unknown possibilities that day. I couldn't live my life for someone else. I knew he was being sincere with everything he was expressing to me; I had known it for years, but at the end of the day, he still went home to her. In a way, I already was the other woman, though it was on my terms, not his. I didn't do ultimatums and in my dreams, he was always with me; but in reality, he was with her. I didn't leave him that day, but I also didn't stay. You can't lose something that was never yours to begin with; I wasn't foolish enough to believe otherwise.

I'm just not made like that.

CHAPTER 33

It was August 2007, and it had been two years since Ysabelle had come to Miami. I kept my eye on her the entire time, just waiting to make my next move; the time had finally come to make her mine. I got all the VIPs together to go to the bar she worked at. As soon as we walked in, I saw her pretty little face watch our every move; she wanted it. I reserved the entire private room in the back of the bar. I had been around this lifestyle my entire life and the look on her face was recognizable, she was mesmerized. Her eyes absorbed every last bit of us, I owned her body, mind, and soul before she ever knew my name.

This was the day that changed her life; it's the day she met her Madam.

I knew she had a break coming up and I went to the bathroom, purposely leaving it open. I knew my Bella Rosa like the back of my hand; you don't become The Madam without knowing every detail of everyone you surround yourself with. I took out my vile of cocaine and poured some on the side of the bathroom sink. I was in the middle of doing my second line when she walked in.

"Shit, I'm sorry the door wasn't locked."

She turned to leave, but I quickly grabbed her by the arm and turned her around, wanting the door to shut behind her. I stared intently into her green eyes and placed my left arm beside her head, then I proceeded to do the same with her other arm after locking the door; I caged her in. I turned my face to the nook in her neck and inhaled. Her body tensed up and I knew that she had never experienced anything of what I was doing to her; she didn't know what to feel or what to think. Although, this pretty baby did try to remain calm. "You smell almost edible. If I lick you, will you melt in my mouth?" I asked with a sultry tone.

She didn't say one word. She stood deathly still while I smelled the side of her neck. She halted her breathing when I started to lay light, soft kisses from her neck to her collarbone. Very subtly and slowly, I took out my tongue and glided it down to her cleavage. She started to slightly hyperventilate. It caused her chest to noticeably heave. I still lightly kissed and licked her cleavage. I took my left hand and started to twirl the hair that hung on the side of her face. I twirled it around and around in my finger several times, until I finally placed it behind her ear.

Using my first two fingers on the same hand, I glided them down from the side of her face to her collarbone. With those fingers, I proceeded to lightly trace the cleavage at the top of her shirt; with both hands, I pushed her breasts up and began to kiss them firmer. I could tell she wanted to laugh and I knew it was from nerves, or maybe even arousal. This was new and foreign to her; I knew that instantly. She could tell my demeanor changed, we were that in tune. I stopped and looked straight into her eyes.

"Are you nervous, beautiful girl? Hmmm...? I think maybe you are also slightly aroused." She knew I could read her mind, and I'm sure it made her curious.

"Do you want to tell me your name?"

She tried to catch her breath. "Ysabelle," she managed to say in a voice that sounded slightly erotic, yet terrified.

I took my face out of her cleavage and looked right into her eyes. "Beautiful name for a very beautiful girl. Ysabelle, how old are you?"

"Twenty-three," she replied.

I smirked and looked her up and down from head to toe. Ysabelle was also a liar; that pleased me.

"Ysabelle, do I look like a stupid woman to you? Now, I don't want to start this relationship based on lies. So, let's try this again, how old are you?"

She was caught off guard. I would bet no one had ever doubted her age, I told you she looked older than what I had originally thought.

"Eighteen."

I smiled and my eyes lit up. She couldn't lie to me; that pleased me more. I knew I was crossing the line but I had to have a taste, I needed to test the merchandise before I bought it. I moved closer and lightly started kissing on her lips, almost goading her to see a reaction.

"What are you doing?" she asked with the same nervous voice from before.

"Whatever I want, Ysabelle. Would you like to be able to do whatever you want? Would you like to know how it feels to be in control of anything and everything around you? Because, I can guarantee you that. I can make that happen for you." I opened my mouth and used my tongue to trace her lips, again enticing her more, trying to read her reaction to the power I had over her.

She couldn't stop me...and better yet, she didn't want to. She responded by opening her mouth. I took that as an invitation, and slid my tongue inside. She moaned slightly. It wasn't the initial reaction I thought she would have, but the second she felt my tongue in her mouth it was a natural instinct for her to moan. I loved every fucking second of making her see that she was made for this. I caught her off guard again as I backed away from her completely, turned, looked into the mirror, and reapplied my lipstick.

"I was right, you do melt in my mouth," I proudly admitted.

She stood there stunned, not just because she was just assaulted by a woman, but also by the fact that she didn't want me to stop. She wanted me to keep going. She wanted to see how far she would have allowed me to take it. Or maybe she wanted to see how far she would have allowed me to seduce her. She knew that's what I was doing. I was seducing her to be with me, and she had never felt someone have that power over her. From the moment I caged her in, she wanted me, not because she was aroused, because she wanted the power.

I didn't have to be in her mind to know this...I know because I lived it.

I have told you from the beginning VIPs aren't made, they're born.

She immediately wanted to know how to have the same power I had just apprehended from her. She wanted to know what I meant by her being in control of everything around her. She hesitantly walked over to the mirror. She could see her own reflection as well as mine looking back at her.

"What did you mean by me being able to have control?" she asked.

I smiled for everything that I already knew she was capable of. "My, my, a small little kitten one minute and a tiger the next. I think we are going to form a beautiful relationship, my Bella Rosa. Do you have any idea how gorgeous you are? We could both gain something miraculous from our relationship together."

She was still giving me some quizzical look through the mirror, "What do you mean?"

"I mean, a mutually beneficial relationship, one where you and I both gain something. I could be like a mother to you. Do you need a mother, Ysabelle?" I asked.

I was treading a thin line, I knew it would have pissed her off to remind her of her mother, but I wanted to see all of her emotions. See, emotions make you weak and she needed to learn how to control hers, and I was going to teach her; but first I needed to learn them.

"Listen, lady, I don't need a mother. I have one of those and I haven't seen or heard from her in two years. I can take care of myself. I've been doing it for a very long time. So can you cut the shit and theatrics now, and just tell me what the fuck you meant." And then, I fucking smiled at her, a big, huge, shit-eating grin smile.

"You're absolutely perfect, Ysabelle. You're everything that I look for in my girls. You're the epitome of innocence, seductress, and feisty. All you would need is some guidance, and you would make me so proud," I said with so much enthusiasm, I was visualizing everything I had in mind for her. "You would have men crawling at your feet, just begging you for some attention. I can see it now. You would be my favorite girl."

She had no fucking clue what I was talking about. I could tell I was getting on her nerves and that she wanted to get back to work.

"Okay, lady, you're obviously wasting my time and I need to get back to work. Thanks for feeling me up in the bathroom. I hope you had a great time! I can now add first bisexual encounter to my resume of fucked-upped-experiences." She turned to get the hell out of there. My mood and demeanor instantly changed, she needed to know now that she should never piss me off. I grabbed her by the hair so fast, and with enough force, to jerk her head backwards.

"Don't bite the hand that will fucking feed you, Ysabelle. That's the first rule that you need to learn, you also need some goddamn manners." I jerked her head back some more, causing her to whimper. "Are you done being a little bitch, or do I need to re-evaluate our relationship?" She nodded her head. I was vicious, ruthless, and didn't give a fuck that I may have hurt her. Bella Rosa needed to know where to march in line and to never move out of place. I let her go with a genuine, motherly smile.

"All right then, let's try this again." I made my personality instantly change back to being prim and proper, like I wasn't just about rip her hair from her head. I could be whatever you wanted or needed me to be, and she would learn how to do that as well. I reached into my purse, pulled out a black VIP business card, and handed it to her. She looked at the front of it and then flipped it over.

"Be there tomorrow at three," I demanded.

"I have to work tomorrow." I looked at her and cocked an eyebrow.

"I'll see you at three, Ysabelle, have a good night." I kissed both her cheeks and left the bathroom. She didn't leave the bathroom for several minutes and I knew she was just looking at the card and wondering what the hell had just happened. I knew one thing for sure; she would be there tomorrow at three.

CHAPTER 34

I had no doubt in my mind that she would show up when I told her to, but I hadn't expected her to be five minutes early. It was a feeling I couldn't describe...still can't. But there she was, dressed in a silky white gown that left very little to the imagination. She was a goddess. It was like a dream come true. I watched silently as she stared at the fireplace in the room, so I clicked it on, surprising her. She turned around, eyes growing wide as she saw me. I told Hector to get some champagne; I knew she would need it as I watched her nervous ticks. Her knee was bouncing rapidly, and I could practically hear her heart beating against her chest.

"You know, beautiful girl, I have been following you around for quite some time. You have several men and women who are very taken by you." I watched, as her eyes grew wide, I knew I had scared her some, like a frightened kitten.

"That night at the bar was the first time I had ever seen you." Her voice was timid, even though she was trying to sound strong. I could see through it. I could see right through her.

"It was the first time I allowed myself to be seen. I realize that you like your privacy, which is something I admire and respect. You don't have many friends. They're more like acquaintances, another trait that I look for. You wear your sexuality on your sleeve, and unlike most women, you know that when you walk into a room, people turn. You thrive on that attention, which I admire also. Although, I am concerned about your boss. Is Devon going to be a problem?" I wasn't worried about Devon...The Madam doesn't worry about anyone. It was her response, "not at all" that made the sky open and the rays of sunshine shine down on her. She was perfect. I couldn't wait to try her out to see just how perfect she was.

"Well then, I am sure you're wondering why I asked you to my home today. I want to begin by saying that you look beautiful. Almost, like a sacrificial lamb in that white dress. Is that what you think this is, Bella Rosa, am I the big bad wolf? Are you trying to tell me you're an innocent, little virgin?" She didn't say anything and it irritated me a little; I wanted her to respect me, not fear me.

"You know, I'm not fond of this cat and mouse game, I feel like you're playing with me. You are free to speak your mind, ask me anything you would like to know."

She raised her eyebrows. "Why am I here?" I laughed internally, Ysabelle didn't like to be pushed, and if she was, she would push back. That's a quality that I have always admired about her.

"Hmmm direct, I like that about you. You don't like to putter around; you want to get to the point and that's that. In my line of work, that's a very good quality to have. Would you like to know what I do?" She nodded.

"I am a Madam. Do you know what that is, Bella Rosa?" I asked and she shook her head no. This was practically a scene I could have played out without a script. All the girls always responded the same. It didn't matter to me, though it made my job easier.

"Well…it's a French word for a lady. It could also mean queen, or a mistress, or it could mean a woman who owns a brothel. Do you know what that is?" My mother's words spilling from my lips as if they were mine to begin with.

She looked down at her lap. "Like a place of prostitution?" That response pissed me off but I couldn't show her that. My girls are never to be called prostitutes and I would bury whoever tried to say so.

"Tsk, tsk, tsk, prostitution is such an ugly word, and it's highly illegal," I said in a high pitched voice.

"What I run here is very much a legitimate business. I pay my taxes like any other American citizen. Nevertheless, I'd like you to call this place The Cathouse; I have some very important high society sets of clientele, who are looking for only the best. My little black book is filled with names from all around the world; politicians, celebrities, sheiks, princes, kings, doctors, men, and women, all looking for the same thing." I cocked my head to the side. "You name it and I probably have it. My place of business provides services of all kinds, Bella Rosa, not just sexual. We provide companionship, you *escort* a client for a duration of time and they pay."

"Ok…what does that have to do with me?" she asked with piqued interest. I had her…I could have stopped there and she would have come back, but I didn't want her to just come back. I wanted her to live, breathe, and love VIP.

"It has absolutely everything to do with you, Bella Rosa. You are what makes me so successful. You could be powerful! Do you know what kind of power you hold with that tight little thing between your legs?"

I could see the wheels turning behind her eyes. She couldn't process everything that was happening all around her. Her mind wasn't processing what she heard me say as fast as she would have liked. She stood up and walked over to the fireplace. I would give her a minute to think about what I was propositioning her with and let it sink in. I didn't want her to think too much about it and I knew subconsciously her mind was already made up. Society can fuck you up with what they think is acceptable and what is not. I wanted her to know that she could make her own rules, and not give one damn about what people thought.

What's life without a little controversy…

She turned when she heard the clicks of my heels coming up behind her. She froze when she felt the tip of one finger stroll up and down her spine. I watched her throat work hard to swallow the saliva that had built in her mouth.

People say they see their lives flash before their eyes just before they die…I saw mine just before I felt alive. I saw my mother with Taylor on that fateful day. The day I realized how it all worked. I saw it as vividly as I saw Ysabelle in front of me. I didn't need to think about my words. I didn't need to plan my next moves. They just came to me as if I was meant for this one moment in my life. As if I was born for this one purpose.

"Bella Rosa, do you understand what I am telling you? I want you. I want you more than I have ever wanted any other woman."

She was too frightened to turn around. "You want to fuck me?" she asked nervously.

"Yes I do, not for the reasons that you think." I continued to rub her back as I kissed the left side of her neck. "I want to fuck you in order to teach you." I kissed the center of her neck. "I want to fuck you to please you." I kissed the right side. "I want to fuck you to taste you." I whispered in her ear, "More than anything, I want to fuck you…to make you."

She closed her eyes, trying to soak in my words just as I had seen Taylor once do.

"Make me what?" she managed to ask.

Moving my fingers from her back, I cupped her chin, beckoning her to turn toward me. She did. I looked deep into her eyes and spoke with more conviction than I ever had, exactly like my mother.

"I want to make you a VIP."

⁂VIP⁂

She called the next morning. I didn't even have to be told it was her on the line when the intercom spoke, I felt her in my bones. It was as if we were one person. Ysabelle was my means to an end. I would stop at nothing to get her, and keep her.

Remember that…

"Bella Rosa," I said. She was caught off guard that I knew it was her. She didn't say anything.

"Are you there?" I asked. She still didn't say anything.

I had to calm her nerves, ease her fear and trepidation. I was her Madam with or without her consent, but I would much rather have her hand it to me freely.

"My Bella Rosa, I can hear you breathing, my beautiful girl," I declared.

"I'm here…I thought about it last night and I want to do this," she blurted out. Her words came out rushed as if she was saying them before she had a chance to change her mind and hang up. That hurt and offended me.

"I know that I could make you proud." And just like that, it went away.

"I know that you can, too. I never had any doubts. Do you work tonight?" I asked.

"I quit, before I came to see you yesterday." She didn't have to tell me, I knew the moment she walked into my house that she was a VIP.

"As I knew you would. I'll see you at six this evening."

CHAPTER 35

"Bella Rosa…" I turned around and took her in, I gestured for her to sit on the settee.

"Please, make yourself comfortable and sit wherever you feel at ease."

She moved to the couch in the middle. I moved to sit opposite of her, thinking she may want some space before I disclosed what was on the itinerary for the night. I handed her a glass of champagne, I knew she would need it.

"You're nervous, darling. I can feel it all the way over here. Please, don't be nervous, nothing is going to happen that you don't want to happen. You need to remember, that you run the show, Bella Rosa. I am a mere spectator." She downed the entire glass of champagne in one gulp. I wanted to tell her that ladies don't gulp, but I held back. We would get to that; we would get to everything.

"Why is there a camera set up?" she uttered. I cocked a smile at her.

Ysabelle was also impatient; definitely something we would need to work on.

"You are an eager little thing, aren't you? Before we talk about that, let's talk about the logistics. By you coming here today, you have agreed to move forward with my proposition, I assume?"

"Yes," she replied, she wanted to say something fresh…but she didn't. Smart girl.

"All right then, let me begin by explaining how all of this works, Bella Rosa. Oh, and please feel free to interrupt me at any time if you have questions."

I moved to sit right beside her; I brushed the hair off her shoulders, and held both of her hands in my lap. It was something that I wished my mother had done with me, I learned a lot from what my mother didn't do, and it made me a better Madam for it. Call it a blessing in disguise.

"I would be your Madam. The most important thing that you need to remember is that you never discuss anything about being a VIP to anyone. This is a legal business; I require the utmost discretion from my girls."

"How many girls do you have?" she asked.

"You would be my lucky number eight," I replied. I didn't tell her that she would be my number one girl, she would find out soon enough. I was salivating with desire to have her here. It was worth the wait to have her seated next to me. I wished I could tell her everything, though I couldn't. The possibility of her hating me would to be high and it wasn't a chance I would ever be willing to take. She was too important to me and VIP.

"I would have complete control over what you do and whom you are with. My clients contact me and I choose the woman that I feel is best suited. You would be with both men and women, sometimes it would be a party of two, and sometimes it would be more. All of my clients are tested to make sure they are healthy and safe. Condoms are not permitted, and you would be put on birth control."

"Why aren't condoms permitted?"

"Because, my beautiful girl, some of our clientele have relationships…we are not here to judge; to each their own. Given that most of our clientele are men, they can be rather…how do I see say this…careless. I don't want drama. I avoid it at any given costs. Therefore, not having to worry about any hiccups such as a condom left in a pocket, makes things run smoother, don't you think?" She nodded again.

The truth was, I would never have another hiccup like I had experienced with Brooke. It was my own fault to put the responsibility on someone else. I was careless to think that anything could get done without me; if you want it done correctly then you need to take care of it your damn self.

"I use the Depo-Provera shot on all of my girls, which is the most effective type of birth control. You would get it done every three months, here in my home. I take care of all of it. I don't like to mess around with the possibilities of forgetting to take a pill, it keeps the clients and I at ease. I also take care of everything that you need- your clothing, shoes, jewelry, transportation, food, and living expenses. I give you your own personal credit card, which you're allotted a certain expense each month for your private things. You would immediately be moving into one of my condos, this is your home, and clients do not come to your sanctuary. The meeting arrangements are pre-determined."

I stopped myself, knowing that she would have questions. It was a lot to take in, but she would live like a queen. I would make sure of it. She would never go another day in her life without knowing how valued and appreciated she is. I wouldn't allow her to step foot in anything that wasn't glamorous or exclusive. She had absolutely no idea what awaited her, and I had the pleasure to say that I was going to show her everything. I was giving the ultimate gift of life…to thy own self be true; VIP.

"I have my own place and my own things. Why can't I just continue as I am and only use your things when needed?"

It was endearing to hear that she was proud of her accomplishments, as she should be. However, there were greater things in store for her that only I could show her; I would open her eyes to the world. It was something that only I could offer her, and in return, she would give me everything I ever wanted.

"I am your Madam, and with that, comes my responsibility to take care of you. I wasn't lying when I said I am a mother figure to my girls. I feel more comfortable knowing that you are kept up to the standards that I feel that you deserve and are entitled to. Do you understand?"

"My lease on my apartment is still good for another eight months and what would I do with all my furniture and my car?"

I wanted to laugh and chastise her, but it quickly reminded me of my mother. I didn't want to be anything like my mother, although the older I got, the more I felt like there were things about her that I was turning into. I was fortunate enough to catch them and immediately change it. It didn't stop them from occurring though.

"Those are easy things to handle. Learn now, beautiful girl, that money talks in all languages, so let me worry about that. You worry about nothing." I smiled.

"You are absolutely gorgeous, therefore there won't be much need for a makeover, but we will be scheduling one anyway. You will be waxed, polished, and primed. A diet plan will be established, as well as a workout regimen that you will follow extensively," I stated. I know she was having her doubts about me, which was expected. I would change her mind and it wouldn't take long to do, Ysabelle wanted control...that was the gateway to VIP.

"Keep in mind that not all of the dates will be sexual, it all depends on the wants and needs of the client. It could vary from being arm candy for the night to a week away on business, to just a good ole fashion orgy. The cost for you would vary, again on what the want and need is from the client. All prices are pre-established, and profits are split evenly between you and I. I tell you what is expected and you follow. There are times when the clients seize the moment and arrangements change, pricing changes after that as well. You let me worry about that. It's all very simple, Bella Rosa. The more you learn the easier it will be for you. Within time, you can determine your own pricing and desires."

"Ok...how much does a blowjob cost?" she asked.

I laughed so hard that it echoed in the room. She needed to learn the finer things in life began with a proper vocabulary. I would be scheduling her to take an etiquette class as soon as possible. My clients had a taste for the finer things in life and she would learn that when the time was right. That didn't stop the yearning for it to be now. I was like a kid in a candy store just waiting...

"My beautiful girl, blowjob, really? *Oral sex*, as you so articulately called a *blowjob* is not what this is about. You aren't rented per hour in a Motel Six, Ysabelle. You're not a whore; you're an escort. You need to realize that you, my dear, are a treasured jewel, not some slut sucking cock. The clients have you for an allotted time and if sex is requested then you will always be pampered and treated like a queen. My clients know how to treat a lady. You will never feel degraded or cheap. You have the authority, you run the show, you govern the room, you hold the power...do I make myself clear?" I questioned. I never wanted her to believe that she was anything less than perfect.

"Yes," she replied with a little more ease. Her demeanor had changed; she was enticed.

"To answer your question so eloquently put, nothing costs less than $5,000, Bella Rosa."

She choked on her champagne and I handed her a napkin.

"$5,000?! Are you for real?" she stuttered. "How...why...what...? Why would anyone pay that much?"

I needed to nip this in the bud now. I wouldn't have the patience to keep explaining myself over and over again. I am fully aware, that to a girl raised like Ysabelle, all of this would sound surreal and shocking. I needed to have my best foot forward with her. As much as it pains me to take baby steps, I would do it for her. She was that important to me and coming from me, that means everything.

"Because they can. You need to get into the mindset that this is not your average run of the mill man or woman. This…my darling, is a craving for wanting the best, which is you. I know that you know you're stunning, let's stop playing coy, okay? I am very good at what I do, that's why I am the best, and I'm not just referring to Miami. I am the best all over the world. I know how to pick my girls, this isn't a sorority that anyone can pledge to, and I chose you…"

She looked down at her lap. I grabbed her chin and made her look back up at me.

"With the training that you will receive, you will be unstoppable, you have no idea what success awaits, and I cannot wait to witness it." I leaned over and whispered in her ear. I didn't want Brooke to hear me; she was in the other room waiting to be announced. I never pinned my girls against each other, but Ysabelle was different. I wanted to make her know and understand that now, so there would be no confusion about her place with me and VIP.

"You're going to be my favorite." I smiled, kissing her cheek. She smelled good enough to eat.

"To be quite honest they pay a lot more than $5,000. That is the minimum; it changes with the want or need. You hold the power and control of every date. The clients are aware of this, if something happens that is not supposed to, or you do not want to happen, trust me when I say that I will handle it. Nothing, and I mean NOTHING, goes over my head. You will never be in harm's way. You will always be safe; do not fret over that. You do not discuss your personal life, or whom you have been with. Discretion is mandatory on all accounts. You are whoever you would like to be for that night, a seductress in her own way. Any other questions?" She shook her head no and I knew she was lying. I could sense she had a million questions, but she either didn't know how to ask them, or she didn't know which one to ask first.

"You need to stop being so nervous. I need the cat to stop grabbing your tongue. I need to see the strong confident woman that I have appraised from afar. Do you understand?"

"Yes I do, I don't know what is going on with me. I am normally very comfortable with my surroundings and myself. I'm just very overwhelmed with everything that is going on, I think. I know that I can do this though."

"I know you can, too. I have full faith in you. Are you nervous, because you think I'm going to pry for information about your past? As you know, I am well aware of your past, your present, and your future." I raised an eyebrow at her. I didn't have to go into full detail about how I got her here; most things are better left unspoken.

"I think it can go unsaid that I am a very powerful woman, Bella Rosa. Have peace of mind to know that there is nothing you need to tell me that I don't already know. I did a background check on you, both legal and personal. I know all about your past, it doesn't ever need to be discussed. Let's bury it; from this day forward, you are now anything you want to be, my beautiful girl." I pecked her on the lips and moved over to the camera setup.

"Now that we have established a comradery, how about I answer your question from earlier," I suggested. "This camera setup is for you, darling." I smiled. "Well...not just for you, it's for you, and Brooke." It was show time; this was the moment that separated the VIPs from the regular women.

As soon as I said her name, in walked my beautiful Brooke. She was wearing the same silk robe that was lying on the couch, only hers was black. She was completely naked underneath which made her nipples hard as stones. She sat right next to Ysabelle, poured herself a glass of champagne, and refilled Ysabelle's glass.

My two most valued girls together at last. We were finally one big happy family. If I would have died that second, I would have left a very fulfilled and happy woman. My life had always been leading to certain points, certain moments in time and I knew with everything I had that this was one of them. This would make or break her.

"Ysabelle, this is Brooke. She is another one of my beautiful girls; she has been with me for almost four years now. You two will make friends. You will essentially make friends with the all the women, however, tonight she will be an instructor for you." Brooke took her glass and handed Ysabelle hers. She clinked their glasses together and then each took a sip.

"She is going to teach you how to please your clients. The camera is going to record this scene in order for you to watch what you look like when you're with a client. It will be sort of a tutorial that you can study and grow from. Brooke is very good at what she does. She is actually one of my top girls." I turned to Brooke.

"Brooke, baby, will you go get that robe." She slid from the couch to retrieve the robe.

"I know that Brooke is a woman, and although we have mostly men clients we also have a few women. Plus you know how men work…a threesome is a very popular demand." Brooke and I snickered at that statement, I moved back to sit behind Ysabelle.

"Now, I also want you to learn how to be with a man. It will be crucial for your success. I know you have only been with one sexual partner; by the way, it makes me so proud that you would sacrifice yourself for such a good cause. Poor boy needed you and you were there for him, I think you knew then that you were meant for a life of pleasure."

"What do you mean? What guy?" she asked confused. I was letting her know too much, however she needed to know how long I've wanted her. Ysabelle had never been loved and she was about to get a crash course on everything. I was eager to get it started.

"Bella Rosa, my love, I am going to elaborate on this one piece of information from your past and then we are going to move on from that. Do I make myself clear?" I asked in an authoritative tone that she knew meant business. She nodded.

"Like I said, I've been watching you for a long time. I just happened to be there the day that you started at the club. I watched you get out of that old blue Ford pickup. Once you thanked the boy for the ride and left his presence, I stood in front of his car, keeping him from moving.

"I wanted you then. I know a VIP when I see one, and you, I wanted. The young lad volunteered all of the information I was after for a dime bag of weed. He told me that you had graciously taken his virginity. What a noble soul you are, my Bella Rosa.

"Like I said, I do extensive investigating on all of my VIPs, way before you are even aware that I even exist. I talked to five of your fellow…what did you call it?" I asked, tapping my chin in deep thought. "Oh, yes, blowjobs. Pro bono blow jobs if you will. Every one of the boys that I spoke with assured me with attitudes that there was something wrong with you. They informed me that you gave a hell of a hand-job, and a mean *blowjob,* but that you wouldn't put out for anything. I like that about you my sweet girl. You stand your ground.

"You were a young lady when you came here; I needed to wait until you were a woman before I made my move. I am aware that you have not been with a single man since you have arrived here. I am also pleasantly surprised by that…impressive."

"How did you know where I came from?" I could sense she was starting to feel a little apprehensive about it all. I'm sure I wouldn't trust anyone that told me they knew everything about me either. But she needed to know that I wasn't just anyone.

"Bella Rosa, where did we agree to leave history?" I felt disappointed that I had to repeat myself.

"In the past."

"Good girl. You did a boy a favor and gained a little pleasure for yourself. Let's leave it at that."

"Well that's not the only reason I did it, and I wouldn't exactly call it pleasurable."

"Now now…I know that. Let's call it baby steps toward the right direction." I kissed her shoulder in an effort to calm her some.

"So in essence, being with a man might feel uncomfortable for you the first couple of times. I would like to leave that for another day, from my experience, being with a woman first is much easier. It's better."

Brooke brought me the robe. I took it and began to lower the zipper of Ysabelle's dress. I felt lost in the moment, like it was a dream. I had waited what seemed like an eternity for this to become a reality, and now it was. I was on a high, feeling euphoria that I had never in my life felt before.

"I don't want you to think of this as taboo, or put a label on it. Straight, gay, lesbian, bi-sexual, it's all so gauche. We're in an open-minded era, Ysabelle. This career will let you embrace all of life's pleasures, the pleasure of pleasing your clients, and most importantly…the pleasure of pleasing yourself." I paused to let it all sink in. She needed to understand that in this life, there were no labels or boundaries.

"Are you ready?"

She took in a deep breath at the same time I let one out. It was a symbol of me giving myself to her and her breathing me in.

"Yes."

CHAPTER 36

I moved to sit on the opposite side of the couch and handed Brooke the robe, while she sat beside Ysabelle. She glanced at the camera that was now pointed directly at them and she noticed the little green light blinking. Brooke knew exactly what her role was, I had trained her for years, and this was truly the time that she was going to prove herself to me. It was as much of a test for Ysabelle as it was for Brooke.

Brooke grabbed her chin and brought her attention back to her.

"Don't worry about the camera, Bella...just focus on me, okay?" I had seen Brooke do this plenty of times with other VIPs, but this was the first time that it really meant something to me. The way she looked at Ysabelle with such want and abandonment wasn't anything that could be learned, it was innate. Brooke was my pride and joy, and watching her take control of naïve Ysabelle was a gift.

"I like the name Bella, too," Ysabelle rattled with a nervy voice. I hated that voice.

"Great! I can tell already that you and I are going to be amazing friends. I started off a little like you. You remind me a lot of myself." My mind wandered to Taylor and how I had used those exact same lines on her; and to watch Brooke pull it off so effortlessly was like watching someone take candy from a baby.

"Phew...you are going to make clients very happy...your body is a paradise," Brooke praised.

I couldn't agree with her more. Ysabelle was gorgeous. Her body was made for sex; it was sinful. I praised it from afar; Ysabelle reminded me of myself at her age, it was like looking into a mirror.

Brooke's hands skimmed the sides of Ysabelle's body until she stopped at the edges of her panties. With her index fingers, she began to slide them down. Ysabelle slipped out one leg at a time.

I couldn't help but feel excited. A part of me wished this could go in slow motion, because I wanted to capture the moment; I didn't want it to end. I couldn't wait any longer...

"Spread your legs, Bella Rosa," I demanded in a soft tone. She did as she was told. Ysabelle's face always disclosed everything- the glow on her skin, the light in her eyes; she was feeling the thrill of it all. She felt our gazes on every inch of her body. She could feel the yearning and hunger in the room. It didn't matter that I was sitting across the room; I could tell it made her pussy throb.

"Your pussy is sweeter than I thought it would be, you're just the right shade of cream. It's a nice surprise that you don't have any tan lines. Your caramel skin color is natural. That pleases me," I assured her while inspecting her pussy.

She loved every second of it. It was a necessity for her to know that she was adored, she was wanted, and she was loved. I pondered the thought if my mother felt like this when she watched me with Taylor. I intimidated my mother; it had always been that way. That's the main difference between me and her. I knew that VIP needed to be handed over to someone; I don't think my mother would have ever let go if I hadn't taken it. My girls make me proud. They show me all that I have taught them.

They shine, I shine, we all shine...

What happened next caught me off guard; Ysabelle turned to Brooke and twirled her hair, as I had once done to her. There was an overflow of emotions as I watched her take control. She was surpassing all my expectations tenfold. It was one of the most beautiful sights I have ever seen. Ysabelle took to being a VIP like a dream. It was inbred in her. She wanted the control like she wanted her next breath, and it was apparent how far she would go for it.

"I knew you would be like this, Bella Rosa. I knew, once given the chance, you would surpass any thought I would have imagined," I proclaimed.

The rest of the scene continued just as I had instructed Brooke, and Ysabelle responded to each and every test with nothing but perfection. She took control when she needed to and she let herself be seduced when it was appropriate. A mere vision of such flawlessness was enough to bring me to my knees. She had me. I would have paid any amount of money to fuck her and that's exactly the attitude that she needed for success as one of my girls. I knew then, just what I know now…

Ysabelle is and will always be a VIP.

✳VIP✳

Over the course of the next few days, Ysabelle got pampered and acquainted with her new luxuries. At first, she was dismayed, though she quickly adjusted. I woke up early one morning, eager to get Ysabelle started on the day's tasks. I had a full schedule and itinerary planned for her. I usually loathed this part of the preparation, and although it was necessary, it was also tedious. But it was different with her; I wanted to be a part of every step in her journey. I felt like God had given me a chance to have a daughter, and I was not going to take that responsibility lightly.

"Thank you, love, yes right over there by the breakfast bar." I ushered the concierges with a tray of every breakfast food designed by man.

"Good morning, Bella Rosa." She didn't have to tell me that she wasn't a morning person. It was clear across her face how much she hated the fact that I was there that early.

"Darling, good to know that you still look just as amazing in the morning as you do when you're put together. That will come in handy. Come on, don't fuck around, the day awaits," I said as I smacked her butt to get her to move.

"El café con leche is on the table. Drink some, it will make you feel better."

"Mmm hmm," was all she could muster to say.

"6:30 am. Really? Couldn't this have waited, till I don't know, noon maybe?" she asked. I handed her a strong cup of coffee. I knew she would need the espresso.

"Early bird gets the worm, Bella Rosa, and we have a mighty big worm to conquer today." She shook her head, looking over at the array of breakfast items that were sitting on the breakfast bar.

"You should have asked me what I like to eat, Madam. That is way too much food. I usually just like coffee and granola bar for breakfast.

I mean maybe oatmeal; that over there is ridiculous. You could feed a small army." I smiled.

"Well yes, it is a little extravagant, isn't it? Darling, it isn't from me. It's from Gabriel." She looked away from the food and looked over at me.

The night before, I couldn't believe how fast Ysabelle had reeled Gabriel in; he was smitten with her the second he saw her. I knew that look in his eyes and I can't lie and say it didn't worry me, I had seen that look in men's stares before. There was nothing I could do about it. My clients loved my girls. I would be out of business if I had to cater to every bad feeling I had when it came to them. I would have to watch Gabriel closely…I wouldn't have another Brooke situation. I didn't have time to babysit and it annoyed me that I felt like I had to when it came to him.

I had known Gabriel for years by that point. The son of a bitch got sexier the older he got, and several of the girls were smitten with him as well. Ysabelle, on the other hand, didn't give a shit…all she wanted was to have a good time and I could show her one every time.

The limo ride home was interesting to say the least. I purposely wanted Ysabelle to stay wet and ready. When I told her she needed to take care of her ache, the first emotion I saw on her beautiful face was one I wouldn't dare her to ever show me again.

Defiance.

There would be NONE of that. I made sure of it.

She listened to me like I knew she would, and the look of her coming was one of the most erotic sights I have ever seen.

Abandonment.

I noticed something kept happening to me every time I made Ysabelle experience something new. I would think of my mother. I would wonder if this was how she felt or what she thought about. I don't know why it was happening, but it wouldn't stop. It haunted me. It was like the ghost of Christmas past, except my mother was the ghost. Over the years, I saw and talked to her less and less; by that point we were talking maybe twice a year and I hadn't actually seen her in three years.

I truly believe I have a sixth sense…more to that later. But it's coming.

The doctor had arrived and I made my way outside; I knew Ysabelle would want some privacy and I didn't want to make her uncomfortable. There wasn't anything he or she could have told me that I didn't already know. I busied myself with taking phone calls for the girls and made sure everything was in line for Ysabelle's big night, which was days away.

I hated the fact that I needed to keep repeating myself every single fucking time we had a conversation about her future. I knew I needed to have patience with her, though that was easier said than done. I looked in through the screen door and saw that the doctor was packing up; I went inside and paid him.

I couldn't believe that she was wearing the cheapest looking clothes I had ever seen. Especially because she had a fortune just sitting in her California closet. I needed to hold back my temper. After she gave me her reasons, I didn't give it a second thought before I went under the sink of her kitchen and grabbed garbage bags. I went straight to her "old" wardrobe and threw away everything that would never belong there.

After I was finished, I turned to her and looked directly into her eyes. "Understand something, Ysabelle, don't you ever take my gifts for granted; as quickly as they come they can go," I confessed, wanting to strike her for being ungrateful.

"Wait, what? No, I didn't do that. I appreciate it all; I just wanted something of mine. I worked very hard for all of my things, Madam. I'm not used to being taken care of, can you understand that?" she responded with the same amount of attitude I gave her, another conflicting emotion for me. I wanted to punish her and praise her all at the same time.

I internally took a deep breath…this was a power exchange.

"Ysabelle, that life is over now. You receive extravagant things and don't wear sandals from Target. Everything in that closet is for you. You exude money and power, learn it, live it, and fucking love it. Yes?" I demanded with an edge to my voice. She nodded.

"Great! Now take off those fucking clothes, and put some real goddamn clothes on. Ladies wear heels, even if they are walking to the dumpster." I grabbed the garbage and left.

The minute she stepped out in her designer attire, all was forgiven.

"There, don't you feel better? Honestly…you can't tell me you don't feel like a million bucks, because you sure do look it," I said. I love being right and by the look on her face she knew I was too. She would learn that I am never wrong, it's going to take time, but we will get there. I was sure of it.

"Actually, I do, Madam. I can see where you're coming from. I'm sorry."

"It's already forgotten, silly girl." She grabbed her purse and we were out the door. She followed me to the parking garage, I had her next gift in my hand and I couldn't wait to see her face. I stopped her as she started to walk to the passenger side.

"Wow, that's one hell of a car," she said right on cue. I slid my hand into hers with the keys.

"Great, because it's yours."

"What the fuck? Are you kidding? I haven't even made any money yet."

"Ysabelle," I said in a frustrated tone.

"Thank you, Madam." I smiled and started to walk over to the passenger side.

It would have been an understatement to say how much I enjoyed being able to give Ysabelle all that she deserved. I felt pride, excitement, and fulfillment.

The saints had given me another.

Redemption.

And it came in the form of Ysabelle Telle.

CHAPTER 37

The next few days Ysabelle got acquainted with the girls, though I could immediately tell she got along the best with Brooke. I wondered if I influenced that. Girls get attached to those they experiment first with.

The second we made it to The Gala, Brooke took Ysabelle to the bathroom, just how she was supposed to. I circulated the room, mingling with everyone, and then I saw him.

Mika.

I ignored him and turned to find the girls. As soon as the three gentlemen saw Ysabelle, they wanted her. It was going to be a great night...unfortunately, I spoke to soon.

Ysabelle made a complete fool of herself and, God, if it didn't make me want to put her over my knee.

"Can you excuse us, gentlemen?" I announced to them, not looking at Ysabelle.

She followed me to an office where I leaned against the desk, crossing my ankles. She wrung her hands and dropped her head, waiting for the storm. And it only further pissed me off.

"What are you doing? Drop your hands and look at me. Do you want to be here, Ysabelle? Have I not made myself perfectly clear about everything, and what is expected from you? Do you think for one second that any of this behavior you're exhibiting right now, will be tolerated? If you would rather go back to earning not even half of what you are truly worth, then the damn door is behind you." I let out a loud frustrated sigh and composed myself.

I didn't need to make her feel any worse than she already did, even though I wanted to. I had to hold back and not be too hard on her, and it was one of the toughest things I ever had to do.

"Now…are you ready?" I tested. If she answered no, I couldn't be held responsible for what I was going to do.

"Yes. I'm fine. I promise."

I smiled a deviant little smile as I walked toward her. I circled her and moved her hair from the front of her shoulder to her back. "Who's holding the control, Bella Rosa?" I asked in my domineering tone.

"I am," she replied.

"That's my girl, now you're going to put these nerves to rest and show these men how confident you are. You've got the looks. You've got the body, and you need to have the confidence, my beautiful girl. I want to see you express that authority. Do you understand me, Ysabelle?" I asked, raising my voice and causing her to jump a little.

Learn one thing; your children need to fear you. It's a part of parenting.

"I'm sorry, Madam. Of course, I understand everything," she replied with more confidence.

"You are in control. You don't ever forget that. These men do not pay for a little girl."

She learned right then and there that I was to be respected. I didn't fuck around and she needed to pick and choose her battles. She decided at that moment that I was her Madam.

"I'm ready, Madam," she promised.

"Follow me," I ordered.

I left her in Brooke's room to observe her, but also to get her wet.

A hand grabbed my upper arm and pulled me into the adjoining room.

"Who the hell-" I shouted and stopped when I saw Mika's smirking face.

"I'm working. Can I help you?"

He leaned on the dresser and crossed his arms and ankles. "You know, Angel, I'm not going to say that my feelings aren't hurt a little because they are."

I rolled my eyes. "What the fuck are you going on about?"

"Why didn't you offer her to me?" he questioned.

"What?"

"The new girl, Ysabelle. I want her." He smiled.

I laughed. "Well you can't have her. She's already taken."

"I'll pay three times as much as her suitor did."

"No," I hastily responded.

He cocked his head to the side. "Really? Since when do you turn down money or give a fuck who I play with. Our relationship is supposed to stay the same, says you. Well guess what? I want her. Make it happen. I'll even let you watch. I know how much you love to watch, Angel. "

I swallowed the lump in my throat. "I don't have time for this. She is already taken; it has nothing to do with you."

"All right, then I want her tomorrow or the next time she is available," he spoke with conviction.

"No," was all I could reply.

"Why?" he countered.

I walked right up to him. "Because, Ysabelle is made for other things. I will never allow you to have her."

"I don't understand. Since when do you give a flying fuck where I stick my cock? I have been with almost all the VIPs, she's up next."

"I don't have time for this. It's not happening, now or ever. Don't worry about it, Mika. I'll make it up to you, and I will throw in free VIPs just for you."

"Why are you being so possessive over her?"

I leaned in close to his lips, and seductively traced them while looking into his eyes. "Because...she's mine." I turned and left.

As soon as I closed the door, I leaned my entire body weight on it, feeling like my legs were going to give out. I took three deep breaths and composed myself before walking back to get Ysabelle.

She turned and saw me quietly wave for her to join me from the cracked door.

"Are we good now, Ysabelle?" I didn't have to ask. Her eyes were dilated and dark.

"Absolutely."

"Fabulous. Darling, we had a little bit of a bidding war with our men this evening. It seems as though the gentlemen all want a piece of the action," I boasted, raising my eyebrows.

Up until Mika decided to cloud my judgment, I was thrilled with the outcome for her first time. I couldn't wait to watch her in action, not because of the arousal, but from the power and control she was about to realize she held all this time.

"I didn't want to overwhelm you too much for your first time, so we came up with a happy medium. Gabriel wants you more, he paid top dollar for you. Here's the catch…the rest of the men get to watch." I paused for a moment to let her soak in my words.

"Don't you worry your pretty little head; it's only the three suitors you met downstairs. And me of course. I wouldn't leave you alone, my pet, at least not your first time, don't fret." I paused and looked at her directly in the eyes to make sure I was understood.

"No one is allowed to touch you other than Gabriel," I explained.

She was intimidated. I knew she didn't want to make the same mistake and disappoint me again. It pleased me that she was more nervous about me than she was about the men.

I needed to reassure her. "Bella, my love. Stop worrying about pleasing me, and focus on pleasing yourself. This is about you, and nobody else."

We walked into the room and the three gentlemen sat center stage waiting for her. I never said a word. I went to a bistro table in the corner, trying to make myself as invisible as possible. This wasn't about me; it was about her.

I watched with an incredible amount of pride on my face, I was sure. The way she took control but submitted to him all at the same time was absolutely perfect. I couldn't have asked her to do a better job.

All three men were stroking themselves.

"Yes…yes…just like that…I'm coming…I'm coming…" she begged while coming undone.

I smiled. I know I have said this time and time again; however, you truly need to understand. I couldn't reiterate it enough.

VIPs aren't made; they're born.

He moved her to the bed and laid her on her back in the middle.

This was it. She could never go back from this.

She opened her eyes to find Gabriel smiling above her with the most satisfied smirk on his face. She turned her face and caught me leaving through the slits in her overactive eyes. I smiled at her with a wink as I exited the room.

I didn't have to watch to know that he fucked her and she loved it.

❋VIP❋

Our limo ride home was quiet. Ysabelle's mind was racing.

"Penny for your thoughts?" I questioned.

"Mmm hmm."

"Care to share, Bella Rosa?"

"I was just thinking I feel pleased…excited. I'm on a high right now. Does that make sense?"

"Perfectly." I reached into my clutch and retrieved a white envelope. This was going to make it so much better.

"This, Bella Rosa, will make you feel even higher." She opened it and there, before her very eyes, were hundreds and hundreds of bills. She had never seen that much money before.

"It's $80,000." Her mouth dropped open.

"You made $160,000 tonight; Gabriel paid $100,000 to be your first client. I charged the other suitors a measly $20,000, forgive me for that, Bella Rosa, I had to entice them regarding the price. I promise you, they will pay more for you later; that I can assure you. Enjoy it, as you will never forget your first time."

And I meant every fucking word.

CHAPTER 38

Time had flown by, VIP was everywhere, and I do mean absolutely everywhere. Ysabelle brought in tons of business; I was actually turning clients away because she was always booked. Men and women loved her; I even started charging more money for her. She always let me handle the financial and booking details for her, she could have taken it over, but she wanted it to be my responsibility. She said it made it easier for her.

That only proved to me that Ysabelle wanted to be taken care of, and I didn't mind doing it.

It all happened so fast and I wish that I had seen it coming; I wish I could tell you that I felt it or something, but I would be lying. I haven't lied to you yet, so I'm not going to start now. I didn't ever think that it would happen, not one fucking bit of it.

I was ecstatic when he finally called.

Sebastian Vanwell was one of the biggest power players in Miami. He was the top rated yacht dealer all over, and devastatingly handsome. I was thrilled when I heard he got a card for Ysabelle- see, that's who she was. That's just the type of people she brought in.

Only the best.

I always knew he was married. Did I care? What do you think?

Just in case...I didn't give a shit about him being married. Here's what threw me off though. He was happily married- and by happily, I mean he was head over heels in love with his wife and child- and we didn't get a lot of those. That's just the magnetic pull that my girl has...I honestly didn't think he was going to call; it was like a silent test for Ysabelle. A test she passed with flying colors. I was the one that failed, not her.

"Mr. Vanwell, so nice of you to finally call, darling," I proclaimed.

"Oh…wait– I think you have me confused with someone else. You don't know me," he explained.

I learned a long time ago how to work a man, you stroke his ego.

"Oh no? You're not Sebastian Vanwell, Alejandro's friend? I apologize if I have mistaken you for someone else," I said and he laughed nervously.

"I do know Alejandro. I don't think I would call him my friend. I didn't know he would speak of me to you. I'm caught a little off guard by that."

As he should be, I wouldn't want my acquaintances talking about me either. Appearances were the only thing that mattered in this town. I needed to reassure him that I meant no harm and that he could trust me. Fuck, all he had to believe was that I was his new best friend.

"Mr. Vanwell, there is nothing to worry about. My business tailors to clientele through referrals. All clients know this, and they also know not to refer unless they know the person can keep the upmost anonymity. Alejandro just let me know that he gave you a business card."

"Right. Listen…I don't even know why I'm calling. I'm sorry I wasted your time," he said as he was about to hang up. I would never let him get away that easily.

"Sebastian…may I call you Sebastian?" I asked.

"Umm…yes."

"Great. Sebastian, I can sense your nervousness over the phone. You're not doing anything wrong, darling. Just relax. We're two consenting adults talking. Now let me begin by telling you how excited I am that you called. I heard you were quite taken by my Ysabelle. She is a beautiful thing isn't she?"

"Yes," he whispered as I chuckled.

"Ysabelle is my prized possession, Sebastian; she is very special to me. Do you understand that?"

"I do. Can I speak freely?"

"Of course."

"I'm not quite sure what you mean. She belongs to you? I don't understand."

"Oh yes…I have gotten a bit ahead of myself, haven't I? Please excuse my carelessness. Ysabelle works for me, Sebastian. She's my girl, she's an escort."

He didn't speak for several seconds, but I heard his breathing so I knew he was still there. I needed to reel him back in. I didn't for once second believe he didn't know what Ysabelle was, that piqued my interest that much more.

"Are you there?"

"I'm sorry to have wasted your time. I had no idea. I'm a happily married man. I just thought...I– I don't know what I thought," he stuttered.

"It's all right, darling. I keep my business discrete for several reasons. You have nothing to be ashamed of, Sebastian, you haven't done anything wrong. Ysabelle provides several different forms of companionship. This isn't what you think it is. My girls are not prostitutes, they are prized jewels and not just any man can be with them."

"With all due respect, I am fully aware of what an escort entails, Madam," he addressed with a tone I didn't approve of.

"Really? Well then, Sebastian, why don't you put your money where your mouth is? You're obviously taken with my Ysabelle, or else you wouldn't be calling a month and a half later. You could have Ysabelle for an evening and you could do with her as you please. I promise you won't regret it."

"There would be no need for sex?" he hesitated.

"Sex is not a need, it's a want. Unless you want it, then no; you can talk, and just enjoy one another's company. There is no harm in that, now is there?"

"How much?"

Got him.

"My girls aren't rented by the hour, Sebastian. Since I can feel your hesitation, I will allow it this time. How about $5,000 for two hours?"

"$2,500 an hour to talk to someone?" he blurted.

"I never said my girls were cheap, Sebastian. My girls are ladies and expect to be treated as so."

"Whatever. When can I see her?"

"Well...that's up to you. How fast can you come in to see me?"

"I don't follow."

"I know you're not planning on being intimate with Ysabelle, however, there is still a process that needs to take place before you can have her."

"Which is?"

"You would need to come in and have a physical, and be tested for any discrepancies. Also, I would need your social and fingerprints to run a background check. I also need to keep a card on file. I protect what's mine, Sebastian, I'm sure you can understand that," I proclaimed.

"I understand. I can come in tomorrow afternoon, let's say around noon."

"Perfect, it won't take long for the results. If everything clears, you could see her this Friday. Her appointment for that night canceled. His loss is your gain. I can tell her once everything comes back, and put you on the schedule. Now where would you like to arrange to meet her?"

"I'm not quite sure. I'm married and I don't think my wife would appreciate what the hell I'm even doing; this will be a one-time thing, I just need to see her this once and I will be done. I won't need more time with her."

"Of course." I smiled; this was not going to be the last time. It never was when it came to Ysabelle.

"Well, may I suggest a hotel room? There's privacy and the discretion that you need."

"Have her meet me at The W at 6 pm, I will confirm the room number as soon as it's booked," he replied, trying not to sound uncertain.

"Have a great evening, goodbye." I hung up before he had a chance to change his mind. Not that I thought he was going to.

I had no clue what the future would hold. Nothing could have prepared me for what was to come. It was the first time in my life that I understood what my mother felt like when she wasn't in control.

I really was my mother's daughter, and that scared me more than anything.

CHAPTER 39

I had invited Ysabelle over a few months later to catch up and have lunch. We usually tried to every other week or so. There we were, talking about her recent trip to Australia with a client, when my phone rang.

"Sebastian, darling, what a nice surprise. How are you?" I said into the phone. I looked over at Ysabelle and her eyes widened for just a second, but I caught it.

"I'm great, thanks for asking. How about yourself?" She smiled at me and there was a certain glow to her, she seemed tense. At the time, I thought that maybe she was nervous or something had happened between them. I would investigate that later.

"Lovely, I'm actually having lunch with our beautiful Ysabelle as we speak."

"Oh…really. Um…let me…" he hesitated.

"Don't be silly. I always have time for you. Now what can I help you with?"

"Right…it's just, I umm…have this thing," he stuttered.

"Sebastian, relax. Ysabelle is absolutely glowing right now. Seems like you have made quite an impression on my girl, Mr. Vanwell," I stated, trying to make him comfortable and at the same time remind him who Ysabelle really belonged to.

"She's made quite an impression on me. That's why I'm calling. You see…I have this yacht delivery I have to make to the Virgin Islands and I wanted the company of Ysabelle for the duration of that time."

"Hmm…that sounds like quite a trip. I'm assuming you're trying to mix a little business with pleasure, seeing as you haven't thus far?" I was definitely fishing for something.

"Wait…what?" And he just answered my question.

Why little Miss Ysabelle gave away a freebie. I had to brace myself from being upset with her; I didn't want to be like my mother. So I left it at Ysabelle trying to be independent and ended it there.

"Please, I know you enjoy your little chats with my Ysabelle, I'm to assume that this will include more than companionship?" I may let her give her pussy away for free…one time.

"Umm…you are assuming correctly. I mean-"

"Sebastian, I am in the business of making people happy. Let me remind you that I'm not here to judge. My Ysabelle was made for you. I know what effect she has on men, you're not the first and you won't be the last," I subtly implied; I knew he wanted to tell me to go fuck off but held his tongue. Smart man.

"Mmm hmm," was all he replied.

"When is this little rendezvous scheduled for?"

"A week from Thursday, we will set sail at 9 am and should be getting back Sunday evening. I will provide the airfare for the return."

"It just so happens that Ysabelle is free for those dates. You know that the expenses will change?"

"I'm aware. How much?" If he wanted her, then he would have to pay. I upped the ante.

"Well this is more than an overnight request. It's going to be costly, I would say somewhere around $80,000."

"Madam!" Ysabelle shouted from afar.

"Excuse me, Sebastian," I said, putting him on hold.

"Since when do you ever rudely interrupt me, little girl?" I asked.

"I'm sorry, I didn't mean to. It's just that price seems kinda steep, don't you think?" she said with a smile. She was hiding something from me. I didn't know what it was and I would find out.

"Since you want to tell me how to do my job, then by all means, Ysabelle. How much?"

She nervously licked her lips. "$40,000."

I got back on the phone with Sebastian, "Well, Mr. Vanwell…it seems as though Ysabelle is feeling generous today. She will do it for $40,000," I stated through gritted teeth.

"Done," he quickly replied. I knew full well that he would have paid $80,000.

"I'll have the money deposited this evening. Have a wonderful day." I said and abruptly hung up.

"What the fuck was that, Ysabelle?" I demanded.

She hesitated for a brief second, trying to contemplate how to address me. "Madam…with all due respect, I'm allowed to set the bar for my appointments, or am I not? Let me know if I've overstepped my boundaries and it won't happen again. I was under the impression that I could make my own decisions," she informed me, standing her ground.

This reminded of what I went through with my mother decades ago, except now I was sitting on the other side of the desk. And let me tell you something, the grass isn't always greener on the other side.

I raised my eyebrows at her. "Do I need to worry about your involvement with this client, Bella Rosa? Is there something you're not telling me? Do I need to remind you of who and what you are, and of our business arrangement?"

"Of course not, if it makes you feel better, take all of it. I screwed you out of your money, therefore take mine."

This is the exact moment where our relationship changed.

It didn't matter what she was saying or how she was trying to portray herself.

Ysabelle lied to me.

"Shit," I said with disgust. "I never thought the day would come. You're attached to him. What the fuck, Ysabelle? Have I taught you nothing? Do I need to call him back and cancel this event? Must I make you walk away from him?" I didn't want to believe what I was asking or what I was thinking and it didn't make it any less true. She was falling for him. She would rather be with him for free. She had never been with someone for no monetary compensation. That's what made her so perfect. This was serious.

"Madam, it's nothing like that. I know how to do my job and you have nothing to worry about. I have this under control. But just to keep the record straight, you can't tell me what to do. You are aware of that?" she hissed.

I needed to think about my next words. They could make or break us.

"Bella Rosa, you're closer to me than any daughter I could have had. DO NOT get emotionally attached to a MARRIED man, do you understand me?"

I heard the hypocritical words come out of my mouth and they made my head swirl and my stomach upset. I was no better than she was, but I spoke from experience. It didn't matter for shit. The more you tell someone they can't do something, the more they want to do it. It's called freewill. I was going to lose her, however, and trust me on this- I wasn't going to go without a fucking fight.

"Perfectly," she responded as she turned and walked out.

⁂VIP⁂

A few months went by and several things changed; my relationship with Ysabelle was the most extreme. We didn't see each other as often and when we talked, she seemed distant and distracted. Sebastian, the bastard, was also paying for all of her time. I know what you're thinking…how could I allow that…right?

I didn't allow anything. I have told you, I don't call the shots, my girls do. I am a mere spectator. Besides, if I didn't "allow" her, I would have lost her a lot sooner than I did. I had to play nice, I had to seem like I cared and wanted what was best for her.

I did.

I do.

⁂VIP⁂

I went to her apartment that day, fully expecting to talk it out with her; I knew we could get past this. I needed to have her see it my way; she had to understand that I knew what was best.

"What the hell, Madam," she said with her hand on her chest. "You scared the shit out of me. Can't you knock?'

"Since when have I ever had to knock, Bella Rosa?" The simple fact that she even suggested that I knock on a condo that I pay for infuriated me. I have never knocked before, and I had no intentions of ever knocking in the future. She was beginning to step out of line.

"I don't know…never mind. What's up?" She dismissively walked over to her refrigerator and bent down to grab a bottle of water. The moment her hair fell away from her neck, my blood went ice cold. I could feel all of my veins tightening. I saw red and lunged at her.

She tried to back up, but I held onto her arm, keeping her in place.

"What the fuck is that, Ysabelle?" I yelled. My mind was too far gone to show any other emotion, other than pure rage.

"What are you talking about, let go of me, you're hurting me."

"You let him fucking mark you!" My voice rose to a level I hadn't heard in years. It had been a long time since I last felt that kind of anger toward another person. But the purple marks all over her neck gave me reason to.

"What?" She shook her head.

Ysabelle wasn't a dumb girl. You know what they say; love is unconditional. I say, love is obtuse. A person in love is blind. The phrase "see no evil, speak no evil, and hear no evil" applies just as much to love as it does to life.

I roughly escorted her to the mirror in the living room so she could see for herself each colorful emotion that was displayed for the world to see. She tried to pull away from me, but it only made me hold on tighter. I didn't care if I bruised her; she was already marked. And a mark from me was far worse than any kind of "love" mark.

"What the fuck are you doing, Ysabelle? What the hell is going on?"

"I don't know what you're talking about. Nothing is going on. Let go of me."

"This is complete bullshit. You NEVER let a client mark you. You aren't someone's goddamn property," I yelled, tightening my hold on her more.

"Really, Madam? Not even yours?" That was it…that was the last straw. This ungrateful girl had pushed me to my breaking point. I crudely pushed her away with such disgust, that she fell to the floor. It took everything I had not to lunge and beat the shit out of her. I wanted to beat some sense into her, just as my mother had done to me. But I couldn't…it hadn't worked for me, and I knew damn well it wouldn't work for her either.

I was at a loss. I didn't know what to do, so I did the only thing I was accustomed to, I used my words.

"You ungrateful child."

"I'm not a child," she argued. I disagreed.

"Oh really, Ysabelle, then why the fuck are you acting like one? Have I taught you nothing? You have been with an infinite number of men and not ever have I had to worry about you. I made you who you are; remember that. Where is your loyalty? You're going to lose it…for a fucking married man!" I didn't even bother trying to control my temper. None of my girls had ever made me react this way. But Ysabelle was different. I couldn't lose her. I needed to make her see what she was doing, and get her to wake the fuck up.

"You know what your boyfriend does when you're not around? He makes love to his wife, he tells her he can't live without her, and that he loves her. You know what you are? You're his whore! That's what he's paying for, that's what he wants from you. And you're handing him your heart on a GODDAMN silver platter." I shook my head at her, knowing that no matter what I said, it would never make her see the truth. She would have to see with her own two eyes. She would have to experience it firsthand.

She was a woman in love.

"You stupid, stupid girl…you know nothing."

She sat in silence while I only stared at her. For the first time since she had come to Miami, I couldn't read her mind. I couldn't sense what she was thinking. It was possibly because I was trying too hard to make her understand, that I couldn't see the look in her eyes. Now I know, she had already been having those thoughts. And no matter what I said or didn't say, it wouldn't have changed the outcome. I had to sit on the sidelines and wait…the time would come, it always did.

I extended my hand and helped her up. I fixed her hair and towel, much like any mother would have, and embraced her in a hug.

"Bella Rosa…my darling girl…don't let this be the end of you. Do you understand me?"

"Yes," she quietly replied.

I kissed her on the cheek and left the apartment.

CHAPTER 40

I got in my car and just drove around for a few hours, trying to clear my mind of everything that was happening. I found myself at Mika's home and I had no idea how I even got there. I turned off the engine of my car, took a deep breath, and walked up the steps to his front door. I knocked and when he opened the door, he had the most perplexed look on his face, like I had done something wrong.

My eyes widened because I finally realized what I had done.

This was his home, the one he shared with his family. I backed away, trying to leave and he grabbed my wrist.

"They're out of town," he said. I nodded and we walked inside.

This was the first time I had ever been to Mika's home. It was beautiful, there were pictures of them all over the walls, and toys scattered here and there. The furniture was simple but lovely. The home definitely had a female touch to it. My fingers ran lightly on every piece of furniture and I could sense Mika's confusion. But this was my reality…I was also in love with a married man. I was no better than Ysabelle; we were one and the same.

I never thought that I would find myself in a situation that I couldn't control and now it felt like it was everywhere around me. I was suffocating in it.

No one can hurt you as much as you can hurt yourself. I was punishing myself by going there. I wanted to feel the pain, to know that I was valid in all the arguments that I had with Ysabelle. I didn't want her to feel this, I wanted better for her, but it didn't fucking matter. It was the first time that I felt like I knew what it was to be a parent. You want what's best for them…you put them first…

I am capable of love…and that scared me more than anything.

"What are you doing here?" Mika questioned, taking my attention away from the colored pictures on the fridge.

I looked at him and shrugged.

"Did you come here to fuck?"

I shook my head no.

"Then why are you here? That's what we are to each other, Angel. Your words, not mine," he viscously spewed.

This was Mika now. He was angry, resentful, and bitter toward me. I hadn't seen him be vulnerable since the day at my office when he confessed everything to me. I walked out of my office and him and he has never forgiven me for it.

"Do you want me to make it go away?" he tested, walking over to me. I nodded.

He deviously smiled and put his left hand on the fridge by the side of my face. With his right hand, his fingers touched my cheek and then my neck. He gripped my throat and my eyes closed as my head fell back against the fridge. His hand continued its way down my torso, he was being tender with me, and I needed it so. He finally made his way to my pussy and lightly rubbed back and forth. My breathing slightly escalated and his mouth found my ear lobe; he bit and then sucked on it.

"You know, Angel…" he panted. "Every time I touch you…" I moaned, as his fingers slipped into my skirt and inside my panties. I could feel the moisture and wetness he was creating with his touch.

He nuzzled my neck with his nose. "Every time my fingers or cock touches your glistening cunt…" I groaned, I was on the verge of climaxing. "I see…her face…I see…Ysabelle." My eyes immediately widened and all was lost.

I pushed and then slapped him across the face as hard as I could. And then the fucker smiled.

"If you wanted it rough, *Madam*, then all you had to do was say please." He pushed against the fridge and his mouth attacked mine. At first, my body gave into him, until I couldn't take all of the confusion anymore and I bit his lip, hard.

He backed away. "What the fuck?" he angrily yelled.

"Exactly! What the fuck?" I replied.

He walked over to the sink to rinse off the blood. "You know, I don't fucking understand you. You can't have it both ways and you can't have everything you fucking want. I'm not made like that," he roared, shaking his head.

"This was a mistake I shouldn't have come here." I quickly ran to the front door and he aggressively caught me by the waist and turned me around.

"You chose this! NOT ME!" he shouted, shaking me.

"I have given you everything, Mika!"

"Bullshit. You have given me nothing but your fucking pussy, and you give that to everybody."

I pushed him again but this time I threw a right hook at him. He stumbled back and grabbed his cheek. I shook my hand from the pain.

"Have fun explaining that one to your wife," I taunted and turned around and left.

Hell hath no fury like a woman scorned.

❋VIP❋

Seven months went by, and mine and Ysabelle's relationship was getting worse by the minute. I knew it had something to do with Sebastian; the bastard was probably feeding her lie after lie about me. What I would have done to be alone with him, little did I know I would get just that.

I smiled when I saw her name come up on my phone, "Bella Rosa," I answered.

"This is Sebastian," he replied. I didn't respond; something was wrong, I could feel it.

"Listen, I'm really sorry that I'm calling you. Ysabelle is burning up, I tried to break her fever and it's getting worse."

"I'll be there in twenty minutes," I replied and hung up. I immediately called the doctor on payroll to meet me at her condo. I was incredibly worried, a million thoughts raced through my head; the first, of course, being pregnancy. I sped all the way to her condo.

I waited in the living room as he checked on her, busying myself with a client on the phone. I called Mika but he didn't answer.

I hung up as soon as I saw them emerge from the bedroom.

"Ysabelle has pneumonia. I got here just in time so there will be no need for hospitalization, someone will need to stay with her for the next few days, she won't be able to fend for herself. Here's the list of things that I have written down that need to be taken care of in order for her to heal," he said, handing me the paper.

"I gave her shots for right now and they will have her out for most of the day; I called in the medication and antibiotics, someone will need to pick them up." I nodded and handed him an envelope of cash. I shook his hand and he left without even looking in Sebastian's direction.

He needed to know his place was not in Ysabelle's life.

I turned to him, finally acknowledging him. "You can go now," I demanded.

"Excuse me?" he remarked.

I could see in his eyes he was ready to have it out. He had no idea who he was fucking with.

"I'm here now, Mr. Vanwell, you're excused."

He shook his head. "I'm not leaving." For some reason, I knew he was going to say that.

"Oh really…" I mocked. "And what is it exactly that you will be telling your wife? You're held up with your whore?"

He needed to get off his high horse and realize he was no better than me. We were each fighting for her, except I would play dirty; I would do anything to win.

"First off, Ysabelle isn't my whore; and second of all, you will need to call the cops to get me to leave, and even then, I'd like to see them try," he declared.

"You amaze me. Aren't the lies getting a little much, I mean how stupid can your wife be that she hasn't caught on to your little discretion yet? How much longer do you possibly expect this to continue?"

"I don't have to explain myself to you." He was right; he didn't have to explain himself to me. However, Ysabelle pretends like she is strong and capable. That's what she's conditioned to do, and I could see right through it. I saw right through her, because we were exactly the same person.

"No, darling, you don't. Ysabelle isn't as strong as she lets on; who do you think will be here to pick up the pieces when she's no longer of use to you? I will! I have been here since the beginning, I have made her who she is, and I am not about to see someone with a midlife crisis take her away from me, do you understand me? I have let this go on long enough."

"All that matters to you, Madam, is if the credit card clears. If you truly cared about her you would have never let her sell herself to these so called gentlemen that do nothing but use and abuse her," he angrily replied.

The fucker had balls of steel; I'll give him that…

I cocked my head back in laughter, aiming to intimate the bastard. "And you think you're any fucking different, Sebastian, what the hell do you think you're doing? You're nothing but another man having an affair on the woman he has a child with. What? You didn't think I knew…I know everything about the men that are with my girls," I shouted, stepping closer to him.

He covered the shock on his face well. I could tell that he felt defeated though, and I needed to keep pushing those exact same buttons. The only thing that will make a person change is guilt and remorse; he had both.

"You think you're the first man that has fallen for one of my VIPs? MY girls are the epitome of class and beauty, that's why I choose them. Don't think for one fucking minute that you're any different than my so called gentlemen, as you so call them."

"Ysabelle matters to me, I care about her more than she'll ever even know. You know nothing about our situation."

I knew everything about their situation. He had no clue how much I could relate to everything that they were both going through.

And here was my one big chance to prove my fucking point…

"Okay…I'm game. Leave your wife, Sebastian. Tell her and choose Ysabelle and I will happily release her to you," I taunted.

I laughed internally because I already knew the answer; it's always the fucking same.

"What's the matter, Sebastian? Can't come up with any excuses fast enough? I love Ysabelle like she was my own. Are you aware that she's in love with you? That if you asked her, she would give this all up for you? I love her, but rules are rules. She can ask to be released anytime, and it would never occur to her to want to walk away from this, until she fell in love with you.

"If she didn't want you to be paying for her time then she would be working and you would have no say in the matter. I'm letting this continue because she hasn't said one goddamn thing about it. I'm not a monster, although, I am a business woman…in that sense you are right, I'm still fucking getting paid."

Everything I spoke was the truth, I swear on a stack of bibles. If he had told me yes, I would have released her. I wouldn't have given it a second thought.

He wanted to say so many things, but he was at a loss for words.

"Where's your wife, Sebastian? I have been in this game longer than you have even been alive. You love your wife; I can even see it now while you're standing here in your mistress's home. It doesn't matter which way you paint it…Ysabelle's the other woman; she will always be the other woman. Now what you have to ask yourself is how you're going to end it," I cautioned.

Sebastian's face reminded me so much of Mika's in my office that day. I knew he loved Ysabelle, I won't deny that. You always have a choice in life- always. He chose his that day. I knew it, he knew it, and soon, so would Ysabelle. It was coming; this wouldn't last much longer.

"You're wrong. I love her too. I fucking love her too. Don't for one second think that I don't. I know what I'm doing is wrong in so many ways, I don't need you to remind me, I remind myself every day when I'm standing in front of the mirror.

"I do love my wife and I love my son, but what I share with Ysabelle surpasses anything that I've ever experienced with anyone, and that includes my wife. I'm at a loss, I have no fucking idea which way is up anymore. When I think about not seeing her beautiful face every day it destroys me. Call me whatever you want, but that doesn't change the fact that I can't walk away from her, no more than she can walk away from me."

We stood there in a staring match before I finally broke the silence, "I have a nurse coming this evening; you have until then. I imagine that's enough time."

"I want to stay here the entire time, Madam."

"I am not a marriage counselor, Sebastian, but you're already rocking the fucking boat; how about we keep it in shallow water," I said in an annoyed tone while grabbing my purse. "I'll let myself out. Give Ysabelle my love and let her know I'll be stopping by tomorrow."

I knew I left him with a lot to think about. Sebastian wasn't a bad person; he was just a man.

Selfish.
He wanted to have his cake and eat it too.

CHAPTER 4

I didn't expect it to happen so quickly, but a few days later, there she was, waiting for me in my office.

"Bella Rosa," I greeted with a hug and a kiss. I took a real look at her. "It doesn't matter how much makeup you put on, I can still see that you look like shit."

"Thanks, Madam, I didn't come for the pleasant conversation. I need you to do something for me, and I will do something for you in exchange, which I'm sure will make you ecstatic," she stated in a sarcastic tone.

"Oh yeah."

"I need you to change my number and move me to another location."

I nodded. "Hmmm…trouble in paradise, I presume?" I was secretly jumping for victory inside. It looked like the ball was in my court, and the tables had finally turned.

"After you do this for me you can put me back on the schedule. I just need some time to clear my head and get my shit together."

"Well…I'm not much for gloating, but I think this needs to be said-"

"I'm fully aware that I fucked up, all right? There is no need for the I told you sos, call it being young and careless, and trust me when I say it will never happen again." I nodded. Though it didn't take away the urge from wanting to say, "I told you so."

"Are you all right, darling?" I empathized. I didn't want her to feel this way, but it was a must for her to change.

"I will be."

I left the room and returned with a new phone and two sets of keys. Presents always make everything better.

"I'll have all your contacts transferred to that phone and the movers will be there first thing in the morning. That's the set of keys to your new condo, it's located in Marquis Residences unit 1613; it's already fully furnished, and all you need to pack are your clothes and whatever personal belongings you would like to bring. I imagine you want to start fresh, yes?" she nodded.

"All right…well consider this a lesson learned; and a gift from me for coming to your senses," I stated, handing her another set of keys. I wanted to believe, but too much had happened.

"It's an Audi A8, it's parked in the garage; you can leave the set to your current car and home."

"Thank you, Madam."

"Of course, Bella Rosa, I'm always here for you, you know that. Now enough of the melodramatics, it's not our style; we're far too pretty for it. The White's Annual Gala is exactly four weeks away; do you think you will be better by then?"

"Mmm hmm," was all she could reply with. I knew that she was thinking no other man other than Sebastian had touched her for at least a year. She was nervous, it was radiating off of her and it infuriated me. Where did my strong independent woman go?

"Lovely, I know the perfect gentleman, darling," I snickered.

"Great. Well then, I don't want to take up too much of your time, I'll be going." She got up to leave.

"Ysabelle."

She turned. "Hmmm."

"Don't ever *fuck* with your heart again. Do you understand?"

"Of course."

I nodded and she was excused.

I opened my drawer and brought out my vile. I broke up two thick lines and snorted one up each nostril. I was going to need it for what I was about to do.

This is where you will hate me, again. I blame my mother; she fucked me up. I placed a call.

"Slavic," he answered.

"Good afternoon, darling. It's Madam," I replied.

"Oh yes, I have been expecting your call. How are things?"

"Just peachy," I exclaimed. "I heard through the grapevine that you were interested in a VIP for The Gala next month. Did I hear right?"

"Yes."

"Well, Slavic, I have the perfect girl for you. But I need you to do a little something for me. Can you do that?"

"Of course," he asserted with a devious tone.

"See, when my girls are bad, they need to be punished. You think you could handle that for me?" I warned.

He didn't say anything; he didn't have to, because I knew he was rock hard on the other end.

"What do you have in mind, Madam?"

"I trust you to know what to do." Slavic has been on my payroll for some time now, he usually handles the dirty work so my hands stay clean.

"I need some boundaries; you know there are no limits to what I can do when teaching lessons," he stated.

"Don't kill her and don't hurt her too much."

I know you're hating me as you're reading this, but I don't care. You aren't in my shoes; you don't live my life.

I don't judge you.

You shouldn't judge me.

My mother did something similar to this to me once. I didn't understand it and I hated her for it. I do believe it made me stronger, though. It gave me the perception I needed to take on VIP. And I don't think I'd be the same Madam without having learned that lesson the hard way.

You pick and choose your battles; I chose mine that day. I hung up the phone feeling more confident, yet despondent at the same time. It wasn't until she came to me after The Gala that I knew I had fucked up.

❊VIP❊

The day she called me to tell me we needed to talk; I already saw it coming. I had her followed throughout that time and I knew where her head was at. She was lost. I had lost her. And she proved it to me the minute she walked into my office. I didn't want to hear the words that were going to come out of her mouth. Although I prepared myself for it, it didn't make it any less difficult to hear her say them. If I could go back

and change things, I would; but the damage was done.

I greeted her like I always had. She didn't need to sense my apprehension and devastation over knowing what was to come.

"We need to talk," she cautioned as I kissed her cheek.

"And what about, darling?"

She moved to sit on the couch. I followed her, placing my hands in her lap.

"I can't do this anymore," she spoke.

My heart broke, it was shattering, and I hid it all behind the façade that I am. I hid it behind The Madam. "Do what, Bella Rosa?"

"I can't be a VIP," she quickly stated before she lost the nerve.

I nodded. "And why is that? For the married man?"

"No, for me. That's over. I appreciate everything that you have ever done for me. I'm not the same person anymore. I don't know when it happened but I've changed. I don't need or want the same things that I used to. I hope you can understand that."

"And what is it exactly that you're going to do now?" I sarcastically questioned.

"I'm not quite sure; I'm going to travel for a while. It's amazing that I've been almost everywhere around the world and I never really took it in. I'd like to do that now," she explained.

"All right. So you will do a little sabbatical and once you're done, you'll come home."

"I don't think so. Better yet, I know I won't."

"Ysabelle, I've been doing this a very long time. You'll come back, you'll get bored, you'll need excitement; you'll be back. Women like us are made like that, it doesn't just stop because you want it to, it's in our blood," I stated. A part of me believed what I was saying, I told you I play dirty, but always keep my hands clean. I would get her back if it was the last thing I would do.

"I want more, Madam, I want it all."

I chuckled. "You want the white picket fence, the 2.5 kids, and the husband. Jesus Christ, Ysabelle, have you learned nothing these last few years? I mean how many married men have you been with? Have you ever seen a happy marriage?"

"What happened to you? What happened to make you this way?"

Everything. She had no idea who I was, nobody did, and that's what made me powerful.

That's what made me The Madam.

"Oh...now we're sharing sob stories? Nothing has happened to me, I'm a fucking realist. This is the real world, Ysabelle, I showed it to you."

She put her hand on her chest. "Oh my God, you knew?" She affirmed, "You knew what Slavic was going to do. You set me up."

I rolled my eyes and moved back to my desk.

"Why?" she demanded.

"You're acting like a spoiled child, you've learned nothing."

"Were you trying to punish me?"

I wanted to tell her everything. She had a right to know, but I didn't. I used my words. It was who I was.

"I've told you since day one not to fuck with me or my business. You think I wanted it to come to this? You were my favorite and you repay me with letting all of it go for love. Well, Ysabelle, how'd that work out for you? Was it worth it?"

She hesitated a moment, taking in my hurtful words. "Yes, it was. I learned the meaning of my self-worth. I'm better than this, Madam, I know that now."

"You'll be back, they always come back."

"I'm not doing this out of spite, Madam, I can't sell myself anymore. I'm thankful for everything that you did for me, because I would be nowhere without you. You gave me what I needed, but I'm done with it. It's time for me to try something else. Please understand that?"

I sighed deeply. "You will always have a family here, Bella Rosa. I will help you in any way that I can." Even though I was saying the words, she knew I truly didn't mean them.

She smiled. "Thank you."

She hugged and kissed me goodbye. I went to the window and watched her walk out of The Cathouse.

I shed one tear.

This was not game over.

This was just the beginning...

CHAPTER 42

My hands were shaking so badly that I had to place them under my arms. My whole body felt like it was giving out on me. There were too many emotions happening to me all at the same time. I couldn't control any of it. I screamed and grabbed the vase on the coffee table, throwing it across the room. I went for anything I could see or was in my way. I screamed the entire time at the top of my lungs. The servants began knocking on the door.

"Leave me the fuck alone!" I screamed.

I ran across the room to find more things to shatter and stumbled on the broken glass, falling face first. I was thoroughly shaking as I tried to get up; there was broken glass all over my hands, arms, and legs. I couldn't see the damage I had done to my face but it hurt like a bitch. I slowly crawled to my cell phone that was on the floor and dialed.

"I need you," I wept.

"Angel, what's wrong? Are you all right?"

"Please."

"I'll be there in ten minutes." I hung up the phone and rolled over onto my back, just staring at the ceiling.

I didn't think of anything. I was numb. I sat there in my own self-pity and blood. I heard Mika gasp when the door opened; he ran over and kneeled beside me.

"What the fuck? Who did this to you?"

A moment of clarity was all it took for The Madam to come back.

I smiled bright and big because I just won.

He helped me up and tended to all my wounds for the next hour. Everything would heal; I would be fine, just like I always have been.

I lay sideways on the couch with my head resting on the back. Mika sat beside me with his arm on the back of my head, playing with my hair.

"What happened?" he questioned with caution and sincerity.

"She's gone," was all I could say.

He looked confused. "Who?"

"The VIP you so desperately want and remind me of every chance you get."

"Ysabelle," he softly whispered.

"Mmm hmm."

He chuckled, "Angel, you know that's not true. I don't want Ysabelle. I wanted to hurt you, and for some reason that I can't fathom, Ysabelle is your weak spot." He grabbed the side of my face. "I want you. You know that."

I propped myself up on my knees and then straddled his lap. I began unbuttoning his shirt. "Show me," I coaxed.

I started to grind myself on his cock and he pulled me in to devour my mouth. I sensed that he wanted to be gentle with me so I bit his lip, not hard enough to draw blood, but enough for him to know what I needed. He grabbed a hold of my hair at the nook of my neck and yanked. I whimpered in pleasure and pain from the force.

"You know who sets the rules, Angel. I have what you want…let me hear the words." I scratched at his chest and he flipped me over on my front, his knee plunged into my back, holding me there, while his hand once again pulled my hair back.

He got close to my ear and licked the side of my face. "Only good girls get to come," he dared.

I saw him grab the pocketknife from his pants and I trembled. He opened the blade and gripped the back of my shirt away from my skin and cut it open. My shirt rapidly came off, along with my bra, and he tied my wrists together behind my lower back. He locked me into place and I couldn't move if my life depended on it. Which is exactly the way Mika always wanted me, at his mercy.

My skirt was next to be pulled down and then off. He slowly took off my panties and then brought them up to his face and inhaled.

"Mmm…I love the smell of your pussy." He pulled off his belt and whipped it in the air. I jumped at the sound.

He struck my ass with the belt a few times, making me sweat and pant. I was expecting another blow and clenched for it.

"Nah uh, you will get ten more just for clenching. Count!" I did as I was told and by ten, my ass felt like it was on fire. His hand massaged my cheeks in a soothing motion.

"You're cunt is fucking dripping on the couch," he teased as he tied my ankles together with the belt.

"Hmm…now what to do with you? Huh?" He smacked my ass and grabbed me by my upper arms to place me over the side of the couch, the top half of my body was hanging off the armrest and my ass was in the air. His hand slipped from the crevice of my ass to the opening of my heat.

As soon as I felt his fingers sliding forward and backward on my clit, I moaned. I hadn't felt liberated like that in such a long time. I lived in the land of confusion for the last year. I was never going to go back there again.

The Madam was back.

I accepted and welcomed every one of Mika's demands. He fucked me with abandonment that only he and I understood.

When his cock pushed into my wet core, we simultaneously moaned.

"God, your pussy is mine. You know that don't you? That's why you always come back to me and why I come to you. Only you can do this to me." He thrust in, deeper and harder.

"You're mine, Angel," he huskily groaned.

"Ahh…harder…fuck me harder…" I demanded.

He grabbed a hold of the middle part that held my arms together, like he was holding onto the reigns of a horse, and plunged in and out. I felt the sting from my arms being pulled and it added to my pleasure.

I was a masochistic bitch.

My legs were tied together and it made my pussy even tighter for Mika. I knew how he operated; he wanted to control my orgasm. But I was on another playing field. I was back…The Madam held her throne once again, and I called the shots.

I released in ecstasy, feeling it ripple through me as if it were the first time. I came with so much force I nearly stopped breathing. He followed me over the edge of ecstasy, and I knew that he was feeling it just as much as I was; otherwise, I would have been punished for calling the shots.

EPILOGUE

Time never stands still, and before you know it, three years go by. Here I am lying on my deathbed in a hospital. The decisions and choices we make in this world can alter not just your life, but also those around you. The impact you can have on others can easily go unnoticed, that is until you make yourself heard. That is by far the most beautiful thing in this world; the ability to alter one's mind in a split second. I learned everything that I knew from the most powerful woman I knew-my mother. She was the top of the hierarchy; she aimed to change your perceptions and behaviors without you even knowing it. She was underhandedly deceptive and used any and all tactics.

Never underestimate the power of a Madam.

Manipulation is all about how you present yourself; it has everything to do with how you act. How you control yourself and your surroundings. That is the key to everything. The biggest enemy you'll have when trying to manipulate someone else, is doubt. It all starts with you. There are several types of manipulation and the one that works the best is emotional; you have no idea how much power you can have over someone with emotion.

And it all goes back to four little letters.

L-O-V-E.

The one term I loathed in this world, was the one that would end up getting me back what is rightfully mine. Time really was on my side.

Now here I lay.

This time I am the victim.

Pity me…feel bad for me…come to me…love me…

I want you to.

I hear the door open and my beautiful Brooke walks in with fresh flowers. She has been bringing me flowers for the past two days.

I smile. "Are you ready, darling?"

She nods. "I still don't understand why you think I need help running VIP. I can do this on my own, Madam."

I grin sympathetically at her. "Brooke, you have heard the doctors, even they don't know how long it's going to take for me to heal. I was badly beaten and I'm lucky to be alive. Please, don't argue with me. Just make the call."

She sighs, "Okay."

She dials the number and I think I may have stopped breathing for a second. Brooke put it on speaker and I could hear it ring a few times before I finally heard her voice.

"Hello."

"Bella." Brooke hesitates, trying to hold back the tears. My beautiful girl is worried about me. Just as I wanted her to be, and soon Ysabelle would feel the same exact emotions.

"Brooke? Are you are all right? What's wrong?"

"Bella, it's Madam. We're in the hospital and she's been badly injured. I don't know what to do and I need you to come home. I need your help with everything. I can't do this on my own. Please, please tell me you'll come home."

"What? Is she okay?" Ysabelle asks with desperation in her voice.

"Yes…but the doctors don't know how long it will take for her to recover and VIP can't run itself. I need you to come home and help me. Bella, we owe everything to VIP. We can't let it go down because Madam is helpless. Tell me you are coming home."

"Brooke…"

"Please…for me." Brooke whimpers.

"All right. I'll book the next flight out," she says and I silently scream a victory in my mind.

"Don't worry about it. I'll have the jet come get you. It should be there by tonight."

"Okay."

"And Bella?"

"Yes."

"Are you coming alone?"

She hesitates. "Yes."

"Okay, I love you."

"I'll see you soon," She says and hangs up.

Brooke embraces me in a hug. "I don't know what I would have done if I would have lost you. Oh my God, I have never been so scared."

"It's all right, darling, I will be fine. It will take some time but I will be better than before, you will see. Everything will fall into place. I promise."

We both turn when the door roughly pushes open. Mika barges in; I have never seen that look on his face before.

Brooke looks over at him and then back at me. "I'll leave you two alone. I will be right outside," she announces.

As soon as she steps out of the room, Mika rushes over to me and grabs my hand, bringing it up to his heart. He kisses all over my face, my neck, and my chest.

"Jesus Christ, Angel, I thought I fucking lost you," he pleads.

"Wha-"

"No, don't talk. I fucking love you. I love you with everything that I have. It has always been you; every day, every minute, every fucking second; it has been you. I can't go another day in this life without you by my side. This has been the ultimate wake up call for me. I will never lose you again. Do you understand me? Never again," he adds with conviction.

"Mika, I'm all right. Calm down," I reassure him.

"You are all right because I'm here and I'm not going anywhere. I filed for divorce, Angel."

I feel my eyes widen and my jaw drop. "Oh my God. Mika, I can't do this right now, everything is falling into place."

"I'm not going to let you push me away. It's not fucking happening. We belong together, I know that now," he urges, squeezing my hand.

"My MVP is coming home, she's finally coming home," I try to explain.

"What? What are you talking about?"

"Ysabelle. She's coming home."

"Why? Why are you so obsessed with her? It doesn't make any sense."

"She's my MVP; my Most Valuable Pussy. She's the future of VIP, Mika," I rationalize, knowing I'm not making sense to him.

I am finally going to say the three words that I have never shared with anyone, and it took sixteen years from the first time I looked in her bright green eyes.

"She's my granddaughter."

The end...for now.

(Keep reading for MVP Prologue)

MVP
m. robinson

Book 3 of the VIP Trilogy

Prologue

Be careful what you wish for...

Life can change drastically over the course of a few hours; can you imagine how much it can change over the course of a few years? I wanted to find myself, I wanted self-worth, I wanted love; I wanted it all.

Was I expecting too much?

Was it my fault?

Can someone truly have a happy ending?

I didn't know...I didn't know anything anymore.

My life ended and began when I met Sebastian Vanwell, and there I was, three years later; alone, confused, frustrated, and angry.

Trust and resentment, two completely different meanings on such opposite ends of the spectrum. I didn't know which way was up anymore. I had no idea who I was or what I was doing. I was just as lost, as I was the moment I stepped out of The Cathouse.

I love him, but was love enough?

Can love truly conquer all or is that just in fairy tales?

I was so confused.

All I knew was that there I was, leaving Sebastian a Dear John letter on the kitchen table, with my suitcase all packed and ready to go.

I walked out of our home, the place we built together out of dreams and love with Chance by my side.

I walked out on Sebastian.

I got into the taxi that took me to the tarmac. I took a deep breath and stepped out on the street to make my way toward the steps to board the jet.

Could I do this?

Am I making the right choice?

Is this who I am?

Is this what I want?

They say what goes around comes around…did everything finally catch up with me?

I grabbed my suitcase and boarded the plane.

There I sat with my hands folded in my lap and my dog by my side.

The only thing that I knew to be true, was that I was going to Miami.

I was going home.

Back to VIP.

S

I had only ever loved one woman. From the first day that I stared at those mesmerizing and entrancing bright green eyes, I was lured in. It was a magnetic pull that capsized me to live and breathe for her and only her. She was soul mate, the one person in this world that was made for me and only me. I wouldn't let her go without a fight…

I lost her once.

I wouldn't make that mistake again.

I had so many regrets in my life and she will never be one of them. It didn't matter how we met or started out. I knew it the moment her tiny frame fell into my arms. We were meant to meet and be together, it was all for a reason; a greater purpose that I knew from the second she told me her name.

Mine.

The instant connection we shared and the gravitational pull we had toward each other was inevitable. That's what happens when two halves of a heart come together and become one. They're bonded for life. The errors of my ways had finally caught up with me, but how did you prove to the other half of your heart that it beats for only her and her alone?

How did I make her understand that I would die before I ever hurt her again? There was no Sebastian without Ysabelle.

She was my everything…

My girl.

I am not an honorable man and I knew that. I had paid for my mistakes tenfold. I had hurt women that I had held dearly in my heart for as long as I could remember. However, I thought I was doing the right thing. Call me a coward, call me selfish, call me a cheater, call me a bastard; I deserve it. There wasn't anything that you can throw at me that I wasn't already aware of. I've waited thirty-four years for her, this I knew. I did love her, I still love her, I'll always love her.

Though, there I stood, holding a letter from the woman who owned my body, heart, and soul. *Fuck that.* She was much more than that. The human body needed water to survive; it could go three days without it before it started to shut down. Ysabelle was my water.

Sebastian,

I love you. Don't for one second think that I don't…I just don't know if that's enough anymore. As much as I want to, I can't forget the past. My heart says or feels one thing and my mind is spinning telling me another. I've listened to my heart once before and I can't go through that again…I won't.

We want different things.

I'm sorry. Don't hate me.

Yours always,

Ysa.

It was taking everything in me to not fall apart. I couldn't do that. I needed to stay levelheaded and hold my ground to get her back. I needed to stay strong. I was not the same man I was three years ago…

I was over to the front door in six strides and what I found breaks my heart.

Fuck me.

There was a torn picture of Olivia on the floor. I ran my fingers through my hair, wanting to pull it the fuck out. This was so fucked up. How would I fix this? How would I get her to understand that I wanted her?

Just her.

I would fight for her if it was the last thing I would ever do.

And I would like to see someone stand in my way because I'd take them the fuck out.

The Madam didn't know whom she's fucking with.

Mine.

And now I had to prove it to her, once and for all.

Connect with M. Robinson

Website:
www.authormrobinson.com

Friend request me:
https://www.facebook.com/monica.robinson.5895

Like my FB page:
https://www.facebook.com/pages/Author-MRobinson/210420085749056?ref=hl

Follow me on Instagram:
http://instagram.com/authormrobinson

Follow me on Twitter:
https://twitter.com/AuthorMRobinson

Amazon author page:
http://www.amazon.com/M.-Robinson/e/B00H4HJYDQ/ref=sr_ntt_srch_lnk_1?qid=1417487652&sr=8-1

Email:
m.robinson.author@gmail.com

CPSIA information can be obtained at www.ICGtesting.com
Printed in the USA
BVOW06s1921050516

446959BV00011B/129/P